Claiming Addison

Book #1

Claiming Addison

BOTTLES 69 — Book #1

By

Zoey Derrick

Cover Design completed by Parajunkee and is copyrighted 2014 by Zoey Derrick. For more information on Parajunkee and to see her amazing work, please visit her page, www.parajunkee.net

Editing completed by Mandy Smith and Lorraine Montuori from RawBooks Editing - They've done an amazing job and I couldn't do this without them - if you need editing services - check them out: http://rawbooksonline.com

ISBN-13: 978-0990326496

The following is a work of fiction - all reference to persons, places or things is strictly coincidental. Some parts (though small)are based on fact or actual events that occurred for the author and are portrayed fictionally here for Dacotah and Orion.

To Friends, Fans, and Lover's of a good story - This one is for you!!

Acknowledgements

Z-Team: Thank you to my beautiful Street Team. You ladies are the best and I love you for everything you do.

Rachel - My BFF, my Numero Uno Beta Reader. Thank you for always being ready, able and willing to read my raw craziness and for loving every word! P.S. Tell your husband he's welcome!

Mandy and Lorraine: Ladies, without you, this book wouldn't be in everyone's hands. You're amazing at everything you do. Stay Raw!!

To my beautiful Beta Readers: Lisa, Danielle, Vickie, Kali, Liliuokalani and Amy - Thank you for your kindness and willingness to read my mess of a beta copy. Your feedback has been instrumental in creating the story in your hands. Your love of Addison, Talon and Kyle is amazing. Thank you for everything!

To Emily - your words, your encouragement, and your love of my work keeps me going and it keeps me pushing my boundaries. Thank you for being such an inspiration.

For my Fans - Thank you for always wanting more, for reading, and for reviewing my work. Without you I'd have no reason to keep going. Thank you for loving my work.

To Rachel, a.k.a. Parajunkee - Your creativity is an inspiration. Your work is beyond amazing, Thank you for the cover of Claiming Addison and for everything you do to bring my stories to life.

To Debra Anastasia - Thank you for being an amazing woman!! *Boobie smash, tackle hug* And thank you for writing Poughkeepsie, and for letting Addison read it, she loved it just as much, if not more than I did.

Zoey Derrick's Other Books

The Love's Wings Series - Contemporary Romance:
Finding Love's Wings
Chasing Love's Wings

The REASON Series - Paranormal Romance:
Give Me Reason
Give Me Hope
Give Me Desire
Give Me Love

Standalone Novels:
One Week

Coming Soon:
Craving Talon - 69 Bottles Book #2
February 17th, 2015
Redeeming Kyle - 69 Bottles Book #3
March 31st, 2015
Taming Dex - 69 Bottles Book #2.5
Coming Spring 2015
Without Regret
Coming Summer 2015

chapter 1

"Good morning, Addison."

"Hi Raine. I have an appointment with Trinity. Do you know where her assistant is?"

"Uh, no." Raine looks around like she's stalling then finally looks at her watch. "Oh sorry, I forgot she had an appointment. Do you want me to let Trinity know you're here?"

I try very hard to not give her the 'duh' look. "That would be great."

I step back and find a seat. It's been a long time since I've been up on the executive floor of Bold International, Inc. The reception area is pretty modern-posh with a bit of swank thrown in. To be honest, you can tell a man designed it, or at least picked out the furniture, and he certainly wasn't gay. But if you compare it to the rest of the building, including the actual building itself, it freakin' fits.

So I'm guessing you're wondering who I am? Well, that's easy, I'm Addison, a twenty-nine year old, out of the box redhead from Kansas City. I've worked as a PR Rep for

Bold International since I graduated from NYU over seven years ago. I was recruited straight out of college and I've never looked back. I work strictly with musicians, and let me tell you, it's the best job in the world. Plus it keeps me on my toes.

"Addison, Trinity is ready for you."

"Thanks, Raine." I pick up my bag and head down the hall toward Trinity's office.

When I get there, her door is closed. I pace back and forth for a moment then see Raine peering around the corner from her desk.

"Go ahead and knock," she tells me. I turn and face the door, hesitate, then knock gently.

"Come in, Addison," I hear Trinity say from the other side. I open the door and peek my head in. "Hi Addison, come in." I push open the door and step inside. "Go ahead and close the door."

There is a woman with black and blue hair sitting in front of Trinity's desk. I can see her shoulders are covered in tattoos and there's something peeking out of the collar of her sleeveless top. "I can wait outside," I say rather calmly, despite the fact that I have a pretty good inkling of who this woman is.

Trinity smiles. "Absolutely not. Addison, I'd like you to meet Cami Michaels."

Oh shit! I was right. I watch as Cami stands then turns around to face me. She offers me her hand and I take it. "Hi Addison, it's great to finally meet you. I've heard a lot about you."

I smile, releasing her hand. "All good things, I hope?" I'm not a big girl by any means, but my lowly five feet seven inches practically dwarfs her. Then again, I'm wearing four inch heels. "It's a pleasure to me you, Mrs. Michaels."

She smiles. "While I love my married name, please, call me Cami."

"Yes, ma'am." She flinches. "Cami." Okay, she doesn't like ma'am either. Mentally noted. I look toward Trinity. "What can I do for you, Trinity?"

"Take a seat." She gestures toward the chair next to the one Cami vacated. "Don't worry about Cami being here, we were talking about the same thing I need to discuss with you when you arrived."

What the hell is going on? I take my seat, thankful for the distraction to stop myself from completely freaking out. "Am I being fired?" I blurt.

Trinity and Cami both laugh. "Goodness, no," Cami says with a wide smile, "In fact, you're being promoted and we desperately need you to do something for us."

I look at Cami and then back to Trinity. "Anything!" I say without thinking, my entire brain to mouth filter is completely busted.

"I hoped you'd say that." Trinity smiles. Her smile is warm, genuine and friendly. She's an older woman, maybe in her late fifties, but she's definitely got a lot of youth left in her smile. "Addison, we brought you in because we have an emergency situation."

Emergency, okay, this I can handle. "Is it with one of my clients? I haven't heard anything." I look to Trinity for my answer.

"No, no. Well, at least not anyone that's currently assigned to you. But before we go into the details, I need to let you know that I'm going to have to pull you from your vacation this weekend." Her eyes dull with sadness.

"Oh, no, no, no." My heart sinks.

"Believe me, I don't want to, but you're the only one who's certified and experienced enough to handle this besides me and Cami. Unfortunately we're not able to make this kind of commitment, so we're desperately hoping you can be our girl."

I look between the two women, dumbfounded. "Uh, I have reservations and concert tickets that I've paid a lot of money for."

"Are you going out of town? Flying somewhere?" Cami asks. From the look in her eyes, she actually feels sorry for having to do this and while it is disappointing, I guess I can make a concession. I always do. Rescheduling with my girlfriends shouldn't be that hard since the concert we're going to will be here in LA in a few weeks. Luckily tickets haven't gone on sale yet. Maybe I can sell ours for San Diego on Thursday and use the money to buy LA tickets. I know the band's concerts sell out in record time, so I imagine selling my tickets won't be that hard. But still, it's the first show of their tour and I don't want to miss it.

"Out of town, yes. Flying, no. My girlfriends and I are heading to San Diego on Thursday for a concert and then we planned on spending the weekend on Coronado."

Cami smiles and looks to Trinity, there seems to be some private joke between the two of them that I don't understand.

"Listen, Addison. We've had an incident with the original rep who was supposed to handle one of our bands. It's because of that last minute change that we need to fill that spot with someone on extremely short notice," Cami says matter of factly, but her confidence wavers when she begins slowly pacing around the room. "Believe me, the last thing I want to do is cancel your vacation. We can make arrangements to reimburse you for your tickets and your reservations. And I give you my sincerest promise that at the end of all this you can have at least an entire month off."

"Excuse me, Cami, it's not about the money, honest. It's just that my girlfriends and I have been planning this for months and every time we seem to plan something, I have to pull out, usually because of work. I just feel…"

"What concert are you going to?"

Huh? I look at Cami, "What?"

"What concert?"

"Oh, um 69 Bottles." Both Cami and Trinity giggle. "What's so funny?"

"Well, here is what I am going to suggest. Because I feel awful about forcing you to cancel your plans, I have no doubt that you can give your girlfriends a better vacation," Cami says. "I will give your girlfriends my plane to San Diego, along with a rental car. Assuming you'd planned on driving down?" She looks at me for confirmation and I nod. I'm more than a little confused. "But, you will have to leave your girlfriends in San Diego after the concert."

I want to scream in frustration because they're being so evasive about what it is that I'm going to be doing, or why I am going to be doing it. Trinity stands up from behind her desk, pulling my attention away from Cami's pacing. In her hand she has a rather thick envelope and a bag, similar to my own. "Inside you will find all the details for your assignment."

I desperately want to roll my eyes at her deflection. "What exactly is the assignment?"

"On Thursday at 11:00 a.m., we need you on a tour bus headed for San Diego, you'll be kicking off the start of a twelve week nationwide road tour."

Twelve weeks, starting Thursday. The puzzle pieces start clicking into place. "For who?" I ask, despite the fact that I think I know the answer to the question, but I need confirmation.

"69 Bottles," Cami answers.

After learning the details of my assignment, I leave her office and immediately slump back against the wall. I'm trying desperately to catch my breath before heading toward the elevator. I'm not normally one to get nervous about much of anything, but I'll be damned, I'm ridiculously nervous about this. Sure, I'm a fan of 69 Bottles. I love their music, but I know nothing about them. Let alone much of what they look like or what has been made of their reputation. I can't let this opportunity slip through my fingers.

After a few deep breaths, I finally manage to compose myself enough to leave the hallway. I straighten my jacket, thank god for it because I was sweating bullets in there. I walk toward the elevator, ignoring Raine. I have my bag and the new messenger bag slung over my shoulder. The envelope in my hands is pressed tight to my chest like a bulletproof vest.

chapter 2

My phone rings interrupting my packing. "Addison," I answer, like always.

"Hey chica, you can save the speech. I already talked to Jess and she told me you're bailing on us again."

"Oh come on, Sam, I am not..."

"Don't worry, it's cool. I just thought that since we were so close you might actually get away with being able to take your vacation this time," Sam says into the phone but I can tell she's disappointed.

"Listen, I'm still waiting on final details, but my boss's boss is arranging for you and Jess to fly down to SD and have a rental car. I will meet you guys there and we will still be able to do the concert and then you guys can head back to the beach house," I tell her.

"Yeah, it just sucks."

I give the phone a half smile. "On the plus side, when I'm done with this tour, I will be getting an entire month off. I will figure out how to make it up to you both."

"Addie, come on, girl, spill the beans. Who are you going on tour with?" she says with a conspiratorial tone in her voice.

I smile, but I refused to tell Jess when I talked to her, which I know Sam knows, so why ask again? "I'm not telling. Actually, I can't tell you, not yet anyway. Give me a couple of days and I can indirectly spill the beans."

I can hear her childish huff and pout on the other end of the phone. "Fine."

"Thanks, Sam. You're the best."

"Uh huh, I know it and damn it, Addie, you owe me. Drinks tonight?"

I look at the clock, it's already after four and I still need to go shopping. "Actually, yeah, listen, I need a favor."

"Anything."

"You want a break from the roommate from hell?"

"Oh my god, yes, please."

"Then why don't you pack up a few things and come stay at my house while I'm gone," I tell her.

"Addie, seriously, I can't do that."

"Shut up, Sam. You can too. It will give you a nice break from mega-watt-bitch and you can eat up all the groceries I just bought this weekend. Plus, it will give me peace of mind knowing that someone is watching over the house besides my housekeeper who only comes once a week."

I know she's rolling her eyes. Sam isn't a broke girl by any means, but for some reason, despite all the bullshit with her roommate, she's never moved out. I've met the roommate on more than a few occasions and she's just pissed off at the world, at least from what I can tell. Despite all her bitching, Sam doesn't do anything about it.

"Alright, I'll do it, but I can't promise I'll leave when you get back," she says.

I smile. "I'm hoping that's the case. Meet me at the haunt, say seven?"

"You got it, see you there. Should I bring Jess?"

"Uh, sure, why not? Then tomorrow night you can start staying here."

"When you leaving?"

"Thursday," I tell her.

"Your house will be alright while I'm gone in San Diego, right?" she asks.

"Yeah, Maria will be here Friday. I'll let her know that someone else is staying here so she doesn't freak out on you and I'll make sure the house is locked up tight for the weekend."

"Sounds good, see you in a bit."

"Absolutely."

We hang up and I dive back into packing. Hoping to god that neither one of them pressure me too much about who I'm going on tour with. Then again, they both know what industry I work in and they have no clue who any of my clients are or have been. Though it will be hard to keep the 69 Bottles thing from them once we're in San Diego, which is why I plan to indirectly tell them what's what.

In the big bad scary envelope are two exclusive VIP badges, usable for each show. I intend to have them given to Jess and Sam when they pick their tickets up at Will Call. Their suspicions will already be high enough as it is when I don't show up to meet them outside the theater before the show.

My phone goes off with a text.

Sam: Where r u?

I look at the time. Shit! It's already seven. CRAP!

Me to Sam: I'm running out the door now. C U in a few.
Sam: Hurry up woman!

Okay, okay, I get the hint. I grab my purse and bolt for the door. Crap, I didn't want to be late, where the hell has today gone? God, I hope tomorrow isn't like this or I'm screwed.

chapter 3

Despite the monumental amount of alcohol we consumed last night and that I hardly slept, I feel great this morning. Maybe that's why I feel great? Still drunk. When I did finally manage to pass out, it was nearly four and I didn't wake again until after eleven.

Which means I have been running around nonstop since noon, and I am finally ready to go. Suitcases are packed, laptop, iPad and new work cell phone are on the charger. Calls from personal phone forwarded to work phone, though I am still taking it with me since I don't have time to transfer my contacts. My personal phone is partially paid for by Bold, one of the perks I guess, but some months that stipend is hardly enough to cover the actual work related use. Being a PR Rep means I am on call 24/7, 365 days a year. I've actually only been awoken in the middle of the night once, but I have had more than a few weekend calls. For the most part, between 7 in the morning and 10 at night, I'm fair game. All of my clients and their 'staff' are given explicit instructions about what constitutes an after 10 or weekend emergency. Though I guess, going on tour puts me at their beck and call all day every day.

Sam is on her way over with Chinese takeout, and I have two bottles of wine ready to rock. We chatted a lot last night at the bar and Jess did a great job of making me feel guilty about ditching the vacation plans. But once I told her this is a major career boost for me, she dropped the guilt trip. Miraculously, it only took me one time of reminding them that I can't discuss my job with them and they let it go after a promise that at some point they will figure out what the hell is going on.

"Addie," I hear Sam call from the front door.

"In the kitchen," I holler back.

"Girl, you need some help with that?" I ask her as she lugs her suitcase up the steps.

"Nope," I hear her grunt followed by her suitcase falling on my hardwood floors. I come around the corner of the kitchen and she is standing at the top of the steps, huffing.

"You're so full of shit. We could've gone down for your stuff, you know?"

"Nope, I got it." She gives me a wink.

"Is that all?"

She looks down at her suitcase dubiously then back at me. "Uh yeah, why?"

"You're staying here for twelve weeks, remember?"

She rolls her eyes. "This is mainly for this weekend. I told bitchface that I'd be back on Sunday. I haven't told her that I am disappearing for three months. Besides, my apartment is ten minutes away from here. Not like I'm leaving town for twelve weeks like some people." She sticks her tongue out at me.

I laugh and shake my head at her. "You do realize that while I'm gone, you're more than welcome to move all your stuff in here."

She looks around the apartment dramatically. "Like I can afford this place."

I shake my head and roll my eyes. "Wine? Then we can discuss your moving in."

"Yes, please." She grabs the two bags of takeout that I can smell all the way over here. It smells really good. Reminding me I haven't eaten much today.

Once we're in the kitchen, I grab plates and pour the wine into two very large goblets. Hmm, maybe I should've bought a couple more bottles. That one bottle fit into two glasses. "Trying to get you drunk," I say sliding the glass to her.

"That will definitely do it, though with Chinese food, you never know."

I hold up my glass. "Cheers." We clink and dive into divvying up the food. "So is Jess pissed you're staying here?" I ask her as we both reach for the egg rolls. I hold my hand out for her to go ahead.

She shrugs and takes a bite of her egg roll. "I don't really care if she is or not. She's got her own place, no reason for her to stay here."

"Well, you have your own place too," I remind her.

"Yes, but it is occupied by bitchface."

I roll my eyes again. At this rate my eyes are likely to freeze looking at the back of my head. "So if it's so bad living with her, why haven't you moved out already?"

She gives me a half smile. "I feel bad because I know she couldn't afford it on her own. I think half of the time she's just pissed off because her grandiose plans fail. Either that or her latest fuck toy screwed her over. Ultimately, I just think she's a really angry, jealous person. Hence why I didn't tell her I was staying here. She'd get all whiny and I'd rather fill her head with bullshit, like having a new boyfriend and I'm spending all my time with him."

"What would happen if you moved out?"

She shrugs. "No clue. The lease is up in two months and lately she's been prattling on about moving back to Michigan or wherever it is that she's from. Says that this acting bullshit is exactly that, bullshit."

I snort. "Is she any good?" I ask honestly, not that I'd do anything about it. Sam looks at me like I've lost my mind. "That bad?"

She nods. "Something like that. Not to mention the fact that she keeps asking me to talk to you and hook her up. She thinks that if she can get an agent, she'll have better luck. But she can't get an agent because she either sucks or she's a bitch to them. She has an entitlement complex, thinks she's entitled to whatever she wants."

I scowl at Sam, "Entitled? Ha! Hardly. You don't just get handed acting jobs or celebrity, you have to work your ass off for them. She wants you to talk to me. You're kidding, right?" She shakes her head. "Okay, first of all, I don't do actors, so I haven't a clue what they even look for. Second of all, if she really sucks, it comes back on me and she'll turn around and blame you. Lastly, as much as I hate to admit it, Hollywood thrives on good looks and she…"

Sam cuts me off with a fit of laughter. "Oh my god, you have no idea. I heard her mumbling something about getting into porn, just to make ends meet…"

I interrupt her with my own laughter. "Tell me you're joking. The porn industry rejected her?"

We both break down into a full on giggle fest that lasts us more than a few minutes and a couple of stomach cramps. Don't get me wrong, bitchface, as we lovingly call her, isn't all that ugly. But she isn't attractive either. She has a very plain Jane style and she gives off the wrong vibe. Her name is Liz, and we really shouldn't make fun of her, but if you knew half of the shit she's done, you'd agree with us.

After a long night chatting with Sam, I settle into bed with my thoughts roaming around 69 Bottles and the tour. Though the tour lasts for twelve weeks, there are a lot of open dates between shows. For the most part, the shows are all on Wednesdays through Sundays with travel days being Mondays and Tuesdays. The travel time is minor considering how many cities the tour is stopping in. Top that off with the fact that all 30 of the 32 shows that have gone on sale, sold out in less than fifteen minutes. Whoever put this together did it right. I wouldn't have put so many cities, like Oklahoma City, Kansas City, Des Moines, Minneapolis and Chicago, so close together date wise. Each city is within reasonable driving distance, I might have just expanded to multiple shows in Des Moines and drew in people from Minnesota, Illinois and Missouri.

However, the Minneapolis show has me most excited. The band is playing their smallest venue, First Avenue, which anyone who's anyone, or trying to be anyone, plays there. In fact, 69 Bottles has played there before, just not as the big names they are now. Plus they have the coveted Sunday spot. The venue is small, so tickets are expensive. I know, I looked. The cheapest ticket was like $345. The most expensive, including VIP experience, was over $1500.

The packet contains information on each venue, including size, number of tickets sold, number of band owned tickets and number of VIP tickets available. Being a

VIP means exclusive front row access along with backstage passes. Most venues limit these tickets to less than 200 people. Some have more or even different levels.

I don't make it much further into the package because the next thing I know, my alarm is going off and it is four in the morning. Hello, hangover. You nasty, nasty bitch.

chapter 4

I knew when I opened that third bottle of wine that I was really going to be in trouble, and now I need to get my shit in gear and get the hell out of here. Shower, check. Hair- I flip my hair in the mirror in front of me, check. Make-up, fabulous as always. Professional attire, for today, double check.

I wouldn't say I'm an overly attractive woman, in fact, I'd say I'm average. With ice green eyes, and luscious, kissable lips. I'm five seven and I weigh about one forty-five, a little over weight, but it gives me some nice curves and a fairly decent ass. The only thing fake about me are the D cup sized tits that enhance my chest. Believe me, I needed it. Before I went under the knife for implants, I barely registered an A-cup and with my height and size, it was awful to look at. At least it was for me.

After Dan's death, I needed something to help boost my confidence, so I got them done. Think what you want, but it was a huge boost for my confidence. If you're wondering if I'd do it again, my response is mixed. If I knew the pain

I'd endure, I wouldn't have done it, but because I know the end result, even a few years later, it was all worth it. Besides, since then I've gained a little weight and they're no longer the super firm, totally fake tits you see in porn.

Anyway, enough about my boobs, moving on. Today I'm wearing a dark gray pencil skirt with a white button up silk blouse, open to show just a little cleavage with the sleeves rolled up to my elbows. It is March in Los Angeles, so the weather is chilly. For now, I'm planning on wearing my jacket. I have no doubt that once the press conference begins, I'll still be wearing it.

Regardless, I manage to sneak out of the house with my luggage in tow after triple checking that I had everything I needed. I threw the fat envelope of death into my messenger bag. Since it's still dark outside, I doubt I will get any reading done in the car on the way over. I'm taking a car because I'm not leaving my car downtown for three months. I'd rather leave it downstairs in the garage. Plus I left the keys with Sam, she said she'll drive it a couple of days to and from work for me. I think she just wants to drive the blue devil.

Despite my ginormous salary, I drive a brand new Nissan Rogue. It's not the most expensive car and I could certainly afford something bigger, better and fancier, but fuck it. I chose to spend the money on my condo instead. Ironically, I spend more time in my car than I do my condo.

God, I am off track today or at least subject to zoning out. Something I like to do when I'm nervous. Why would I be nervous? That's easy, I haven't a clue what I'm stepping into, what is going to happen at the press conference and well frankly, I'm freaking out about spending twelve weeks on a bus with five men... the only female, with five men... Yup, let's just leave it at that.

"Good Morning, Miss Beltrand."

"Oh, hello, you're early."

"I'm Darius, I'll be your driver today. I understand that we're headed downtown to LA Live?"

I nod, "Pleasure to meet you Darius, yes."

He bends down and takes my luggage from me, putting it into the trunk of the sleek black town car parked in front of my building. I keep my messenger bag and purse with me as he opens the door so I can slide in. "We're going to avoid the highways this morning. There is a lot of traffic out already."

I smile at him. "You're the driver, so whatever way you think is best, have at it. We have plenty of time."

"Yes, ma'am." He smiles and closes my door. Within a moment, he is sliding into the front seat. If I wasn't hung over, I'd think that Darius was quite attractive. Caramel colored skin, very black hair and a wicked sexy goatee. Not to mention tall and well-built and if I didn't know any better, I'd think he was packing. I take comfort in that.

"There's some water in the pull down on the console, help yourself," He says over the seat.

"Perfect, thank you." I open the compartment and pull out a nice cold bottle of water. I manage to down the entire bottle before we get out of my neighborhood. Stupid wine. Now I remember why I prefer the hard stuff. At least I can wake up without much of a hangover, like I did yesterday morning. I certainly drank more Tuesday night than I did last night.

"Miss Beltrand, we're here," Darius says and I look out the front windshield at a mob of people. It's not even seven in the morning and already the horde is out in full swing.

"Can you get me close to that gate, where the security guys are?"

"Yes, ma'am."

Darius begins his approach and compliments of the deeply tinted windows and the swanky car, people part the mass, screaming at the car. Obviously they think that I'm someone important. I watch the security crew at the gate as they make a circle, pushing people back and one of the guys approaches Darius's window. He rolls it down. "I have Miss Addison Beltrand in the car." The guy does a check of his clipboard, flips a page. Jesus, how many people are coming through this gate?

"Does she have her credentials?" I hand my badge, compliments of the massive envelope of death, to Darius who hands it to the security guard.

"Okay, you can pull through; to your right you will see other cars, go ahead and park there. You'll need to come back through here when you leave." He gives my credentials back to Darius who hands them back to me. I tuck them back into my bag.

"Yes, sir," Darius replies and the guard waves his hand. I watch as the gate manually swings open then I finally see the "rent a fence sign." Obviously this isn't normal for this area of town. When you live in LA, downtown isn't a place you visit very often, but this is a great open location to kick off a bus tour because the highway is only a few blocks away.

As we come through the crowd and the gate, I can see two buses. Neither are openly marked, which is a good thing if you ask me. But it also leaves me to wonder which bus I am supposed to be on. They're exactly the same. Except that one of the buses is pulling a trailer that's nearly as tall and wide as the bus itself. Must be equipment.

Darius does as the guard asked and pulls off to the right with the other cars. "Let me go ahead and pull your luggage, then I will come open the door for you."

"Sounds great, thanks, Darius." I busy myself with putting papers back into my messenger bag and grab another bottle of water from the pull down. I might need it. Downside to joining so late, I don't know what's going to be on board the bus.

Once I'm done stuffing my messenger bag, I take a look around. At one of the buses, the one without the trailer, standing on either side of the door are two, rather tall, muscled up men in black suits. The Ray-Bans they're wearing complete the ensemble and I feel like I've walked onto the set of Men in Black. I wonder which one is J and which is K. One of the guys has a deep, dark complexion and looks oddly familiar, but I can't place him.

I feel the car shift and hear the trunk close. Darius is at my door, pulling it open. Ironically, the crowd goes crazy thinking that I'm someone important and I roll my eyes. "Oh sweethearts, you're about to be completely disappointed," I mumble to myself.

I climb out and almost instantly the crowd dies down, though there is still a dull roar of murmurs from the waiting fans as they realize that I am me and not one of the band members. Darius laughs.

"I couldn't agree more." I slip a hundred dollar bill into Darius's hand. I included a tip in the credit card charge for the car, but meh. He's done good. "Thank you for your company, your service and for putting up with this madness."

He smiles, not looking at what's in his hand and I commend him for that. Most drivers peek. "Anytime, ma'am." He slips me his card. "If you need anything at all, don't hesitate to call. For curiosity's sake, who's in the buses?" I see him smile slightly.

"That would be 69 Bottles." I watch his eyes get wide and a smile spread across his lips. "A fan, I see?" He just nods. "Thank you again, Darius, it was a real…"

"Addison?" I hear someone shout.

"It was a pleasure, Darius."

"The pleasure was mine," he says with a grin and off he goes around the front of the car. I turn, looking toward the voice that hollered for me. Given that the girls' cheers have picked up some, but not to an overwhelming amount, I assume that whoever has called my name isn't a member of the band.

Coming toward me in long, confident strides wearing ripped jeans, a tightly fitted 69 Bottles t-shirt, a pair of shit kickers and a wolfish grin is someone who is vaguely familiar to me, but I can't quite place him either. I know him from somewhere, but where? He's extremely good looking.

Darius pulls out from in front of me just as the man approaching reaches the opposite side of the car. "Hi Addison, welcome to the madhouse that is 69 Bottles." He smirks. "I'm Kyle, the band's manager."

chapter 5

"Hi Kyle. So I take it, this," I gesture toward the waiting crowd, "is normal?"

He laughs with a beautiful boyish grin, a faint blush in his cheeks, weird? "This is minor. I was on the bus and when I heard the collective downshift in the volume of the crowd, I figured it had to be you pulling in." I cock my head at him, my hair falls over my right shoulder and his eyes light up. "Let me help you with your stuff, I'll show you to your rack, help you get settled."

I nod. "Are they all here?"

He shakes his head, "Not yet. We're still waiting on Mouse."

"Mouse?" I ask questioningly.

"Uh, sorry. Calvin, he's the lead guitarist."

"Oh," I say, trying to pull back the surprise I feel at the name.

"We call him Mouse, actually everyone does."

"Why's that?"

He laughs. "You'll see."

Well, okay then. Kyle bends down, picking my duffle bag up off the ground, throwing the strap over his shoulder and pulls up the handle on my suitcase. "I need the duffle on the bus, the suitcase can go…"

"No worries, we have room on the bus for it."

"Oh, okay," I say surprised.

"This way."

He leads me toward the closer of the two buses, but I notice that his pace slows until we are more side-by-side and I catch him peeking over at me. I keep looking at him because there is something very familiar about him, but I can't place it. I know it's going to drive me nuts until I do. He, on the other hand, keeps sizing me up, looking me over and I want to roll my eyes. Keep wanting, buddy, because you aren't ever gonna touch. *Nobody touches anymore.* I think sadly.

"Hello boys," Kyle says to the two on door duty. "I'd like to introduce you to Addison, she'll be tagging along on this here tour." I watch as Kyle smiles widely at his fake southern hillbilly accent. "Addison, this is Beck." Agent K in my mind, "And this is Leroy." I smile at the name because well, it fits, but yet it doesn't. Leroy is huge and I hold my hand out to him first.

He takes it and my pale skin looks paler up against his, and tiny as hell. "Pleasure to meet you, Leroy. Have we met before?"

He smiles. "No, ma'am, though I've seen you before. I was assigned to Mrs. Michaels for some time a few months back."

I nod in recognition. "That's right, I remember now."

I turn to Beck, extending the same greeting. Though his facial features are not unattractive, he has a very hard demeanor about him. Why? I'm not sure. He softens enough to take my hand. "Nice to meet you, Beck."

"Likewise, ma'am." He pulls his hand back and returns to his position. I see Leroy giving him the stink eye and I smile.

"Well, gentleman, see you later," Kyle says as he ushers me toward the three stairs onto the bus. I climb up and get a full shot of the interior and holy crap. It's such a masculine space, filled with blacks, chromes and reds. Immediately in front of me is an L shaped couch with a couple of tables in front of it. The couch is on the right side of the bus, behind the driver's throne. Across from the couch is a kitchen that looks rather state of the art with an overly large dorm refrigerator on the far end wall. On the wall opposite the fridge is a large flat screen that literally has half an inch to spare between the bus wall and the hallway that leads toward the back of the bus.

I can see three curtains, open, stacked on top of each other and there are two men standing in front of them putting stuff away.

"Hey guys," Kyle says.

"What, dick?" One of the guys replies, laughing and turning toward me and Kyle. They both stop dead in their tracks, staring at me. They make no secret of the fact that they're looking me up and down.

"You brought a pre-road snack I see." And he starts moving in my direction in a rather unsexy yet provocative advancement.

"Shut it, Dex," Kyle snaps.

"Oh but Kyle, she isn't here for you. She'd take me over you any day."

"Don't hold your breath," I blurt. Dex is tall, maybe six two or six three. He's not overly large, but he has well-muscled arms that are completely covered in ink. I can also see a couple of tats popping the top of the collar on his t-shirt. He is also in a tight fitting white t-shirt and snug jeans, only he's swapped his shit-kickers for well-worn brown flip-flops. He keeps eye-fucking me. My hand twitches with the impulse to punch him.

"I can tell, this one's gonna be feisty, but just you wait-," he says to Kyle but he's still looking me up and down. He never finishes his sentence, but the look of 'I'll get her first' is there. I want to roll my eyes.

"Addison, this is Dex, the drummer, and regular fuckwad. The big guy behind him sporting what would normally be a hawk is Peacock, or Eric or shithead. He usually answers to each one."

Peacock sidesteps Dex to come toward me; he extends his hand. "Nice to meet you, Addison."

I smile and take his hand. "Same here." He extends a smile to me. Peacock, as he seems to be affectionately called, is a big man and based off of the name Eric, he's the bassist. All in all, he's pretty good looking. I can see tattoos and while he's a bigger guy, he's not unfit. I can see the outline of his pecs through his black t-shirt. Ironically, the jeans and shit-kickers seem to be the norm around here.

"Addison is replacing Dylan."

"That fuck-tard. I must say that his replacement is already a million times better on my eyes." Dex gives me that bad attempt at being seductive again.

"Forget it, Dex. You ain't got nothin' I want," I tell him straight out. His eyes light up giving me the realization that I've just given him the ultimate challenge.

"We'll see about that."

"Dex!" I hear someone bark from behind him. "Knock your shit off." I look past both Dex and Peacock to see a tall man, very tall actually, taller than I am by nearly a foot, with light brown shaggy hair with natural highlights and a scruffy beard. But what I'm hypnotized by the most are his vibrant green eyes that have an almost glowing effect. He's wearing a white t-shirt that's cut off at the sleeves, a black leather vest, and he has an outrageous amount of tattoos covering his arms. Looking at him makes my mouth water and my pussy weep. Jesus. "You must be Addison," he says in a sweet, sexy, and completely panty melting voice as he parts the sea of Dex and Peacock. "I'm Talon."

chapter 6

Oh boy, I'm in trouble. Get your shit in gear, Addison, don't blow this shit now. Turn off your fucking hormones. He doesn't want you. He's just being friendly. "Hi Talon, it's a pleasure to meet you." I hold out my hand.

He takes it gently in his. "Likewise," he says without much confidence. God, his hands are huge and warm and callused on the pads of his fingers. There is an electric zing that passes between us when we make contact and my hormones go back into overdrive. If I'm not mistaken, he feels it too. "Likewise," he says again in that sweet voice. I can feel a collective huff of the men around me and I wonder idly what that's all about, but I'm having a hard time giving a shit. At least until he lets go of my hand. Good, maybe that means Dex will drop his shit.

"So, Red?" Dex queries. "What the hell possessed you to take this damn gig?"

I snort a laugh. "Honestly, I have no fucking clue." Thankful for the distraction from Talon, I look to Dex, but

36

that same raging heat is still burning in his eyes. In fact it is in all of their eyes and I suddenly feel like I'm on display as a buffet ready to be eaten at a moment's notice.

"Alright, guys, let's let her get settled while we wait for Mouse."

"That fucker still isn't here?" Talon growls. "He should've been here twenty minutes ago. Kyle, call him when you're done." Just then the crowd outside picks up in volume. "Nevermind, he's here."

Kyle ushers me past the men. It's amazing that they all seem to fit on this bus given how big they all are and I can tell right away that Dex is going to be my number one enemy during this tour. I know his type. He's the drummer. Ironically you'd think that the guitarist and the lead singer would out score the drummer on the women front, but no, they all want the drummer. Which of course has made Dex cocky as fuck.

"Here is the bathroom." I peek inside and the small counter is littered with a shit ton of hair products, razors, shavers, and brushes. Jesus, there is more shit on there than in my own bathroom. *Fucking rock stars.* Aside from that, the accommodations are pretty small inside. "The shower is behind the door. It's narrow, but it is longer than most stand ups. I don't recommend showering while in motion. It's a bitch." He laughs and I join him. The image is pretty comical.

He turns around facing the bunks where Dex and Peacock were standing when I came on board. "This is Mouse," he points to the lower of the three bunks, "then Peacock, and finally Dex is up top. The guys usually spend most of their time in their racks and I don't recommend opening the curtains if they're closed, you never know what you're going to find. Each one has a TV that hooks into headphones and believe me, there is no shortage of porn on this bus."

"Fuckin' a Kyle, why you gotta be like that?" Dex says from behind me and I turn in his direction. "Spilling all our fucking secrets and she's been on the bus for five minutes. What the fuck?"

"Whatever, Dex. She doesn't need to open your curtain to you spankin' your junk. Don't need to scare the poor girl."

"You know what dick, who gives a fuck? She's on this damn bus, she can fucking get used to it." I roll my eyes at Dex and he gives me a hard stare. "With you around, my curtain is gonna be closed all the time." He runs his tongue over his lips like he tastes something sweet and I want to cringe. So much for my weeping pussy-- I knew I should've rubbed one out before I left this morning. I mean, come on, they're fucking rock stars. Of course they're gonna be hot. Who the hell was I kidding?

"Just keep your dick to yourself, Dex," I tell him but he isn't shaken. I shake my head.

"Come on, Addison, back here." We turn a very short corner then another one headed toward the back of the bus. Immediately ahead of us is a door, closed. Kyle points to it. "That's Talon's room. And this," he points to a black curtain "is our room."

"Our room?" I say, trying not to scream. Of all the people on this bus I have to share a room... oh. He pulls back the curtain and beyond it are two bunks, similar in style to the ones where Dex and them sleep, but these beds are slightly bigger and there is a lot more headroom between each bunk and the ceiling.

"Top or bottom?"

I turn to him. "Huh?"

"Which bunk do you want?"

"Oh." *Jeez, Addie, get your shit together.* "Whichever you don't want."

He rolls his eyes. "I haven't picked one. I knew you were coming, so I wanted to let you choose." Ah sweet...*gag.*

"Um, I'll take the top."

"Good choice." He looks at me; his eyes are on fire with the words I've just spoken, as if I've just agreed to be on top of him. A shiver runs through me and I can feel my nipples harden. *Fucking perfect, my body has a hard-on for the manager and my pussy is crying over Talon.*

chapter 7

I may have had a 7 year dry spell, but I'm not a prude. I'm sure you're probably thinking that right about now, but honestly, I'm not. There's just too much in my history and in my life to make me want to lie down with any man and spread my legs. In fact, I haven't done that in over seven years. The reasons why are unimportant, but after Dan's accident, men just never looked at me the same. Maybe it was because I got my boob job and it brought out the dogs and drooling idiots, or maybe it's because I put out a 'don't touch her' pheromone that drives men away. Who knows and frankly I'm not sure that I cared, until now. Talon is the first man to ever excite me, down there, and well, Kyle is having an impact too and it's unsettling for a girl who's spent seven years working, not fucking.

"Okay, we get a closet. It's small, but there are some hangers in there. Go ahead and put your stuff away, get yourself settled. Mouse will be in shortly and I can introduce you before we all sit down and talk," Kyle says as he turns to leave our tiny space. To call it a room is an understatement. There is no curtain separating my bunk from the world, but there is a curtain separating our shared space from the bus, so I guess that's a good thing, right?

"Alright, thanks." I take a look around. There's some floor space between the side of the bunks and the walls and a good chunk of floor between the curtain and the long edge of the bunks. I notice too that the beds are wider than the ones the guys have and I almost feel guilty taking the wider bunk, leaving bigger guys to sleep in smaller spaces.

The closet is about two feet deep and filled mostly with shelves. There are a couple of drawers.

"Oh, the top two drawers are yours." Kyle says from the entryway before he ducks beyond the curtain. I can hear the guys talking but it is muffled so I can't quite make it out.

Anyway, thankful for drawers and hanging space, I set about emptying my duffle and some of my suitcase. I'd thrown enough clothes into my duffle bag to get me to Vegas tomorrow where we'd be in a hotel. I don't unpack everything, but I do hang up the couple of my dresses I brought along with me, and put my undergarments in the drawers. I don't wear bras much because of the surgery; it's rather unnecessary. I still pass the old pencil test. You know, the one where you put a pencil under your tit to see if it stays or if it falls. Believe me, it falls.

A few minutes later I'm satisfied enough with my progress. I don't know whether or not I'll get back here before the show. I need to chat with the guys, especially Kyle. I need to know what he needs me to do besides my PR job.

I go back into the main cabin of the bus. Dex, Talon, Kyle and Peacock are sitting around the tables in the 'dining room' and the one I haven't met yet is working on his bunk. I come to stand next to him and he stops dead in his tracks, staring at my black peep toe pumps and deep purple nail polish on my toes. I watch, with a smirk, as his eyes slowly slide up my exposed legs in a very slow manner. I roll my eyes and shake my head. I hear a bunch of laughter coming from the couch and I chuckle.

"Forget it, man, she's got iron knees," I hear Dex say.

"Only for you." I tease back at him, resisting the undeniable urge to stick my tongue out at him. My burst at Dex brings on another round of laughter from the guys.

I'm still waiting for Mouse's eyes to finally reach mine or for him to stand up, but instead I watch his palm twitch like he's desperate to touch me as his eyes continue raking up my frame. "Well, what do we have here?" he finally says, and in an instant, I understand why he's called 'Mouse'. His voice is higher than it should be for a man of his size and he sounds a lot like Mickey Mouse. Frankly, I'm surprised he can fit between the bunks and the wall of the bathroom crouched down like he is. I can also tell that he isn't anywhere near as built as the rest of the guys in the band and if I had to guess, he's barely six feet tall and lanky.

Finally his eyes meet mine. "Enjoy the view?" I raise my eyebrows at him, and then watch as he swallows hard, but all he can manage is a slight nod. "I'm Addison." I hold my hand out to shake his and watch as the fire in his eyes smolders briefly then fades away. He stands and I see I was right, he's not that much taller than I am, in fact we're nearly eye to eye, but the four inch heels I'm wearing are helping that.

"Pleasure to meet you," he says with a sly smirk and I fight the urge to roll my eyes.

"She's rather hypnotic, isn't she?" I hear one of the guys say, though I don't know their voices well enough to decipher whether it was Kyle or Talon who spoke.

"You boys seriously need to get laid," I tease them all.

"We're trying," they all spout back in unison and just like that the sexual tension explodes on the bus and I know without a doubt that I'm screwed seven ways from Sunday, big time.

"My eyes are up here, buddy," I say to Mouse and he shakes himself out of his trance.

"Sorry," he says rather sheepishly. "I'm trying to decide which I want to lick more, your slit or that beautiful bust..."

"Jesus, Mouse, knock it off. Y'all are a bunch of damn pigs," I hear someone say, not seeing who said it, but judging by the tone, I'm assuming it's Talon. My judgment is confirmed when he stands up and stalks towards us, grabbing Mouse's shoulder. "Seriously, back off."

"A bit testy, aren't we, mate? Saving her for yourself?" Mouse raises his eyebrows at him.

"No, she's a woman, she's here to do a job and she deserves our respect. She's been on this bus for all of twenty minutes and every single one of us as already eye fucked her at least once. You've had your turn, now shove off. We have a meeting." Talon pushes against Mouse's shoulder.

I smile at Talon's act of chivalry, but I can't say I'm fooled. I sense a hint of jealousy in his push off of Mouse and I wonder exactly where that's coming from. Then again, like he said, they've all tried to eye fuck me since I boarded. For some reason, the idea of them all eye-fucking me sends a thrill through me.

"Alright, boys. Let's get this over with. A few rules." They all take a seat, except for Kyle who remains leaning against the counter in the kitchen. "First of all, I'm not your mother. I won't tell you what to do or when to do it, but if you step out of line, get your dick stuck in something you shouldn't, I will be the first to jump your ass. I am here for your protection and more than anything; I'm here to keep your noses clean and out of the tabloids. Which, based off of my introduction to you all, is going to be more work than I ever imagined." I look at all the guys, whose eyes are pinned on me, but interestingly enough, not on my lady bits.

"I won't get in your way, I'm here to help in any way I can." I look at Kyle when I say that, trying to convey that I will help him with things unrelated to PR work.

Dex lets out a hot whistle. "Except for the pinky between your legs, Dex," I tell him. That garners some whooping from the rest of the guys, but Dex looks pissed. I smirk.

"It ain't no pinky, sweetheart. It's an anaconda," he bites back.

I snort. "Please, any man who refers to his junk as an anaconda obviously has a pinky in there."

He stands up, grabbing his belt buckle. "Want me to show you?"

Kyle pushes him back into his seat. "Knock it off."

"She started it," Dex argues back at him.

"Great, what are we five?" I'm snarky with him. "I am not here to service your dick, Dex. I am here to keep your nose clean and help you make a name for yourself."

"Yeah, whatever," he sulks.

"Look, I know your last guy was an idiot, and for that I'm sorry, but you've got twelve weeks of hell coming up and all I want to do is help make it easier. I'll be working on some sponsorships that will make you guys even more money, but I can't do that if you go off half fucking cocked

44

and blow a good reputation. If you fuck up, it's my ass that has to deal with it. So a little word to the wise, Dexyboy, don't piss me off."

This meeting certainly isn't starting off the way that I wanted it to, but I think I'm getting my point across. "I don't care who, where, when, why or how; you're fucking rock stars and y'all have the same damn reputation. It's inevitable, but wrap your dicks before you stick it. No girls or guys, if that's what you're into, on the bus within two hours of leaving because I will not enjoy dragging them off the bus by their hair. If something happens that I need to know about or that could potentially turn into headline news, you better suck it up and tell me because once it's out there, I can't do anything about it. I can, however, stop it from happening. This means no pictures, no videos and no giving them your phone number and you sure as shit better not give them mine. If one of your little sluts calls my phone, I will have your balls with a side of bacon in the morning. Got it?"

There is a collective 'yes ma'am' that comes out of each of their mouths, but the trance in their eyes is beyond anything I've ever seen before. I have the feeling that if I asked them to lick the floor clean, they would. But it doesn't make me complacent that this is going to be an easy ride.

"I'm not trying to be a bitch, or come down on you guys, but this is your first major nationwide tour. The fans are going to be crazy, the press starving for anything you want to feed them, so unless it is an approved press conference, no talking to the press. In other words, don't feed the animals," I tell them.

They nod their agreement. "I have a question."

I want to roll my eyes because-well shit-because it's Dex. "Yes," I say calmly.

"What happens if we talk, unapproved?" he asks.

I'm impressed, a logical question. I shrug. "Nothing really, depending on what you say. The problem with talking to one reporter verses dozens at a time is that there is no one to corroborate what was said. Your words can be edited or twisted, or god only knows. Reporters are hungry and relentless jerks that will take anything you say and try to twist it around. Remember too that any chick who's trying to crank your chain-," snickers fill the small space, I ignore them, "has the potential to be a reporter."

"Are you trying to scare us straight?" Mouse asks.

I laugh. "Absolutely. They're a waste of time." More laughter and I roll my eyes. "No, Mouse, I'm not. I'm just trying to make you aware of the fact that you're no longer small town boys playing in a bar in the middle of Podunk nowhere. You're famous, you're rich, you're fucking rock stars, and girls will do anything to get you between their legs."

"You sound like you know from personal experience," Kyle says with a rather straight face, but his eyes are wrinkled in the corners, giving me the impression that he's joking around.

"I've been around musicians for more than seven years, some who are extremely famous and some not so much. With the exception of the females, it's a musician's M.O. And when a girl has that much power over someone rich and famous, they're going to do anything." I shake my head. "Look, I didn't mean to turn this into an anti-sex campaign, but the truth of it is that your dicks are what will get you in trouble every time. So please, just watch yourself, and come to me if anything happens that you can't control."

"You got it," Talon says without hesitation.

"Okay, moving on. We have standing reservations in both Phoenix and Albuquerque; I need to know where you guys would like to stay after the Phoenix show Sunday night. If we take off for New Mexico on Monday morning, we'd be there early afternoon and have all day Tuesday and then Wednesday before the show. If we stay in Phoenix, we don't need to leave until Wednesday morning, so I need to know what you'd like to do?"

"Stay in Phoenix," Talon says and everyone else nods.

"Alright, I'll make the arrangements. Now, onto this morning's press conference."

The rest of the meeting lasts another twenty minutes. I give the guys some pointers on dealing with the press and answering questions. After about five minutes of debate, they finally agree that Talon will be the one to call for the questions. Also there is the matter of a large receiving line of fans standing by for autographs. If they decide to sign, take pictures or whatever, then everyone needs to be back on the bus by ten forty-five in order to get out of here by eleven for the two-hour drive to San Diego. The other plus side to being downtown is we should, with any luck, have less traffic to deal with.

chapter 8

The press conference goes off without a hitch. The band spent the better part of an hour answering questions, most of which revolved around their new album and when it will be released. Weirdly, Talon turned to me to answer that question. It was awkward, but I think I handled it pretty well. "Right now their focus is on the tour. Once the tour is over, the band is scheduled in the studio to work on it. Vicious Records will have more details in the coming months." That was my response and by ten I had an email from Trinity congratulating me on fielding the question. She spent a good portion of the email telling me that she knew I was right for the job.

So now we're on the bus. God, I feel like a second grader being on a bus. I haven't done this in a long time and it is going to take some getting used to. We were on the road five minutes before I traded my heels for flip-flops because moving buses and stick heels do not mix well.

We received a police escort out of downtown and down Highway 5 until we were pretty close to Disneyland, which was kind of cool. Through the two-way radio chatter between the two buses and one of the roadies' campers, we learned that there was a line of cars about a mile in length following behind us. It was at this moment that it hit me how big 69 Bottles really is, and the fact that I am shacked up on this tiny forty foot bus for the next twelve weeks with them is mind boggling.

Around noon I received a text from Sam telling me that she and Jess were at the airport and would be taking off in about an hour. She gushed over how cool the plane was and how high class she felt.

An hour after that, just as we were getting close to our destination in San Diego, I got this.

Sam: OMG UR NOT GOING TO BELIEVE WHO JUST BOARDED THIS PLANE!

Me to Sam: I'm going to take a guess that it's Cami.

Sam: AND TRISTAN FREAKIN MICHAELS! THEY'RE COMING TO SAN DIEGO FOR THE CONCERT!!!

Holy Shit! "Kyle!" I shout from my bunk and I hear heavy feet coming down the bus quickly.

"Jesus, woman, what the F?"

"Sorry, momentary panic." I show him the text from Sam.

"You're shitting me?"

I laugh. "I wish I were. What do we have left of the VIP passes?"

"Just use yours," he says.

"I can't."

He looks at me like I'm crazy. "Look, and if you repeat this to anyone I'll make a new hat out of your balls, but my girlfriends and I were supposed to drive down to San Diego today for this fucking concert."

He busts out laughing. "Of all the things I could've pegged you for, a fan certainly wasn't one of them."

"Huge fan," I say deadpan and he all but falls to the floor laughing.

"What's going on in here?"

Shit, it's Talon. "Nothing." I sober quickly but Kyle has no intention.

"Addison's a fan." Oh my god, traitor. I go beet red.

"You weren't supposed to fucking say anything," I bark at him.

Talon just stares and laughs, "I would've never guessed, at least not with the way you were busting everyone's balls earlier. Most fans don't do that."

I laugh. "No, they don't, but while I am a huge fan of your music, I didn't find out until Tuesday that you're a Bold client, let alone the fact that I've never looked at any pictures or really read anything about you guys before coming on board today." He's shocked at my revelation. "I never really have time for personal investigations of rock stars and once I found out about coming on board, I didn't have enough time to get through the packet of information. Besides, I don't like tainted opinions of clients, I'd rather form my own."

Talon smiles and his cheeks turn slightly pink. "So, you're a fan?"

I look him square in the eye. "Huge."

"You want an autograph?"

"Oh my god." I bust out laughing. "Is that how you pick up the chicks?"

"Hey it works, Red, trust me."

I laugh a little more. "I don't doubt it. But no, I don't want an autograph, I'm sure by the time this tour's over I will run away screaming."

"God, I hope not," he says with that sweet sultry voice of his and I want to melt into a pool on my bed. My nipples tighten and once again my pussy moistens with wanton need, a desperate need for Talon Carver.

chapter 9
talon

"So why'd you scream for Kyle?" I ask her; watching her very closely. She's a fucking knockout and I'm almost sorry that I'm not the only one that thinks so.

"Well, I suppose I'll have to explain the whole story now. Thanks, dick," she says to Kyle and I can't help but smile. That seems to be our name for Kyle and in less than five hours she's managed to figure it out already. "Okay, basically this weekend I was supposed to be off, but after you fired your last guy, Bold stepped in and said they would send someone, namely me, so I had to cancel my plans with my girlfriends. However, Cami, my boss's boss and owner of Bold, offered my girlfriends her plane to bring them to San Diego." She blushes. "We were coming down for the concert."

I can't hold in the laughter. "You really are a fan, aren't you?"

"I was," she says completely deadpan.

Her seriousness is a shock. "And why has that changed?" I ask her, completely ignoring the fact that Kyle is standing right next to me.

"Because I have to put up with you for the next twelve weeks." I'll put up with you, sweetheart, up and in. Damn it, Carver, cut the shit.

"Fair enough," I tell her.

"Anyway, after the show we were going to spend the weekend on Coronado and just have some girl time. Well, I had to bail on them, again, and Cami felt bad. So anyway, back to the point, my friends, Sam and Jess, are on the plane waiting for it to take off for San Diego when all of a sudden Cami boards the plane, followed immediately by her husband."

"Oh, and who is that?" I ask; I honestly have no clue. Kyle has managed most of the Bold dealings, hence why he's our manager.

"Tristan Michaels," Kyle chimes in.

I look at Red and back to Kyle. I shrug.

"Holy shit dude, you don't know who Tristan Michaels is? Where have you been the last four years, under a fucking rock? Even I know who Tristan Michaels is," Kyle says standing a little straighter.

I watch as Red rolls her eyes. "Tristan Michaels is one of Hollywood's biggest celebrities, the whole Love is Burning movie phenomenon?"

I curl my lip. "I've heard of those, but…," I shrug. "I'm a dude, chick flicks don't do it for me."

Red laughs. "Well, okay then. Bottom line is that I called Kyle back wondering about remaining VIP passes."

"Just use yours," I tell her.

"And that is the problem. I was going to give them to Sam and Jess, kinda my payback for ditching them this weekend and having to ditch them during the show.

They're fans and they haven't a clue that I'm now working for you guys."

I can't comprehend why she wouldn't tell her girlfriends. "Why not?"

She gives me an exasperated look. "Because I'm not allowed to. They know the drill, so I thought that if I gave them my VIP passes that they'd get over it and figure it out without me actually having to tell them, because I can't," she says with emphasis.

I look at Kyle. "Can we handle getting this Cami and Tristan VIP access?"

Kyle nods his head. "Though I doubt they'll need it. I'm sure you're the only one on the planet who doesn't know who Tristan Michaels is."

I sock Kyle in the shoulder. "Whatever, dude, just get it done."

"Hey guys, we're here," someone shouts from up front.

"Let's get to work," Red says as she hops down off of her bunk at the same time the bus comes to a stop, throwing her off balance and right into my arms.

Fuck, she feels just as amazing as she looks. She's skinny, but she's not bony. Supple and ridiculously sexy as hell; my cock hardens to a point beyond pain. I'm growing a serious case of blue balls right now and it's driving me nuts. Shut up, that was so not intended to be a pun and I'll be dammed if her hip isn't rubbing up against him.

"You all right?" I ask her. Her eyes widen at the sound of my voice that's filled with lust. God, I fucking want to be buried inside her sweet cunt.

"I'm...I'm fine," she stutters and she tries to stand up, but I'm not ready to let her go just yet. My lips twitch with a desperate need to kiss her.

Someone clears his throat and I freeze. Instantly helping her to her feet just in time to see Kyle staring at both of us and for some unknown reason, my eyes travel down to the bulge in his pants that wasn't there before. And that causes my dick to twitch again.

kyle

In all the years I've known Talon, I've never ever seen him look at a woman the way he just looked at Addison and it turned me on. I'm no stranger to admiring men, but Talon? I've never looked at him that way before. Seeing the look in his eyes, looking at her, fucking turned me on and he saw it.

"Let's get to work," I say, desperate to avoid the fact that while Talon helps Addison right herself, he's still looking at me. The look in his eyes is full of something similar to how he was looking at Addison earlier, lust maybe?

chapter₁₀

addison

"Addison?" Talon calls my name from the front of the bus. I, on the other hand, am still trying to get over what happened in the room a few minutes ago. I jumped down, the bus stopped and I fell into Talon's arms and HOLY FUCK! He was hard as a god-damn rock and it was pressing against my hip. But his eyes were alight with lust and my god, his lips twitched with a need to kiss me. Ultimately, the look that was exchanged between Kyle and Talon was beyond anything I have comprehension for. I could spend months analyzing that look, but instead I need to pull up my big girl panties and get to work.

"Be right there," I shout back.

"Hurry up. There's people waiting for you."

What the fuck? "I'm coming."

Oh fuck, that was the wrong choice of words to use, especially after what just happened.

Thank god there is a mirror in our room. I adjust myself and climb back into my heels, fluff my hair and check my make-up, pinch my cheeks and straighten my skirt. If I didn't know better, I'd think I was straightening up after a mid-day sexcapade on a tour bus. I roll my eyes at myself. It might as well have been.

"Get your shit together, Addison. You've been here for like five hours out of twelve weeks," I whisper, then steel myself as I head back to the front of the bus.

When I come around the corner it's just Talon and Kyle with two more members of the men in black patrol. I smile sweetly at them.

"Addison, these are our two main bodyguards. The one on your right is Mills. He's the head of the team who travels with us. He's also responsible for event security coordination among other things. If you have a security problem or question, he is the man to go to," Talon says with a very professional attitude and I'm surprised given what just happened. Is he not as affected by this as I thought I was? Ah, forget it.

"Great to meet you, Mills. I'd ask you for a first name, but I doubt you'll give it to me."

He smiles sweetly. "No, ma'am."

I cringe. "Addison or Addie will be just fine. None of this ma'am crap, I'm not old enough for that and I'm certainly not your boss." I smile just as sweetly at him.

"Yes ma- Addison."

"That's better."

Mills is a good looking man with an obvious military stature. His dark hair is buzzed short and he's easily twice as wide as I am, but he's decent looking none the less with his tanned complexion. If I had to guess, he's Native American or similar. Now the man next to him is someone more in my league. "You are?" I ask him.

"My apologies, Red. This is Rusty. Mills' second in command. If you can't find Mills, you will most definitely find him roaming around."

"It's a pleasure," I say holding my hand out to him. He takes it gently into his. Rusty is attractive with strawberry blonde hair, its skater boy long on top, short all the way around. He has it pulled back in a hair tie. His eyes are a gorgeous blue-ish green color and he, like Talon, has a rather scruffy beard, but it is trimmed nicely. "Okay, I seriously have to ask this, am I the only damn woman around here?"

All four guys laugh. "No," Kyle says. "My assistant Kate is here too, though she's on the other bus with the rest of the crew."

"And us," Rusty says.

"Oh, you guys don't travel on this bus?" I ask.

Talon answers, "When we leave a major city, like tonight when we leave, either Mills or Rusty will be on board with us. The couch-," he turns around and gestures, "folds down into another bed. We try not to use it if we don't have to. The length of the drive determines whether they will stay on board with us or not. Like from here to Vegas, they'll stay."

"I'll be on board tonight," Rusty says with a smile.

Yeah, I bet you will. I smile back at him and Kyle gets us moving along. "We need to finish off loading the equipment. Addison, this would be a great time to catch up on any work you might have to do. I'll come grab you before the sound check."

"Actually, I need to run my passes up to will call. Are the attendants here yet?" The four men look at each other. "Can we find out so I don't walk all the way up there for nothing?"

"Absolutely. I'll send Leroy up there to check. Actually, I can have him drop them off," Mills says.

"Oh, that'd be great."

I write down the details of the order number and names on the tickets. Mills looks at me kinda funny when I give him my name. So I end up explaining the situation to him again. He smiles and Rusty laughs. So much for keeping that between Kyle and I. Everyone seems to know and I'm pretty sure Mouse, Peacock and Dex already know and that means I am never going to live this down.

The men all leave me alone on the bus and for the briefest of moments I debate on doing what I should have done this morning, but in the end I decide against it, better to not have someone walk in on me. The whole curtain closed policy doesn't seem to apply to my room.

I set about checking my email and setting up the Phoenix reservations and cancel the Albuquerque reservations altogether. The drive from Albuquerque to Galveston, Texas, for Friday's show, is about fourteen hours long so we will spend the majority of Thursday driving across Texas. Then Friday, by two in the morning we are back on the road for Dallas. It's a short jaunt up the highway, but it's better to leave earlier when we have a tight schedule.

After about an hour I decide to climb into the shower, not that I need it, but I might as well get ready for tonight. I don't plan on wearing the pencil skirt to the concert. I am going with a modified version of what I was originally going to wear tonight. I'm swapping the 69 Bottles t-shirt I picked up at Hot Topic for my worn out Nirvana t-shirt. Is it wrong to wear a different band's t-shirt to a concert? Hell yes it is, unless it's Nirvana, I mean, come on!

To complete the Nirvana t-shirt, I am wearing a short red plaid skirt with thigh high fishnet stockings held up by a garter belt. Couple that with a matching pair of panties and lace demi cut bra. Oh, did I mention the Nirvana shirt's been modified? The sleeves are gone, which means all my tattooed glory will be on display, well most of it, for the first time. Also the neckline has been cut to enhance my cleavage.

Ironically, for a chick that hasn't slept with a man in over seven years, I sure as hell dress like a rock chick. I'll be completing the ensemble with my black, ten eye, steel toed Doc Martens, studded belt, and bracelets to match.

chapter 11

"Addison, where are you?" Kyle shouts from the front of the bus.

"In our room, but don't come back here. I'll be out in just a minute." I don't want him walking in and I need him to learn some boundaries when it comes to us sharing a room. I don't need to be freaking out that at any minute he's going to come barging in.

"What's going on?" Great! I roll my eyes when I hear Talon followed by a bunch of other male voices streaming back here from the front. "Come on Addison, we got sound checks.'

"Yeah, you know being a fan and all, it's the ultimate high to be in on sound." Fucking Dex. Damn it, I knew everyone would know.

Oh game on! I am so glad I showered, changed, and am dressed and ready to go. Time to go blow their socks off. I'm leaving my hair down, and more or less in it's natural, post washing and air-drying state of curly-messy look. The only reason my hair is currently fire engine red is because of the new dye job. I'm trying to go from platinum blonde to purple, but the best way to get there is to go with red first. So I did. In about a week, I'll turn it purple.

"Hurry up, woman," I hear one of them shout.

"We don't have all day." That would definitely be Mouse.

"Yeah, yeah, keep your dicks in your pants," I shout back. "Show time," I mumble under my breath.

I walk out of my room, feeling like a slow motion shot in a movie. You know the one where the girl is walking down the beach and all the guys are staring and drooling? I leave the curtain open. I suddenly start feeling self-conscious and wondering if it was too early for this unveiling, then I look at my watch and we're less than two hours from show time. Fuck it.

I come around the corner and their reactions say it all. Dex and Kyle fall dramatically to the floor holding their chests. Peacock takes a step back and Mouse and Talon's jaws are hanging on the floor. I do a cute little twirl and Talon takes a seat. Peacock on the other hand shouts, "Rusty, get your ass in here." What the hell?

I hear heavy pounding footsteps outside and then the bus shakes with force as he bounds up the steps. "What?" Then he catches an eyeful of me. I watch him swallow hard.

"Do not let this one out of your sight. You get me?" Peacock orders.

"Yeah," Rusty breathes.

"Don't you boys have a sound check?" I say but nobody moves. "Oh for the love of god. It's not that attractive."

"You keep on kidding yourself there, girlfriend," Dex says as he pulls himself up off of the floor. "I think I had a heart attack."

I roll my eyes. Fucking men. Then again, this is pretty fun. It's been so long since I've had this kind of attention, maybe I should soak it up. Eventually I'll just become one of the guys and it won't matter what I wear to their shows. "I figured I should fit in."

"The problem with you fitting in is that it comes a little too natural for you," Peacock says.

"Well, I was coming to the show anyway, the only thing I changed was the t-shirt."

Kyle snorts a laugh. "Let me guess." He finally pulls himself up off of the floor. "You were planning on wearing a 69 Bottles shirt." I blush. "Uh huh, don't want to look like a groupie, do ya?"

I roll my eyes again. "Whatever. I might have worn it if I hadn't left it at home instead."

"Aww, you break my heart," Dex says. "I design those t-shirts."

I give him a skeptical look.

"No really, he does." Mouse finally finds his voice. "He's wicked good with the graphics. Come on, let's get this show on the road," He says, corralling Dex, Kyle, and Peacock and when he attempts to go for Talon, he backs off.

"I'll be right there," Talon finally manages to say and the rest of the boys disembark the bus. I start to follow behind them but Talon grabs my arm. I look at him. "Of all the things I pegged you for, this,"-he runs his hand from my shoulder to my elbow-"was not it. They're gorgeous."

I smile sweetly at him. "Oh dear Talon, I am a girl of many secrets."

"I'm gathering that." He shifts, winces and stands rather uncomfortably from the couch. He's looking at the ink on my shoulder. Both my arms are three quarter sleeves of various tattoos, mostly flowers, a few Asian symbols, etcetera. He doesn't move, but I can see he's antsy about something. I look up into his eyes and I'm immediately lost.

Swallowing hard, I find my voice, "Are you coming?"

A wicked gleam fills his eyes. "For you?"

I try desperately to avoid the eye roll thing but his banter has broken the spell. "Rehearsal, sound check? Remember?"

"Oh, yeah, give me a minute. Oh and Red?"

"Yeah?"

"Don't ditch Rusty tonight. Please."

"Why, aren't we a tad over protective?" I try to say it sweetly but it comes out a little more snarky than I intended.

"It's not my fault if you don't see yourself clearly, Addison."

He releases my arm, shakes off his trance and walks straight for his room at the back of the bus. I hear the door slam. "What the hell was that all about?" I mumble.

"Don't worry about him."

I turn quickly to see Kyle standing at the top of the stairs. "I just don't get it."

He shrugs. "I do."

I look at him again, this time a little closer. "I'm still trying to figure out where I know you from."

He gives me a half smile. "You don't know me directly, Addison, but I'm sure you know of me."

I cock my head. "Care to explain?"

He shakes his head. "That conversation is meant for a six pack and another time." He gives me a sweet smile, which tells me to let it go, for now. "Come on."

"I'll be right behind you." I look back toward the back of the bus. "Give me a minute. I owe someone an apology."

"Alright." Kyle descends the stairs and hops off of the bus. I go to the back.

When I come to Talon's door, I knock gently.

"What do you want, Addison?"

"How'd you know?"

He opens the door and he's standing there, shirtless and I can't breathe. His body is all sinewy muscle, well defined abs, gorgeous pecs and dark brown nipples. Not to mention a light smattering of hair right on his breast bone and a beautiful happy trail that disappears into his jeans right along with the well-formed V coming from his hips.

"Most of the guys pound."

"What? Oh, right." My eyes are still traveling downward, down to the massive bulge in his jeans.

"What do you need, Red?" Now we're back to that again.

"I..." I finally look up into his eyes and that burning desire is there once again and I'm lost to it, lost to him, momentarily forgetting what I came to say.

He pulls his hand off of the door jamb and gently brushes the back of his fingers along my cheek. His touch is warm and soft, leaving goosebumps in its wake. I reach up to hold his hand there and close my eyes. Desire I haven't felt in a very long time bursts across my entire body. I've got to get out of here, away from him. "I came to apologize."

"For what?" That sweet, sexy sultry tone is back and once again I find my clit hardening, screaming for attention, desperate to be licked.

I shake it off as best as I can. "For being a bitch," I breathe.

I open my eyes slowly and he's smiling. "I'd hardly call that being a bitch and I meant what I said, you don't see yourself clearly."

With that, he pulls his hand away from my cheek and he straightens. He's calm and collected and all I want to do is melt into a puddle at his feet. Surrender myself to him, but I get the feeling that might not be what he wants.

"Go ahead; I'll be right behind you. I just need a minute."

I pout and nod as he closes the door.

I stand there for a moment before I finally turn and leave the hallway and step off of the bus. When I do, my pal Rusty is standing there waiting for me. I shake my head. "He's really gonna make you shadow me tonight, isn't he?"

He laughs. "Yeah, he is. Come on."

"This is truly ridiculous, you know that, right?"

He shrugs. "Maybe, but from what I understand you gave those boys a pretty stern lesson in keeping their dicks in their pants, I'd imagine they, in their own way, are doing the same for you. Though in this case, keeping the dicks out of you."

I snort a laugh and let it go. Rusty escorts me into the building, despite the fact that the area surrounding the bus is fenced off and hidden from prying eyes. I don't think the guys are gonna give up on me so easily, at least not tonight. I wonder momentarily that if I were to go change my clothes if I could ditch my detail. I feel like I'm twelve, walking with my friends through the mall while my mom shadows behind me.

We come in the back door of the arena that we're playing tonight. It's not the stadium by any means, but it is still a good size facility with a twenty-five thousand capacity. From back here I can hear the strums of a bass booming through the speakers and I know that Peacock is working his magic on those strings. When we come around to the stage all eyes turn to me once again.

"Seriously? Would you all feel better if I changed?" Overprotective fools.

"Yes." I hear more than three say yes at the same time, including Rusty and a voice behind me. I turn to see Talon walking toward me. He seems to have donned some type of stony faced mask since I left him in the bedroom on the bus. Either that or this is just his game face.

"You'll hear better in front of the stage, Red, why not go up there?" I smile at him and nod. Rusty escorts me through a door that leads to the floor of the arena, past the barricades that have already been set up.

I hear Dex pounding away on his drums and Mouse is tuning up his guitar. I don't have to turn and look, I can just tell. Rusty leads me to about the halfway point across the floor before he stops, turns around, and points at the floor. I walk to the spot and turn around. Rusty isn't far behind me, but he slips into the shadows giving me the impression of being alone. Anticipation courses through me as I realize that America's hottest alternative rock band is warming up, and about to run a sound check. A thrill runs through me and my skin is covered in goosebumps as I watch the chaos on stage morph into something sexy and coordinated.

Then, out of nowhere I hear the strains of my favorite song. It's not even their biggest hit, if it's even been a hit, but it's a damn good song, and a love song at that. Well, that's my interpretation of it anyway.

*chapter*12

The guys continue to play and I can hear some adjustments being made to speakers and to the playback to the guys because every once in a while one of them will fall behind. After about three or four minutes of just playing the melody of my favorite song, called Your Eyes. They start again, this time Talon steps up to the microphone and my heart starts pounding. It's one thing to listen to your favorite band on their perfectly recorded album version of a song, but it is something else entirely when it is being played live, in front of you, and for you alone.

The beat picks up and I watch as Talon closes his eyes and when they open, they're smoldering and boring right into me.

Your eyes
Are like nothing I've ever known
Nothing I've ever seen
They bring be here
They bring me home

Your eyes
Are all I can see.

His voice is amazing. Perfect in pitch and my heart melts, my nipples harden, my clit throbs and I'm ready to fall to the floor and jam my hand down my skirt and start fingering myself. Fuck, this is hot and I can tell that Talon can see it too.

To try and stop myself from doing the unmentionable in the middle of this nasty arena floor, I start to dance. Closing my eyes and soaking up his voice. It's a beautiful cross between Daughtry and Scott Stab all rolled into one beautiful sex god package.

A couple of times I catch myself peeking at Talon and he hasn't taken his eyes off of me the entire time. Then the next thing I know, Kyle is standing with me. "Dance with me," he whispers and I look to Talon whose expression hasn't changed. I have this deep-seated, unknown, need to seek out his permission and I don't understand why. Then he grins behind his microphone and I have all the answer I need. I take Kyle's hand and he pulls me into his arms. I sneak a peek at Talon as Kyle spins me around again and his smile grows a little wider. The sultry look in his eyes is there, his voice changes to be more lust filled as Kyle and I begin to dance. The look Talon is giving the two of us reiterates to me that the look on the bus was real. Then a surge of something I can only describe as fear races through my veins. There is something going on between the two of them and I am stepping in the middle of it.

The song draws to a close with the same verse it opens with and I shiver in Kyle's arms as pleasure and desire wreak havoc on me.

"Not many people pay much attention to this song," Kyle says as the band makes some adjustments.

"I love this song. It's one of my favorites of theirs." I smile at Kyle.

"It's not in their set, but it's a great warm up song for them."

"Well, it should be in their set. Especially if he's capable of looking like that. He'll make the girls go nuts." I pull back from him, the fear a moment ago racing through me again. I don't want to upset Talon, if there really is something going on between the two of them.

Kyle grins at me. "I'm pretty sure that look was just for you."

"Really, because it got a little hotter when we started dancing."

Kyle freezes. "It did?" he breathes.

"Is there something going on between the two of you that I should know about?" I try to tease, but it comes out more accusatory than I'd planned. I watch as Kyle just shakes his head. "Do you want there to be?"

"I... Oh hell, Addison, I barely know you and you want to discuss this with me?"

I smirk and shrug. "I couldn't help but notice your exchange on the bus earlier, when he caught me."

Kyle runs his hand through his shaggy blonde locks then rubs at his chin. "Honestly?"

I give him a shoulder shrug, going for nonchalance. "Always," I say.

"That had more to do with you in his arms than anything. The spark between the two of you was pretty hot," he says with a blush to his cheeks.

"Am I embarrassing you?" I ask him, surprised by my own candor.

Then watch as he shakes his head. "I'm just, uh, not usually so open and forward."

"I have a tendency to bring that out in people. Sorry," I tell him, but it's more of a sorry, not sorry kinda thing. I like that he's being honest with me, but yet I feel a stab of disappointment at the fact that it had more to do with me than Talon. Why is that so disappointing. *Because if they're into each other, then they're certainly not into you.* And just like that, all the years of insecurities come flooding back. "Excuse me for a minute." I back away quickly and head back toward the door Rusty brought me through, desperately looking for a bathroom. I find one quickly and duck inside.

talon

"You need to add that song to your set," Kyle tells me as we're wrapping up so that the opening band, Empty Chamber, can set up for tonight and run their checks and warm up.

"Why would we do that? It's like the red-headed step child of songs," I tell him with a glare. Is he kidding me right now? The set has been in place for weeks, now he wants to change it?

Kyle laughs at me and immediately I understand why. God, I just sang that damn song to her like it was written specifically for her. "It's her favorite song," he says back.

"Well, isn't that fucked up."

Kyle snorts. "Well, it's a damn good song and if you perform it with the same heat and excitement in your eyes, you'll have all the girlies eating out of the palm of your hand."

No need to state the fact that the only girlie I want eating out of my hand is Addison, then again, I think Kyle knows that. The moment she stepped onto the bus, she posed a challenge to me, without actually throwing down the gauntlet. Women, to me, are best when they're available for a couple hours, and gone by morning. It works better that way, no strings, no bullshit, and none of that sappy shit. Not my style.

But fuck, when they were dancing like that? A spark of lust runs up my spine just thinking about what I saw from the stage. There is something about watching the two of them together. I find myself drawn to both of them for some unknown reason, and again, my cock is throbbing thinking about it. I don't know whether I should be running to it, or away from it.

Needing a change of subject I ask him, "Where'd she go anyway?"

He shakes his head and shrugs, "No clue, one minute she was there, we were talking and the next she was running off."

"What the hell did you say to her?" My voice is angry and I'm surprised by it.

"Nothing, Jesus, T, chill. I didn't say anything to her. We were talking about honesty and my being so forthcoming with her, then she kinda locked up and ran."

Kyle and I keep talking as we clear off the last of our stuff to make room for EC to set up. But I notice we both keep looking for her, waiting for her to come back.

Finally Rusty comes out. "Dude, where is she?" I snap at him.

"Chill, dude. She's back on the bus, said she wanted to be alone. I left Leroy outside in case she decides to come back in."

Kyle and I both look at each other. "Should we talk to her?" Kyle asks the same question running through my mind. Then he answers his own question. "I think that she's a little overwhelmed, let her be."

I nod in agreement then get pulled away by Adrian, our sound guy and a couple of the roadies with some questions. By the time things are finally straightened out, we're less than an hour from show time and the doors are about to open.

"I'm going back to the bus," I holler at the guys milling around the stage bullshitting with the guys from Empty Chamber. They can go to the bus or the greenroom, where they stay is up to them, I need my personal space. Despite years of doing this gig, the last hour before a show is always my worst. I'm not the puking type, but sometimes I feel like I end up rocking in the fetal position sucking my thumb. Figuratively speaking, of course. They know the drill once the doors open and by the sounds of things as I step back off the stage, I got off the floor just in time, the other guys scramble quickly off the stage and the lights go out.

When I reach the bus, alone, Rusty is stationed out front. "She still in there?"

"Yup, hasn't come out, said anything or really moved around much from what I can tell, but Leroy said she was in there so I just let it go."

"Shit," we hear from the bus. Both Rusty and I turn toward the bus, and I take off, hitting just one of the three steps into the bus.

When I clear the wall separating the stairs and the kitchen, she's sitting at the table, her laptop in front of her, untouched. "You alright?" I ask her, waving Rusty back off

73

the bus, he'd damn near slammed into me when I stopped so fast.

She looks at me, Jesus, she's fucking gorgeous. Who knew that the prissy girl in a pencil skirt had such beautiful ink hiding underneath her blouse? When I saw her in that damn outfit, I couldn't move. I was floored and then I was a little pissed because I had no right to be turned on by it for one, and for two, if I had it my way, there's no way she would have been wearing that.

"Yeah, just burnt my hand." She waves her hand back and forth. "It's not bad, just that initial contact burn." She looks at me and scowls, "Why aren't you inside with everyone else?"

I chuckle. "I came back here to check on you."

"Oh, um, I'm fine. Security detail and all, just hungry. You want some?"

"No, I don't eat before shows. It's a waste. I'll just puke it up. Then feel like shit because I ralphed." What the ef? Where the hell did that come from?

"Ah, gotcha. I'll remember that for next time. Feed you sooner. Got it." She has this puzzled, 'what did I just say' look then she turns back to the stove.

"What are you making anyway?"

She laughs. "Um, mac n' cheese."

I laugh with her. "That's my favorite."

chapter 13
addison

Okay, mac n' cheese added to his list of favorite foods, check. Wait a damn minute, why am I making a mental list of his favorite foods? I roll my eyes at myself. He doesn't stick around while I eat. I feel awful that he can't eat before a show and wish there was some way I could help take the edge off. I noticed as the time passed, sitting here with me while I waited for my food to cook, and the show got closer, he got really fidgety. When I tried to talk to him about it, he just brushed it off.

69 Bottles has played some of the bigger music festivals before going on this tour so I don't know if the size of the audience has anything to do with it. I shrug it off. Something to ask him about later. Here I go again, assuming him and I will ever have that kind of conversation.

I can't believe I got all personal and shit with Kyle earlier and more than that, for the first time in years I was struck down by my insecurities and damn it, I hate that. I haven't felt that insecure about myself since before the boob job. But there is definitely something brewing between Kyle and Talon, I'd just like to know what. It's not like they're new to each other. Kyle's been with them since the beginning. He met Talon in college or some shit like...

SON OF A BITCH!!!

I run to the front of the bus and down the steps, straight into the arena and Rusty is hot on my tail. "Dang, girl. What's on fire?" he shouts from behind me.

I clear the back door and the person I need to talk to is dead ahead of me, being overly flirtatious with a chick wearing less clothes than I am. Time to cockblock.

I stride up to Kyle and place my arm around his waist. "Hey baby," I say in the sexiest voice I can manage.

He looks at me, shocked, then back to the girlfriend. "Hi," he says hesitantly.

"I was waiting for you on the bus and you never came."

The blonde bimbo huffs and stomps off. I can't stop the snort.

"Now what in the hell was that all about? So not fair, you cockblocked me."

I laugh. "I need to talk to you. Outside, please?"

"Now? The shows gonna start."

"Oh my god, are you actually whining?" I cross my arms over my chest.

He pouts. "Maybe a little. You cockblocked me."

"She probably has rabies. You'll get over it." I take his hand and lead him back toward the back door, we pass by Rusty. "He's with me, I'm covered and I need to talk to him, alone."

He nods in acknowledgment as I crash through the back door, scaring the shit out of the door guy. "Sorry," Kyle says.

As soon as we're some distance away from the door I let go of his hand and turn on him. "Why didn't you tell me?"

He looks shocked. "Tell you what, Addison?"

"Who you are?"

"Huh?" He has a genuine look of surprise on his face, but yet I'm still not buying it.

"Don't give me that shit, Kyle Black! You know damn well what I'm talking about."

"Bad timing...?" He says with a shrug of his shoulders, the shocked face is gone, replaced by sadness. Something is flitting in his eyes. Fear, maybe?

"It's worse now because standing in the middle of that bus it hit me like a ton of bricks. I don't see how I couldn't see it before."

"Aw come on, Addison, you've never met me before, how could you have known?"

"But damn it, Kyle, you have his eyes. You look just like him in some ways, but my memory is tainted and fuzzy."

"Shit, Addison, I'm sorry. I hoped you'd never figure it out." He looks so sad. "I really didn't want you to figure it out and I'm not sure I could've brought myself to ever tell you." His voice drops to a whisper, "I didn't want it to come between..." He trails off. His lips move, but I can't quite make out what he's said.

I try to give him a half smile but fail. Tears are forming in my eyes and I know that if I blink, they'll run over. I try to look up to the night sky, but I can't and the tears spill over. The next thing I know I'm wrapped up in the warmth of his arms. "Jesus, I'm so sorry. I should have, I could have..."

"Addison, stop. Please don't cry. It's not a big deal."

"He was your brother, Kyle. How on earth can you say that?"

"Because it was an accident, and accidents happen. I've moved on with my life."

"Did you know who I was when I showed up this morning?"

I feel him shake his head in a silent no. "It wasn't until after I saw you face to face and your bright green eyes that I knew who you were. Mom still has a picture of you and Dan on the fireplace." He takes a deep breath and I don't know how to respond to him. The idea that his mom still has our pictures on display is unsettling. "Look, this really isn't the time or place to talk about this, but I promise you, we will talk about it. Soon."

I nod into his shirt, praying like hell my make-up isn't bleeding all over onto his white shirt. When I pull back I notice that it's not and I'm thankful. I look up into his eyes, "Promise?"

"Absolutely," he tells me with a sweet yet sympathetic smile. "But I need a promise in return."

"Anything," I blurt before I can think twice about it.

"I hoped you'd say that." He gives me a devilish smile. "Promise me that you will keep me and Dan separate in your mind."

I smile. "That I can do, but I still need that talk."

"You got it, I promise, but I have to have the separation because I am not him."

"I know that. It's just…" I brush away a stray tear from my cheek, "I…" I can't finish my thought. I see fear in his eyes, like he's afraid that his relationship to my ex-fiancé is going to have an impact on whatever may be developing between us. I can feel it, deep down, I'm drawn to him and I can't understand why. I pray it's not because of Dan.

"I promise, okay, I don't break promises easily and now that you know, it will be a little easier for me to talk to you about it, but I need some time, okay?" I nod. "Okay, take a deep breath." I do. "Now let's go rock." He grabs my hand and pulls me back into the arena.

We're not inside but a couple of minutes when I duck around the wall to see the VIP area and sure enough, mingling together are Cami, Tristan, Jess and Sam. I look around for Rusty and he of course is right on my heels. "I'm going out there."

"I wouldn't if I were you."

I turn to him and say, "Well, my boss, along with her husband and my two best friends are out there, try and stop me. Oh and call for Leroy, have him slide over here when he gets a chance."

Rusty's eyebrows scrunch up in confusion. I roll my eyes and mouth a whiny 'please; and he melts like butter in my palm then jerks his head toward the door, signaling for me to go. I double check myself, make sure that I have my security badge and then step through the door. The minute Jess and Sam see me they squeal so loud that Tristan playfully covers his ears. I laugh.

"What the hell, why didn't you tell us?" I get the immediate third degree from Jess and look over her shoulder at Cami who winks at me.

"You know better than that, I couldn't and technically speaking I still haven't told you."

Sam laughs. "No, Cami told us." I shake my head and smile, wrapping my girls into a three way hug.

I look right at Cami and say, "Thanks."

"Absolutely." I let the girls go and move to stand in front of Cami. "Nice ink." Oh crap. I subconsciously rub my arms, I've never exposed my ink at work before. "Stop," she says, "now look at me." I do, between my lashes, "I don't care. It's the clients who care and I gather your boys don't mind?"

"Uh, you could say that. I think I caused at least one heart attack already today."

"I heard you put on quite the show at the press conference and then a little birdie told me that you put these boys in their place."

I laugh. "I tried. I guess only time will tell. We're,"-I look at my watch, 7:50-"thirteen hours into this wild adventure, so we'll see."

She laughs then settles. "I'm being very rude, I apologize. Addison, this is Tristan, my husband."

I extend my hand. "It's an honor to meet you, Tristan."

"Likewise." He jerks his thumb toward the girls. "They're quite entertaining and speak very highly of you." I fight a blush. "I agree with Cami, great ink."

"Oh, thank you. It's not all I have."

"Oh?" he says curiously. I hesitate for a moment and decide to say fuck it and I turn around, lifting my Nirvana tee and hear their collective gasps. "Wow, Addison, that's, wow, that's amazing work."

"Huh? Seems like wings run in this circle a little more commonly than I thought," Cami says with a conspiratorial smirk as I turn around. I notice that standing directly behind the two of them is another man, a man I've seen a lot around Bold. But I get no introduction. By the way he's standing so close to Tristan and Cami, the black ensemble combined with the bulge of a weapon that he's wearing is a dead giveaway that Rusty isn't the only bodyguard standing here.

I give her a puzzled look and she turns around, displaying for me her own black and purple wings on her back. Though mine have been done only in black and various shades of grey and attached to a fairy between my shoulder blades, hers are vibrant with color. "Wow. That's amazing work."

"Tristan has dragon wings on his back." I look at him and he smiles, but it seems like that's something that's private to him so I don't push for him to show me. I look again at the guy behind the two of them. He doesn't exactly make me nervous, but curious, not to mention that fact that he's ridiculously good looking. Cami notices my glance and chuckles. "Tyson, this is Addison Beltrand, she's one of mine."

He holds out his hand, but his eyes are ever moving, I take his hand. "Nice to meet you, Addison."

"Likewise, Tyson." I smile sweetly at him.

"Tyson is Tristan's bodyguard."

I smile at the three of them, "I figured as much."

Cami smiles back, "Listen, have they decided about whether they're staying in Phoenix or Albuquerque?"

"They want to stay in Phoenix."

She smiles. "That's great. How about we have you for dinner Monday night? We live in Phoenix and we'd love to have you over."

I'm so taken aback by the request that I don't know what to say. "Just say you'll be there. She'll take care of the rest," Tristan whispers in my ear.

I smile. "I'll be there."

"Perfect." Just then the opening act takes the stage and the crowd gets crazy, making it impossible to talk.

I turn to the girls. "I have to go. Enjoy the show. Come back stage when you're done." They both nod and start rocking out to Empty Chamber. "See you after the show," I shout to Cami and Tristan, they both nod and smile. Just as I turn around Leroy comes to stand in front of me.

"Leroy," I hear Cami squeal and watch as Leroy's face lights up. I put my hand to his shoulder reassuringly and slip out of the VIP area.

Rusty leans into my ear. "Is that who I think it is?"

I laugh. "Yes."
"And you know him?"
I shake my head. "No, his wife is my boss."
"Oh shit," he says shocked.
"Yeah, pretty much."

*chapter*14

Empty Chamber rocks the stage for twenty-five minutes and I have to admit they are pretty good and I don't mind the fact that they're joining us on this western part of the tour. They'll be with us through Albuquerque, then we pick up another band in Galveston who is scheduled to stay with us through Miami, which is toward the end of the tour.

Backstage is a madhouse of activity as Empty Chamber sings their last song. Now comes the switching of gear for 69 Bottles. The crowd is completely pumped up as they round out their song. The lead singer thanks San Diego for being awesome and tells them to hold tight because the band they've really come to see is coming on shortly and just like that the great switch begins.

Empty Chamber is pretty small time because most of our roadies along with the band members are clearing their own gear. It's rather humbling to see when our roadies are doing everything and the boys are still lounging in the greenroom. Or they were.

"Here we go," Kyle whispers in my ear and the butterflies start kicking up. "Are you excited?"

"I'm stoked," I say to him as I watch the band walk through the hallway toward the stage. It's like watching a slow motion movie, the only thing missing is the fog. Dex is in the lead, followed by Peacock and then I'm assuming Mouse because there's too big of a gap between him and Talon.

Dex saunters right up to me and tries to wrap his arms around me. "What are you doing?" I squeak.

"I need a good luck kiss."

"Pfft." Before I can protest he lands a big wet sloppy kiss on my lips.

"That's what I'm talking about." He laughs as he pulls back and I want to gag.

"Seriously, Dex." I wipe the slobber off my lips.

"Thanks, love, that's what I needed." Just as quick as it came on, he walks away and on stage.

Peacock and Mouse look at me as if they want to do the same thing. "What am I, the good luck charm?"

"Yes," They say in unison.

"Oh, for crying out loud. Come here." I spread my arms wide and they both come in, wrapping their arms around me and in unison they both plant a kiss on my cheeks. "Break a leg, boys," I say when they let me go, though Mouse lingers a little longer and I can hear Dex laughing from the stage. I look at him, point my finger and mouth, "This is your fault." He busts out laughing again and takes his seat behind his drum set.

Kyle comes up behind me, wrapping his arms around my waist. It feels comforting and just like that my butterflies are gone. Now Talon is standing before me. "You need one too?"

"Of course." He smiles. I open my arms and he steps forward. Kyle doesn't release my waist, but Talon doesn't seem bothered by what Kyle's doing.

Talon surprises the shit out of me when he takes my face between his hands. His fingers dig into my hair and I can feel Kyle stand a little straighter, his erection pressing into my backside. Talon slides himself closer, pressing his own erection into me from the front and just like that, his lips slant against mine.

My heart skips and my breathing stutters. My entire body goes limp in their embrace. I'm thankful for Kyle behind me, holding me. That is until I feel his lips press against the hollow of my neck and everything else in the world fades away. My lips go slack and Talon steals his chance, sliding his tongue along mine.

I'm melted butter in his hands and I pray this kiss doesn't end; I don't want it to end, ever. My nipples are hard peaks against my bra, my pussy is dripping with desperate need, and my clit feels like it's going to explode. I want to grind my hips against the two men who've captured me in their grasp. But before I can savor every touch, Talon pulls back. "That was, wow," I say breathless from his kiss and their joint hold on me.

He steps back, watching me closely. Then he steps back again and again, finally turning around for the stage as Dex strikes his drums and the crowd goes wild the moment Talon steps onto the stage and the lights explode.

"Where's my kiss?" Kyle murmurs in my ear.

I turn in his arms and he brings his lips to mine. His kiss is equally as breathtaking and heart stopping, but I feel strangely naked without Talon here. Kyle turns me ever so slightly and I can see Talon looking at us with an extremely sexually charged smile.

There is something comforting in that smile, something that tells me that he's enjoying Kyle kissing me as much as I am.

Kyle pulls back and there is a look in his eyes; a look that says that there is nothing he won't do to have me. It takes everything I have not to grab him and drag him back to the bus. Just get it out of our system so that we can work on this tour, but I have a feeling that won't be enough, for me, for Kyle, and it just might make Talon jealous.

Talon and the band finish up their first song. Talon works the crowd, introduces the band and thanks his crew, including Kyle and myself by name. He looks straight at me and Kyle when he says it then encourages us to say hi to the crowd. I fight the blush and step out onto the edge of the stage with Kyle and we both wave.

"Without these two, we wouldn't be here," he says and the crowd gets impossibly loud. It's hardly the truth. I've done nothing to get this tour off the ground. That's been Kyle and probably the one they fired. But I think it's his way of showing me some affection the best way he knows how.

Once we're out of sight of the crowd I turn to Kyle, "I don't feel right taking that kind of credit."

"Suck it up, buttercup. I think it's an expression of appreciation for today, tonight and going forward. You'll keep him in line."

I snort. "I doubt that."

"I don't," he says very seriously.

"What do you know that I don't?" I ask him.

"Nothing."

"I'm calling bullshit, Kyle."

"Look, I don't know much, other than the fact that he's really into you. I've known him a long time and I've never seen him like this." He says with confidence, but I can't help thinking that this isn't going to be the case in a couple of weeks. I'm a cynic, what can I say?

"I'm not the only one in this equation."

"What are you talking about?"

"Oh come on, he kissed me the way he did while you were holding on to me. You made your own advances and he didn't shove you away. Are you really that dense?" I ask him serious.

"No, I'm not, but it doesn't mean he wants me. It could just be the idea of him with you, or the fact that he likes to watch."

I shake my head, "You know what? We could sit here and assume all we want. It's not going to make this any easier."

"Good point," he says just as the band strikes up with 'Your Eyes'.

"You said this wasn't in their set." I look toward the stage at Talon and he's looking at me with that same look in his eyes he had earlier. He only keeps his eyes on me for a moment then he turns to the crowd and there is a collective increase in volume from the ladies in the crowd.

"It wasn't, but I told him he should add it and that look is the key to turning all the women in the arena into putty. It worked. But I think he's really singing it for you."

"Stop that." I bump shoulders with him. He doesn't say anything. "Kyle, are you jealous?"

"Ohmygod. No."

"Oh my god, you're so full of shit."

He shrugs. I roll my eyes and go back to enjoying my song. Then Kyle wraps his arms around me, leaning down to rest his chin on my shoulder and he starts swaying both of us to the music. There is something strangely comforting about his embrace and I sink back into him, letting him sway me to the beat.

chapter 15

The rest of the concert goes off without incident. The crowd was extremely wound up when they came off stage the first time, the crowd went crazy demanding more. Talon looked at me with a big shit eating grin on his face. I nodded and his face lit up as he called the boys back. They returned to the stage for two more songs. I felt an overwhelming sense of pride as I watched the boys play their first encore. It was amazing.

When the guys come off the stage for the final time, they all have the most inspiring grins on their faces. Talon comes straight for me, wrapping his arms around me in a massive hug. "Thanks, Red."

"For what?"

"Being an amazing good luck charm."

I laugh. "Anytime."

"You realize I'm going to have to kiss you every night before we take the stage, right?"

I shake my head. "I'll be here."

"Good. Come to the greenroom." He pulls back from his hug.

"I have guests out front, remember?"

"Oh, that's right. Bring them by."

"Alright, we'll be back in a bit." Just like that Talon follows the rest of the guys back to the greenroom and the amount of VIPs coming through the door is increasing. I shoo Kyle off to the greenroom with the guys and wait for Sam, Jess, Cami and Tristan.

Thankfully it doesn't take them long to make it back.

"Oh my god, Addison, that was amazing." Jess and Sam schmooze as soon as they see me. I smile and hug them.

"You enjoyed the show?"

"Hell yes, we did. I'm buying tickets for the LA show," Jess says.

"No, I'll bring you guys in for the LA show."

"Ohmygod Addie, you're the best," Sam squeals.

I can see Cami and Tristan standing back. "You guys want to meet them?"

Cami is bouncing with excitement. "She's such a fangirl," I hear Tristan say.

"That's a little hard to believe," I tease.

"Well, except when it comes to me." He grins a secret smile that rivals Talon's panty melting grin.

Cami bumps her shoulder into Tristan. "I fangirl over you, I just don't show it, besides, you're mine so I can fangirl in private all I want."

Tristan laughs.

"Alright, follow me," I say and lead them into a room next to the greenroom. Once they're inside I turn to them. "Get comfortable. I'll bring them here. I'm sure Tristan would enjoy his privacy; that room is already crawling with fans. Sam and Jess, you wanna stay here or go next door?"

They both turn to Tristan and Cami. "We don't want to intrude."

"Nonsense, stay here, then when we're done, we're going to leave to avoid the crazies from attacking Tristan," Cami says.

"Okay, we'll stay here for now," Sam says. I nod and leave the room, almost running straight into Tyson who has taken up residence outside the door. I smile at him and he returns it. God, he's really hot. Then I catch the glimmer of a ring on his left hand and I want to pout. The good ones are always taken.

When I recover from my near collision with Tyson, I notice that there is a line out the door for the greenroom and I bypass them all and walk right in, right past Leroy and Beck. The sight before me is definitely one to see. The guys are sprawled out on the couches with girls groveling at their feet. The overwhelming need to roll my eyes overruns my initial irritation and jealousy over the girls climbing all over Talon. I have no right to be jealous.

"Red?" Talon says over one of the girls, looking straight at me.

"I need you guys."

"For?"

"Super VIPs," I say back and he nods.

"Guys?" He gives them a nod toward the door and the guys get the hint. They unwind themselves from their perspective hoard or the night's conquest, depending on what you want to call them. They all come to stand next to me.

I lean into Beck who bends and brings his ear close to my lips. "We have Tristan Michaels and his wife next door. The boys are going over there to say hello, shoot the shit for a few minutes and then come back."

"Roger," he says and sets about parting the masses surrounding the doors. "Ladies. Step back. The guys will be right back." There is a collective sigh from the ladies but when they realize the guys are walking past them they get excited again.

We manage to make our way through the body parts and women trying to throw themselves at the band members. I want to smack some sense into each one of them. When we come to the door, Beck and Leroy take up their posts on either side, right next to Tyson. They're quickly joined by Rusty, who's been following me around like a lost little puppy all night and finally Mills joins them. I open the door; and the guys duck inside. I was going to wait outside, but Talon grabs my hand as he passes, pulling me in behind him.

Jess and Sam are bouncing up and down and I can see immediately that Dex has his eyes all over Sam. I want to cockblock again, but I can't right now. "Gentlemen, this is Cami and Tristan Michaels," I point to each of them, respectively. "Tristan and Cami, this is Talon, Dex, Peacock, and Mouse." Again pointing out each one.

"Excellent show," Tristan says, putting his hand out for Talon to take.

"Thanks, that means a lot coming from you. We're glad you guys could make it." Talon is very polite and professional as he takes Cami's hand. "And you, thank you for sending Addison to us, she's been an amazing asset so far."

Cami looks to me and I shrug. Cami smiles. "We couldn't think of anyone better. I hope she continues to be. You guys put on one hell of a show. I understand you're in Phoenix on Sunday?"

"We are. Looking forward to it."

"Great. We live in Phoenix and Addison tells me you're leaving on Wednesday?"

"Uh, I think that was the plan. It's been a crazy day," Talon says.

"Yes, we're leaving early Wednesday for Albuquerque." I interject.

"Great, then let us have dinner Tuesday evening," Cami says to Talon but looks around to the rest of the guys. "We can send Addison the details."

Talon looks to me before telling Cami, "You'll have to check with our manager, but I imagine we will be free for dinner." Talon smirks at me.

Cami laughs. "It's a date then."

I get around to introducing Jess and Sam a few minutes later. The eye fucking between Sam and Dex has me paranoid, but I decide that Sam is a grown woman and she can make her own decisions. Talon and Tristan seem to hit it off and Cami takes up tattoo conversations with Peacock and Mouse.

After about ten minutes, Cami and Tristan say their good-byes and Dex is quick to drag Sam and Jess back into the greenroom. The women in the hallway have grown in numbers since we left the room. As we walk through the throng, I remind Talon that we have a scheduled kick off after party to get to. He in turn promises to get through the hoard quickly and they do. Sam doesn't leave Dex's side and Jess seems to have taken to Peacock, and it irritates me. For fuck's sake. It's like I've brought them their own personal buffet of girls and I hate feeding the animals.

chapter 16

I'm waiting outside with Rusty, Kyle, Mouse and Talon when the town cars show up to take us to the after party. Dex and Peacock come out of the venue with Sam and Jess in tow and I'm surprised. They don't say anything to me, they're too busy chatting with their 'dates', for lack of a better description.

We pile into the cars and it doesn't take us more than ten minutes to get to the bar where the party is being held. When we pull up, there is a mountain of reporters and screaming girls standing outside.

My car has myself, Rusty—of course—and Kate, Kyle's assistant. She isn't exactly the type of girl you'd picture running around the country with a bunch of rockers. She's very shy and for lack of a better word- virginal. She's about five four with blond hair and she's petrified of the band. I find it kind of funny, but then again, any smart girl would be more than aware of the band's reputation. Her fear makes me wonder if it's actually jealousy. She's jealous that no one is paying attention to her.

In front of us, in another car, are Talon, Mouse and Mills and behind us in yet another car are Peacock, Jess, Dex, and Sam. I'm pretty confident that for Jess, her hanging out with Peacock is tied to Sam's interest in Dex, not her own interest in Peacock. Or at least her own sexual interest. She's never, in all the years I've known her, slept with a guy on the first date. She's all about "like me, woo me, love me, fuck me." So her being with Peacock is okay. He's the teddy bear of the group and I take comfort in that.

Kyle is in the last car with Leroy and Beck. Poor guy got stuck with the bodyguards, though I think he pushed Kate into my car so she wouldn't get stuck with the guys. She's not very talkative and that's disappointing. Her discomfort gives me a strange thrill, but in all honesty I don't want her to feel left out or too uncomfortable. However she still doesn't talk to me.

When we get to the front of the club, I tell the driver to just take us around back. Rusty radios to the other cars letting them know what our plan is. We're not important and because we're the second car in the motorcade, the reporters stacked out front will be disappointed when we step out after Talon. As we approach the back door, another car pulls up behind us.

Rusty turns to me, "Leroy and Beck will scoot through the club to meet the guys out front. They're all waiting to move in and get out until they're in position."

"Okay, good. I need to get out front in case there are any issues, but I'd prefer the guys to be pulled into the club."

Rusty relays my message to the other guards and they confirm they'll behave. I don't want too many pictures of Sam and Jess floating around out there, they both have professional careers to think about and seeing them partying with rock stars is just the kind of thing that could get them into trouble with their jobs. Lucky for me, it is my job.

Rusty climbs out of the car and opens my door for me. I get out and am followed by Kate. She ignores me, skirts Rusty and heads straight for the back door of the bar. If she's gonna be such a prude, I can't understand why she even tagged along. I shrug it off.

"Addison." I turn to Kyle as he comes running up to me. "Are you ready for this?" He asks with a sincere concern in his eyes.

"Absolutely." I smile as Bert, the driver of my car, holds open the back door, unleashing the wild and crazy sounds coming from inside the club. There's screaming along with very loud rap music? Oh for the love of...

"It's great dance music," Kyle says.

Was I talking out loud again? Jeez, I gotta watch that. "Yeah, I guess."

He laughs. "Not a fan of the rap, are we?"

"Um no, not at all."

"Don't worry, they'll change it up once the guys are here."

I shrug and we duck inside.

The club is all shiny black, electric blue and chrome everywhere. The dance floor is sunken and surrounding the main floor are raised platforms of various heights with tables and tons of people standing around. Leroy and Beck lead the way, parting the masses. When you put the two of them shoulder to shoulder like they are right now, they're like a brick wall being moved through a pool of water. Kyle and I are hot on their heels with Rusty bringing up the rear. Beck stands at the door, ready to open it, and I nod, giving him the go ahead. He talks into his mic and just like that, two town cars pull up in front of the bar.

The second of the two car's doors open as soon as Beck and Leroy are next to the car. Out climbs Peacock and Dex, but Sam and Jess don't get out. What the?

"They want to come in the back," Rusty tells me over my shoulder.

"That's odd."

Rusty chuckles. "I think the guys made them do it."

"Oh for the… why would they do that? Wait,"-I hold up my hand- "don't answer that."

There are only two reasons for them to make the ladies do something like that. One, they're ditching the girls or two, for whatever reason they feel the need to protect them. I shake my head as Beck and Leroy shove the guys into the door. Both Peacock and Dex smile at me as they pass.

There are dual roars going on. The crowd outside has reached a fever pitch and the crowd inside has realized that the band is arriving so they're whooping and hollering. I'm trying to see who climbed out of the car, but given that I can't see anything, I assume it's Mouse. My suspicions are confirmed a moment later when the crowd outside grows so loud that I can hear them through the door, then the flashes and reporters jump into action. I push open the door and hear, "Mr. Carver! Talon!" followed by uninvited random questions about the concert etcetera. God, they're loud, but just like the force of Leroy and Beck with the crowd in the bar, Talon, Mouse and Mills plow through the throng of people and are in the door without uttering a word. Thank god.

As soon as the guys hit the club they scatter and I notice that the bodyguards are right there with them the whole time. I turn to Rusty. "Shouldn't you be watching them?"

"I should, but my orders are for you. So unless you want to make nice with one of them and stay near them, I'm left to watch you."

I roll my eyes. "I won't sit or hang out with them, but I can hang near them, will that help?"

He nods. I make my way through the packed crowd, straight to the bar. After all the alcohol the last two nights, this isn't a good idea. But with figuring out who Kyle is and the back and forth with Talon and Kyle, I need about a dozen of them.

"Two shots of Crown and an Irish Bulldog, please," I tell the bartender.

"An Irish what?"

Oh, come on. I give the ingredients to the bartender and he nods his head and sets about making my drinks. When he's done he slides them over to me. "Cash or charge or tab?"

"Tab," someone says behind me and I turn to see Kyle. "69's tab. Anything she wants."

I roll my eyes and slip the bartender a twenty anyway. "Keep it," I holler as the music pick up its beat. The bartender smiles at me then proceeds to look me up and down. What the hell is it with guys all of a sudden? Is my repelling pheromone broken? Do I have 'flirt' tattooed on my forehead?

I shoot back one of the shots, slam the glass back to the counter, grab my other two drinks and turn to find somewhere close to the guys, but Kyle is blocking my path.

"Thanks for the drinks," I shout.

"No problem, where are you going?"

I shrug and slide past him. I walk around for a couple minutes until I find a table that is far enough away, hidden, but in close proximity for Rusty to help the other guards with the guys.

Unfortunately I'm too close to them because I get eyefuls of Sam and Dex making out. Peacock is getting friendly with Jess. Mouse has a very skanky looking chick on his lap and I shoot down my shot. Wrap it up, Mouse, you tap it, fucking wrap it because...I burp into my mouth. Ew, okay and we're over that one.

One problem with moving past Mouse and his skanky piece is that my eyes land on Talon and the blond haired, blue eyed bimbo laughing her way into his pants. I roll my eyes. *Seriously, since when does laughing get you laid? Oh, why all the time* — insert an eye roll here —*...it's too easy, come on, Talon, take on a challenge, damn it.*

Then out of nowhere he looks right at me, almost as if he knew I was watching him. But he turns back quickly, like he didn't actually see me, which is entirely possible. It's really dark over here. Then I'm distracted when Kyle enters the circle of the band with a brunette he picked up on his way back from the bar.

What's confusing me the most about the pre-show ritual, and what happened between Talon, Kyle, and I, is that I'm sitting here alone while they entertain their sticks. I try desperately to ignore them but it's like watching a car accident about to happen and being unable to take your eyes off of it.

"Do you want to dance?" I look up into the face of a cute, but not drop dead gorgeous man who's about my height in heels. He's wearing a 69 Bottles t-shirt and ripped up jeans. All in all it's not a bad package. I look over at the circle of band members and their bevy of bimbos and agree to dance. He holds his hand out to me and I take it. I stand up and he pulls me straight to the dance floor.

Just as we get there the song changes to David Guetta's remix of Usher's Without You and I lose myself in the music, not giving a shit who I'm dancing with or what I look like doing it. Each thump of the bass flows through my veins; and the beat consumes me. My dance partner, thank god, has some skills and he's keeping up with me. The song is slower, but it has a great beat so it's easy to move around.

At one point I turn around so that dance boy is behind me and I'm grinding on him without actually touching him. My eyes are heavy, lost in the music, alcohol kicking in and I see through tiny slits that I have an audience. An audience of five. Talon and Kyle are all but wiping drool from their chins. I work it a little longer, playing it up to what I know they're watching me do.

When the song concludes dancer boy asks if he can buy me a drink. I shake my head. "No thanks, I think I've had enough for tonight. Thank you for the dance." And with that I leave him, walking toward the guys, mainly Sam. I get to her and whisper in her ear. "I need to talk to you, now."

I grab her hand and she comes with me. Dex of course protests. "Girl time," I shout and he scowls at me. I drag Sam through the back door of the club. I need some air.

chapter 17

"Addie, why are we out here?" she asks me.

"Because I'm sending you home."

"What the fuck for?" She's pissed, as she should be.

"Because you're my best friend and I'm not going to let Dex fuck you over."

"That's my fucking choice, Addison, not yours."

"You know what, Sam, you're absolutely right. It is your choice, but let me tell you this. He will fuck you and dump you. He won't commit to you, he won't make you his wife. Seriously, Sam. It will be a one night stand. Is that really what you want? With him?"

"Yes," she says matter of fact and I'm shocked.

"No, you don't. You're better than that, Sam. You don't need to screw the biggest slut in this band, for what? Heartache. I know you, Sam, and I know what this will turn into. When he's done with you, he'll throw you to the curb without a second thought."

"She's right, Sam." I spin around to find Dex has just come through the door. "One night, one fuck, you deserve better than that."

"Wow, Dex, did that hurt?" I tease him.

"Excruciating." He smirks.

"Addie, is it so wrong to throw your inhibitions out the window," Sam says. "To indulge in a fantasy?"

I take a couple of steps closer to Dex. Her question spurs my own desires to have Talon and Kyle, not separately but to have them both, together. "If you do this, with her, I don't want to hear about it, no bragging, no gloating, not a fucking word, you get me?" He nods. I turn to Sam and walk back toward her. "Sam, I swear to god, if you do this, know that come time for that bus to leave, if you're still on it, I will throw you off of it because come Vegas tomorrow night, there will be somebody new capturing his attention and you will be a notch in his bedpost. If you can live with that and leave me out of it, then by all means, have at it."

I don't wait for her to reply. I walk over to Rusty. "I'm going to get into that car and return to the bus. Between here and there I have the driver of the town car and the bus is surrounded by security, plus the drivers and whoever else might be there. Do not come with me."

"It's my job," he argues.

"Don't give me that bullshit, I am a big girl, I can take care of myself." I turn straight for the car and the driver. "Take me back to the bus, then you'll need to come back here."

"Yes, ma'am." He opens my door and I slide in. I don't look at Dex or Sam because I know what's going to happen and I don't want to be a part of it. I also don't want to go back inside to see the girls hanging all over Talon and Kyle like the bimbos that they are. I've had enough for today.

Ten minutes later we are driving in past security and I have the driver pull up alongside the bus. I'm on the wrong side of the car so I slide across the seat. I want to be able to just walk straight onto the bus. I slide the driver a twenty and climb onto the bus quickly.

Within a matter of minutes I have my pajama pants and tank top out of the drawer and I'm in the shower, desperate to wash the filth off of me from tonight.

Luckily by the time I'm done, no one has returned. The driver is standing at the front of the bus looking over a couple of things. "What time do we need to leave?"

"By eight, ma'am."

"Okay, wake me if you need help throwing people off of the bus. Otherwise, make sure you roll on time."

"Got it," he says and he leaves the bus. There are beds on the other bus for the drivers and from my understanding there are two additional drivers tagging along with us for longer trips, but not all. They show up when we need them, like in Albuquerque to get us to Galveston.

I return to my little alcove of a room and climb up into my bed. I pull my headphones and iPod from my messenger bag at my feet. Plugging in and curling up with a good book sounds amazing. I pick one of my softer playlists and settle in to read a great book about a homeless guy, on a train platform, who counts the smiles of the heroine of the story. It's a heartwarming romance and I love it.

Sometime later, I hear muffled sounds of people returning to the bus, but I don't get up, I don't really care. Unless I have to kick bimbos off the bus.

I roll toward the bus wall, putting my back to the curtain, glad I threw my hoodie on before climbing into bed. I try to fall asleep, hoping they don't come back here to bug me.

At some point someone, I don't look to see who, opens the curtain because the room floods with light. The light fills the room for a good minute or two before it falls closed again. Then finally after what feels like the longest day in history, I settle in, comfortable and ready to sleep. Though it's a bit ironic, even a little depressing, that I was hit on, practically drooled on, caused two 'heart attacks', and yet I am the only one going to bed alone.

chapter 18

When I wake up, I don't bother to look at the clock. I can tell it is sometime after eight because we're moving. Good, no one had to wake me up to kick off half naked bimbos. God, what an idiot I was yesterday. With all the shit with Kyle and Talon, I can't believe I let myself get upset over the fact that they were hitting on, making out with and likely fucking two chicks and they paid no attention to me once we hit the party.

I'm even more bothered by the fact that I let myself get depressed over the fact that I was sleeping alone. *You've done it for nearly eight years, Addison. Why is it a big deal now?* That's the million dollar question. Sure, I've been hit on in bars, a lot, but it's not something that has ever bothered me before. I guess maybe it was always their cheesy-ass one liners that were a turn off. None of these guys had anything more to say besides drooling and cheesy one liners, but still.

God, that kiss before the show... I shiver again thinking about it. How they both held me so gently, and the ferocity of Talon's kiss. I shiver again. No, I'm not cold. I just don't know how to describe the excitement running through me when I think about it.

Couple Talon's kiss with Kyle's own tender kisses on my neck, gah!

Now this morning, in a way, I feel used. It's stupid and petty, but it's true. I was there, I was great and I was the good luck charm, at least until the chicks started stroking their egos and eventually their dicks. It was stupid of me to think that it would be remotely possible to actually have something with either Talon or Kyle, or... both of them? Nah, there's no way. Besides, if I had both of them, they'd have to be equally into each other too, right? I mean, I can't have all the glory, right?

My thoughts of Talon and then of Kyle bring the memory of Dan sliding back into my thoughts and I feel like crying.

I met Dan in college at NYU. He was a year ahead of me but he was pre-law so he was going to be in school a lot longer than I was. I didn't mind. We hit it off great, we got along amazingly well and we just worked great together. Dan took my virginity about six months into our relationship. I was so sure that once he got that, it was going to be over between us. I guess that was the cynic in me even then and it was also the reality of how he made me feel. He pushed for it, all throughout those six sexless months, which didn't help make me feel any better about where our relationship was going.

But in the end he didn't run away. After we broke that barrier, not in the literal sense, everything changed for the better between the two of us. We grew closer and that's when I fell in love with him. Well, in the months that followed our slightly drunken, extremely awkward first time. When I say awkward, I mean it was awkward. I knew he wasn't a virgin, but he wasn't exactly promiscuous before meeting me.

After two years of being together, and him graduating, he proposed to me and we had great plans to get married and finish up school. We talked about everything. He was my everything, and he never once held me back from anything. In fact, he encouraged me to pursue the things I wanted most and I did. I'd met his mom, Lilly, several times when she would come to New York to visit Dan and we got along great.

She was helping me plan the wedding and her and my mom, Lori, got along great. But Dan insisted on paying for the wedding, so ultimately I got everything I wanted and then some. The Black's were not overly wealthy, but there was a good reason Dan had money.

Dan and I never talked about Kyle. I knew of him, of course, but we never talked about him. Even Lilly never mentioned him much and when she did, Dan would always get pissed off.

Dan and Kyle's father was murdered during Dan's first year of college. Dan never talked about it, but when he talked about his father, it was never with kindness and I learned that he'd been abusive and an alcoholic among other things. After Dan Senior was killed, Kyle slipped into drugs and alcohol and slipped away from everyone. Dan never understood how a jackass like his father could impact someone like Kyle. But it did and Kyle ran away with the drugs and alcohol, leaving his family behind to suffer. Dan hated him for it. When Dan Sr. was killed, he left behind several large life insurance policies, which is where Dan got his money.

Kyle too, I'm sure. I won't speculate about his drug and alcohol abuse because, well, I don't know what parts of what I was told are true or not. Lilly wasn't exactly mother of the year after her husband was killed. I wonder idly if she's really the reason Kyle ran to drugs and alcohol.

We were two weeks out from the wedding. Anxieties and tensions were running high. I'd started working for Bold, but barely, still learning the ropes, kind of barely, and I had so much left to do before the wedding and I was completely stressed out. Dan and I argued over something stupid, something so stupid that I can't even remember now what it was. We'd talked on the phone before he'd left work, and neither of us said we loved each other, said bye or even a see you soon because we were that angry with one another. Then he never came home. On his way home Dan had been hit and killed by a drunk driver at five in the evening. It was the hardest, most devastating thing I've ever dealt with in my life.

When his family came to California after he was killed, no one paid any attention to me whatsoever. No one cared how I was doing and I threw myself into playing hostess-cooking, picking up after everyone and trying to hold it all together. Dan and I had been together over three years and were about to be married, but it didn't matter.

Because of that, among other things, I wonder if I've ever really dealt with it because even now, seven years later, I haven't gotten over it, or at least it still haunts me. Losing Dan is the reason I've stayed single for seven years, the reason I've kept my legs closed and the reason I've devoted myself to my job. I love my job and I loved Dan.

I keep trying to tell myself that my fear is stupid, that my fear is completely irrational, but when you've lost two men in your life that you've loved dearly, it's hard to put your heart out there for another one. First my dad to illness, followed by Dan's death. I was never able to apologize for the fight, say good-bye or tell him I loved him one more time. I've lived with that guilt for far too long.

Until now, being here on this bus. It was easy to live with it, deal with and some days even forget about it entirely. But coming on this bus, figuring out that Kyle is Dan's brother, on top of the fact that for the first time in a long time, someone is actually capturing my attention has the guilt meter rising much higher and I don't know how to handle it. But I've got to find a way to deal with it and dealing with it means no longer feeding the animals. Throwing myself into work and doing what I do best, what I know to be my best outlet. If I throw myself into work, then I can't get hurt because I won't have time to fall in love.

There's a knock on the wood surrounding the curtain. "Addison, are you awake?"

"No," I groan.

"Liar." The light pours into the room when Kyle comes in. "We're about thirty minutes from Vegas."

"Holy shit. What time is it?"

"Twelve-thirty."

"Fuck. I can't believe..." I rub my face, "God, I've never slept that long in my life." He laughs and I sit up.

Kyle takes a deep, sharp breath and I can't understand...Oh shit. I quickly pull up my tank top and cover my almost fully exposed tits. "Oh my god, I'm so sorry."

He takes a couple steps toward me with lust filled eyes. "Don't be. You're just full of surprises, aren't you?" I blush like a virgin and try to cover myself. "Please don't do that. You're beautiful, Addison." I shiver at the tone of his voice. Like Talon it has dropped to a soft sultry tone that makes my nipples harden beneath my tank top.

His hand wraps around my arm, he tugs on it to free it from the trap of my chest, trying to pull it away. I pull it back. "I can't," I breathe.

He freezes, removes his hand and takes a step back. "I'm sorry," he says, his voice is soft and apologetic.

"It's not your fault, I wasn't..."

"It's alright. I should go. Let you get ready."

"Kyle, I..."

"Shh, it's alright, Addison."

For some unexplained reason, I want to cry. I have no idea why I said I can't, no clue why I can't let this happen, why I can't let him touch me, or...

He slides out between the curtains and disappears. I let the tears consume me. I know why I couldn't. I woke up thinking about Dan this morning and the guilt is back. Radiating from every pore in my body and I hate it. I hate that I have to feel this way. I hate that after all this time, Dan still has this effect on me.

He and I had a great relationship, but it wasn't effortless, it wasn't like breathing and it certainly wasn't love at first sight with him. I remember thinking early on in our relationship that we were good for each other because we let each other live our dreams. But at what cost?

There was a point, after he died, that I felt relief. That relief quickly turned to guilt because I shouldn't feel relieved that my fiancé had died, right? Well, that was what I told myself at the time. I felt guilty for the realization that I wasn't a widow, that I didn't lose a husband, just someone that I was comfortable with. Someone who was familiar. Maybe that's all it was. Maybe all the love I think I felt for him was superficial and I'm just being a childish idiot waiting for something to wake me up to reality and just maybe Talon and Kyle are that wake up call.

It is with that thought that I wipe the tears from my eyes and climb down out of bed. I throw up the hood of my hoodie, hiding myself in my little shell of protection and I get the strangest sense that I am taking the walk of shame, without having done the act itself.

When I get to the bathroom, the door is closed. Damn it. I really have to pee and I don't want to stand here so exposed to the guys in the bunk behind me. I walk into the kitchen, following my nose to the coffee and find Kyle sitting on the couch watching TV. "Is everyone else still asleep?"

He nods. "Or at least hiding in their bunks."

"Did we have any girl problems last night?"

He just shakes his head. There is a sense of shame coloring his features. "Did you have a good night?" I ask him and he nods, but he's not really looking at me. "Get lucky?" I tease, but instantly regret the question when I see him flinch. I take that as my answer and pour myself a cup of coffee.

"So, panda, you're the reason we have coffee on board this bus?" Panda? Huh? Oh my god, my hood. I turn to see Talon standing between me and the bathroom, the light of the bathroom illuminating the rather dark hallway.

"I didn't ask for it and I certainly didn't make it." I try to look at him, only to realize that he is standing there in low riding pajama pants and nothing else. God, even his feet are sexy.

"How'd you sleep?" he asks with genuine curiosity.

"Okay, you?"

He just shrugs and steps around me to the fridge where he pulls out a bottle of Gatorade, opens it and chugs down over half before capping it and putting it back in the fridge before sitting on the couch next to Kyle and watching TV. I turn around and stomp off to the bathroom. What did I do, turn into a fucking pumpkin over night?

I shrug it off, do my business, run a brush through my mess of a head of hair and pull it back into a pony tail. I don't get too dramatic with the make-up, but soon I will be walking into a hotel, I'd like to look decent when I do. When I'm done, I ignore the boys and go straight to my room and start packing up some clothes, my make-up and shoes for the next couple of days.

Then I climb back up onto my bunk after I'm done making it and check my email, check my web searches and I come across some great articles from San Diego about the concert last night. They all make me smile.

chapter 19

"69 Bottles puts on one hell of a show."

"Best concert I've seen in years."

"Watch out world because 69 Bottles is the real deal."

The headlines are all positive and I save several to tell the guys about. In fact, no time like the present. I jump down off of my bunk and grab my laptop, heading toward the front of the bus. Now sitting in the kitchen are Kyle, Talon, Dex (who I can't even look at this morning), and Mouse.

"Where's Peacock?" I ask just as the toilet flushes and the door opens. "Good, take a seat. I have some things to show you guys."

That earns me a raised brow from Peacock who maneuvers past me to take a seat on the couch.

I read the same three headlines and the accompanying story following the real deal comment. By the time I'm done, the boys are glowing with excitement. The last line of the article makes me chuckle. "69 Bottles is so good they brought out Hollywood's Elite couple." Including a picture of Cami and Tristan standing in the crowd.

"Well done, guys," I say and I let them have their moment of glory. They deserve it.

I continue scanning through my emails and come across one from Kyle. Odd. I open it. It's a forwarded message.

It says, "This was forwarded by the label. After last night's show, the owner of a chain of venues that we're already scheduled to stop at is asking for additional shows. Three of the venues already have waiting lists long enough to fill a second night and two of them are asking for two additional nights with accompanying waiting lists. Scheduling will make things tighter, but it is doable. I won't discuss it with the band until you give the okay. All expansion will now include vendor paid hotel rooms for the nights we're there. We also have access to the label's plane if we need to accommodate a faster travel time."

I read on in the email to find out that Cincinnati, Philly and DC want to add an additional night, while Atlanta and Denver want to add two additional nights.

I flip to the calendar I set up for the tour that outlines travel time and time we're in our destinations and I look at those days.

And I email Kyle the following information:

"Cincinnati could add either Friday or Sunday night shows.

Philly would have to be a Wednesday night gig because we're in Boston on Saturday and the time frame gets really tight with a Friday show.

DC we can add Saturday night, and technically Monday night if they want more time. We have plenty between shows.

Atlanta we would have to do a Monday and Tuesday add because we're in Orlando on Thursday, again, another tight time frame.

Denver would have to be a Tuesday and Wednesday, cutting the vacation short.

From a PR standpoint, I wouldn't hesitate. Being open and willing to add more shows will show the bands dedication to their fans. From a manager standpoint, it puts a lot of stress and pressure on the guys. After parties will have to be limited or nonexistent in order to avoid total burn out, but then again, you know these guys better than I do. I can always sleep. ;-)"

I hit send and shortly after I hear a phone chime and watch Kyle pull out his phone, read something, smile, look at me, shrug and reach for the remote, killing the TV.

The guys grunt and groan. "We were watching that," Mouse argues.

"I have more important business to discuss," Kyle says.

"What's more important than the Kardashians?" Mouse snorts.

"Brain cells." I laugh. And that grants me some glares, I fight the five year old need to slick out my tongue.

"Alright, so, I need to discuss a few things with you. Things that will, well, make you guys a hell of a lot more money."

"We're listening," Dex says with a laugh.

Kyle goes into explaining the additions and what it will mean to the guys. He also tells them what it will mean in regards to their vacation, their time and performance expectations. When he's done he puts it to a vote, which I could have told you was unnecessary just watching how animated the guys were about expanding their tour. It's a unanimous hell yes. I laugh at their enthusiasm and Kyle sets about making the arrangements. Because of the tight timeline, the tickets will have to be put up for sale immediately. I, on the other hand, get to write my first press release for 69 Bottles and it's a blast. I would rather write positive press releases all damn day, than to ever have to write a negative one.

Before I can dive into editing it, we pull into the private entrance area of the MGM Grand in Las Vegas.

I hop off the bus and head inside to collect room keys and the important information pertaining to their show schedule, rehearsal time, and all that.

The keys are tucked in envelopes that are labeled with names and room numbers. I find it odd that Kyle doesn't have his own room. Mouse and Peacock are sharing one room. Dex, Talon and myself all have our own rooms, but where's Kyle's?

When I climb back on board the bus, Kyle is the only one sitting on the couch and I can see the three guys gathering their crap from their bunks. "Why don't you have a room key?"

"I usually crash with Talon. He gets the biggest room, which usually means two or three bedrooms."

"Oh."

Just then Talon comes into the kitchen area. "The room here has three bedrooms."

"Ah, okay, that explains why there are two keys."

"They should all have two to three keys. Peacock and Mouse should have three so that they each have one, plus Mills gets his. Dex should have two, you should have two and mine gets three. Unless you'd rather give your room up to Mouse, and stay in mine," he says with that sultry look in his eyes.

"Yes," I blurt before I can install the brain to mouth filter.

"Alright then," Talon says. "Give your keys to Mouse and I'll have Mills get a new one for the suite. Don't worry, panda, you'll have your own room, with a locking door." He winks at me. Not that I really care about that. But I have butterflies in my stomach when I think about the fact that I'm sharing a suite with Kyle and Talon. Then I feel like rolling my eyes at his new nickname for me.

*chapter*20

The suite is gorgeous, I mean, it's Vegas, I hardly think there's an ugly room on the strip.

"Take it," Talon says, pointing to the master room.

"No way, that's your room. You need it more than I do."

He snorts. "Hardly, please, just take it."

"He won't let you argue with him so you might as well get comfortable in there," Kyle adds.

"Fine," I say sulkily.

The room is huge, with its own bathroom nearly as big as the bedroom. There's a wicked awesome bathtub tucked into one corner and the shower has two rain shower heads. A girl could get used to this.

Once we're all settled into our rooms, Talon orders a crap ton of room service for us to all share. We eat and then I set off to get ready for tonight's show. Kyle comes knocking, asking if I want to come to the sound check and I'd love to, especially to watch Talon sing 'Your Eyes' again, but I'm not ready yet.

The bitch about tonight's outfit is that I need to be completely dry to put it on, or at least the pants. I'm wearing my favorite pants in the entire world tonight. My leather ones. With black leather pumps and a double layered tank top and wide studded belt over the top of my shirts. Though Kyle has seen more than I wanted him to see today, I'm not quite ready to show off my back ink yet. Yes, I know I showed Cami and Tristan, but ya know that was in the heat of conversation and I know that it wasn't a sexual show off for them. For Talon and Kyle, it would be.

Ever since I got my back tattoo, I've had a fantasy of showing it off in the heat of the moment and while that might not be the case now, I still don't want to ruin it, should something happen between me and someone else while on board this wild ride of a tour.

During lunch, Kyle got confirmation that the clubs were moving forward with the added shows and that tickets would be on sale by Monday. Talon was excited that they'd be going on sale so fast and though his excitement is palpable, he's the least excited of the band about the added shows. I find it odd, but decide not to press it. For all I know, this is as excited as he gets.

I'm finally dressed in my leather pants, black pumps, studded leather belt, my usual array of jewelry and my badge wrapped around my neck. I go to leave the suite only to find Rusty standing guard at the door.

"Please tell me you're not my babysitter again tonight?"

He smiles. "Not wearing that." He looks me up and down. "You look great, but I don't think the guys are going to keel over this time."

I snort a laugh. "Then why are you here?"

"Because they weren't going to be here to determine if you needed an escort and someone needs to show you where to go."

"Oh, okay, so I pass the 'dressed appropriate' test?" I put my hands up and turn.

"Yes, you do," he smirks again. I follow him down the hall, into the elevator and then into the backstage area. It's rather confusing so I'm glad he came along. I can hear the guys warming up on stage and I hear the now very familiar strings of 'Your Eyes' being played at different speeds and at different points throughout the song. I'm guessing that some last minute tuning and adjustments are being made before they get around to actually singing through the song. With as much time as it took me to finish getting ready, I expected them to be done, but I shrug and am glad I get to enjoy the show.

I don't go out front this time, but I stand back and watch. I can see Kyle leaning against a wall on the opposite side of the stage and while he's not falling over from a heart attack, he is staring at me again. I shake my head and smile at him, but he doesn't move and he doesn't take his eyes off of me.

Then the band stops and I'm distracted by it, only to look on stage and all four sets of eyes are on me. Though Talon portrays the biggest expression of emotion by smiling. The others are just ogling. I roll my eyes.

I think that I look rather plain Jane tonight, but they obviously don't seem to think so.

The sound check goes off without a hitch and once again I found myself dancing as Talon sings 'Your Eyes'. This time I'm off stage so he doesn't spend much time looking at me. But when he does, that lusty heat is burning bright.

This is all so confusing. He looks at me like that, throwing off massive heat, lust and desire, but yet he had some bimbo on his lap all night, one that I'm pretty sure he screwed. I frown at myself. I shouldn't make assumptions and after Kyle's expression when I asked about getting lucky, there's a small chance Talon didn't either.

That creepy chill runs through me when I think about Dex with Sam. I haven't asked for confirmation of their encounter, don't want it, don't need it, but given that I've yet to hear from Sam, I'm pretty sure my assumption is correct. Add that to the fact that Dex had a goofy, overly satisfied smile on his face this morning. Either that or he gave himself a damn good hand job before falling from his rack. "Ugh," I shiver.

I go back to watching Talon, who's looking at Kyle, watching me. I shiver again, this time it resonates in my core.

At eight sharp Empty Chamber takes the stage and just like last night they rock out and the crowd gets riled up for 69 Bottles to take the stage. When EC finishes their set they clear off the stage and the boys come walking down the hall toward me- Dex first followed by Peacock and Mouse, then finally Talon. The four bodyguards are doing their thing because there are some VIPs who only spend their time backstage, not actually watching the concert.

Dex saunters up to me, wrapping his arms around me and planting another 'wet and sloppy' on my mouth. "Ugh, Dex, seriously. God only knows where your mouth has been." He pulls back and winks at me. "Ugh, dude." I wipe his kiss from my lips just in time to be mauled by Peacock and Mouse, both planting kisses on my cheeks at the same time. "Break a leg, boys," I tell them and they walk on stage with their typical goofy grins.

I turn back to find Talon standing in front of me. He's standing in front of me like a shy school boy about to get scolded. His hands are tucked into his back pockets, his head is down and he's kicking at some invisible object on the ground, but he's peering at me through his eyelashes. While I try to mull over why he's so bashful all of sudden, I feel Kyle wrapping his arms around my waist. Just like last night, my body is sent directly into sensory overload between Kyle's touch and Talon's gentle hands on my cheeks. His lips are soft, warm and oh so tantalizingly delicious. There is a delicious scrape of his scruffy beard along my lips. It sends goosebumps flying across my skin, making my nipples hard.

I lean into his kiss, soaking up every touch, every sensation, letting my breath be stolen as my tongue is stroked by his.

Each flick and lick of his tongue against mine is a hot button straight to my throbbing clit and I can feel my panties dampen when Kyle presses his erection into my backside and his lips are on the side of my neck. His goatee bristling my skin, leaving more goosebumps in its wake.

Desperation causes my breathing to become highly erratic. My head starts to spin because of lack of oxygen and Talon senses it, pulling back on his kiss, "Kick some ass," I breathe as Talon backs away, winks and turns to face his audience.

Kyle doesn't let me go, he kisses my neck once more, but doesn't say anything, he just holds me. I wonder idly if it's because he's hard as a rock against my backside, but then I look at Talon and while it's hard to tell from the front, from the side, I know he's hard.

The idea sends a rush of wild excitement through me that I can barely contain. I let the excitement consume me and I start to dance in Kyle's arms. It's becoming clearer to me now. It's only been two days, but I know that I can't choose between the two of them, so my options are to let them both go, or embrace them both. One of them wouldn't be enough for me, but the two of them just might be too much to handle.

The prospect of trying sends a new wave of pleasure to my sex and I really start to dance.

chapter 21

The concert is a major hit and maybe even bigger than
last night's show, is that even possible? I guess it is. The
band just finished up their little private show, it only lasted
about twenty-five minutes and it was a total acoustic set. It
was awesome! The guys went into the greenroom
afterward and while it was crawling with bimbos there
weren't near as many tonight as last night. I'm sure we
have the MGM's ticket office to thank for that with the high
cost of the VIP experience for tonight's show.

The after party is the same tonight as last night, except
I'm not being watched, directly, by Rusty. The band is
surrounded by women and the booze is flowing from
bottles like nobody's business.

Tonight however, Dex seems to be working his talent
on two, possibly three women at the same time and it takes
all I have to not puke everywhere.

I'm in the corner, a dark one at that, desperate to stay
out of sight and hopefully out of mind with my two shots of
Crown and an Irish Bulldog (which I didn't have to explain

this time). And much like last night, when my drinks are gone, I leave the party. Though watching a train wreck about to happen is always nice, I can't watch this, not anymore. After my revelation earlier, it actually makes my chest ache to watch them schmooze the bimbos. God, they could do so much better. I mean, I get it. You're a frickin' rock star and the easy ones always throw themselves at you, but just because they do, doesn't mean you have to dip your sticks.

I am so grateful for the fact that I don't have a babysitter tonight. Before I take off on my own little adventure, I head up to the suite to ditch the leather pants. They're comfortable as hell, but I want to blend into the crowd, not stand out. I pull my hair up into a messy bun and wipe off some of my make-up. A softer appearance is my goal. I swap leather for denim, tank tops for a three quarter sleeve cotton shirt and my heels for my chucks and socks, grabbing my hoodie on my way out the door. It's March, in Vegas, which means it's chilly out.

I slink quickly down the hall to the stairwell, not wanting to risk running into anyone from the band in the elevator and I climb my way down to the lobby level and sneak out of the hotel through the casino and onto the Las Vegas Strip.

The streets are busy, but filled mostly with frat boys. Spring break, Vegas, does this even need to be discussed? The air smells of massive amounts of booze and the occasional raunchy smell of vomit because someone drank themselves sick. Once I get up to the escalator at Planet Hollywood, I cross the street to the Bellagio and the fountains out front.

I stand there for a long time watching the water shoot and dance to the music. The sight is a gorgeous one and

I'm hypnotized by it. I've been to Vegas countless times both personally and professionally. Though I've never actually taken the time to sit and watch the fountains. The downside to being alone, my mind begins to wander back to the MGM and Talon, Kyle and the girls surrounding them.

It's obvious to me now that watching Talon and Kyle sweep women into their beds makes me upset, and maybe even jealous. Hell, there isn't a maybe about it. But despite what appears to be desperation to have me, neither of them are truly making an advance on me. I'm not exactly playing hard to get here. I haven't come right out and straddled their laps, if I'm what they want bad enough, they know where to find me.

Now I'm thinking about what happened on the bus when Kyle backed off immediately this morning. No argument, no explanation, nothing, and frankly I was seriously disappointed by that. Yes, I said, 'I can't,' but I realize that hindsight is always twenty-twenty and the side I'm seeing now is that I wanted him to argue, to fight for it and he didn't. He just backed off. Why did he do that? Most guys would have done or said something, tried to argue, but he didn't.

Then my mind slips to his brother. Is the holding and the kissing okay because it's rather innocent, well, on the outside- no need to remind you of what it does down there. Hell, just thinking about it again makes my clit throb. But is that why? I can see both sides of that coin. I honestly can, but -not trying to sound rude or mean- Dan's gone, it's not like we broke up. He's gone and never coming back for me or for Kyle. Did he back off because while he wants me, he knows that Talon does too?

I can totally see that angle to things because when Kyle and I are alone, it's one way, but when we're around Talon it's a little different. Is he fighting his inner need to give Talon a try first?

The thing that worries me most is the fact that I'm here and I'm right now. Sure, they can get what they want from the greenroom or the bar. Watching them work a room full of eager chickies isn't exactly the best way to draw me in; it's going to push me away. I want to be first in line, not second. Which would make my decision to turn them down even easier. Or is there something more? Do I need it to be something more?

I think the answer to that question is obvious, yes. I need it to be something more than a woman to fill an empty bed. I need it to be about me, not about the women that they can pick up after the show. I need to be the woman sitting on their lap, enjoying their company, not the lonely girl in the corner.

My revelations are interrupted by a huge group of drunken frat boys catcalling at me as they parade down Las Vegas Boulevard with their drinks in hand. It's quite comical to watch and I take a lot of entertainment from them. Though I'm thankful I threw my hood up, I can listen and not make it obvious, no feeding the animals.

Their antics pull me away from the water, breaking the majestic spell it had on me, so I start to look around the fountain. It's not crowded, hell, I don't even know what time it is. There are a couple of individual people, like myself, admiring the fountains, but it's mostly couples and I can't help watching them standing close together or making out at the fountains. I feel a stab of jealousy that me, a 30 year old successful business woman, is standing here, alone.

After another hour or so of the charade and shenanigans going on around me, I give up, taking one last look at the fountain and begin my slow walk back to the MGM.

When I cross the threshold of the casino I check my watch and it is nearly three in the morning. I could have stood there all night watching those fountains and been content. But tomorrow is another busy concert day, followed immediately by Sunday's travel and a concert in Phoenix.

I take the elevator this time, not caring who I might run into on my way up. It is Vegas after all and people stay up all night drinking, gambling and partying. When I reach the twentieth floor I'm immediately assaulted by noises and some yelling. Fucking fabulous.

"Find her!" I hear a deep gravelly voice. It sounds a lot like Talon only deeper and more pissed off.

chapter 22

What the fuck? "I don't care how long it takes, where you have to go or what you have to do, find her."

Is he talking about me? He can't be talking... "All we know is that she left the bar within an hour of getting there. This is Vegas man, she could be anywhere. She's a big girl..."

"That's not the fucking point. Call her, find her, get her back here." I pat down my pockets for my phone. Shit. I never brought it with. For a moment I debate on slipping back onto the elevator and escaping just to make him worry a little more. But I'm too tired to play this whole cat chasing a mouse game so I pull up my big girl panties and turn the corner. As soon as I come into view all the yelling ceases and I see Mills, Beck, Leroy, Rusty, Talon, Kyle and Peacock all standing in the hallway.

I stop dead in my tracks, staring at them. "What?"

"Where have you been?" Talon growls at me.

I scowl at him. "Getting laid, what's it to you?" I'm not a child and I'll be damned if I'm going to be treated like one, especially not by these asshats.

Peacock laughs. "See, I fucking told you."

I roll my eyes. "I went for a fucking walk and you want to send out the cavalry. Real nice. I'm a big girl, Talon. I can take care of myself." I'm actually a little angry with him because he looked hurt the moment I said I was out getting laid. Not like he wasn't doing that a few hours ago. Ugh! Double standards piss me off. I don't need a 'it's okay for me, but not for you' attitude. Then once I told him I went for a walk that anger faded. "Now if you boys will excuse me, I'm tired and I'm going to bed."

The men part the hallway making room for me, all except for Talon and Kyle. "What?" I snap.

"Next time you need to tell someone where you're going or at the very least answer your phone." He's still angry.

"I forgot my phone in my room when I changed. And let me tell you something," I hiss as I get in Talon's face. "I've lived for over seven years in LA, I think if I can handle LA, I can handle Vegas. I am not a child and I am not your responsibility. If I want to fucking go for a walk without a god damn shadow, I damn well will. Now," I puff up my chest just a little bit, straighten my jacket, "if you'll excuse me, I'm going to bed."

He doesn't move, but Kyle steps back. He's wise to keep quiet right now as I skirt around Talon. He grabs my arm, pulling me back toward him. "Let me go, big man. I've done nothing wrong. You're drunk and you're pissed off, but do not..." His hands squeezes a little tighter. "Talon, you're hurting me, let me go."

"Let her go, T." Kyle says to my defense, breaking through the rage in Talon's eyes. He lets me go. I walk the three doors to our room and slide my key into the slot.

When I open the door I am greeted by the sounds of women, yes, I said women - plural, moaning. I flinch and want to be anywhere but here. I can feel eyes on me as I hesitate. No, I'm not hesitating because I'm going to apologize for taking a walk. I shiver in disgust. I make a mental note to avoid sharing a room with anyone going forward. Sorry, Mouse, you're gonna have to suck it up with Peacock.

At least then if I decide to talk a walk, no one will be the wiser. Just the fact that someone stopped their marathon of sex long enough to look for me or kick me out makes the creepy shiver slide through me again.

I take a deep breath and step inside the suite, determined to just walk straight to my room. As I am rounding the corner to the sitting room I get an eyeful of Dex's pasty white ass grinding into some blond bimbo who has another blond on top of her, grinding their pussies together. Then Dex pulls out his tool. Good god, it's huge. I take back my pinky comment, then shutter. He slides it into the chick on top. He pays me no attention whatsoever.

Looking around the room, on the couch are three more half naked chicks prattling on and on about how they can't wait until Talon comes back. I hear the door behind me open and then close again. I make a beeline for my room, desperate to hide the tears that are about to start flowing.

How the fuck can he kiss me like that, sing a fucking rock love song with me in mind, flip his fucking lid because I'm not here and then have three horny cumbuckets waiting for his return on the couch in the sitting room? I can't fucking believe I thought he wanted me, that they wanted me. Obviously I was very wrong. Or

131

at least the want of me doesn't hold a candle to their want of an open, easy and willing woman. The tears spill over before I even get my door closed.

chapter 23

Knock, knock, knock.

"Go away," I growl.

"Come on, panda girl, open up."

Panda girl? "No, go away, go back to your party."

"It's not my party," Kyle says through the door. I shake my head.

"Leave me alone," I say loud enough that I know he can hear me.

"Never."

"Bullshit."

"Come on, panda. Open up."

"You left me alone tonight. What difference does it make if you leave me alone now?"

"Shit. Come on, Addison. I didn't think, open up." I can hear the agony in his voice and my resolve softens.

"It's open," I say softer, but still loud enough that he can hear me.

I roll over onto my stomach, facing away from him, my hood is still up so I can't see him. I hug my pillow close to me, tucking it under my chin. I get settled just in time for the door to click open and then close again. "What do you want, Kyle?"

"You," he says soft as a whisper. I roll over quickly, looking at him standing against the door to my room.

"You can't be serious."

He smiles. "I am. I've wanted you since you gave that speech about the band's dicks. Actually, since you pulled up to the bus in LA."

"I'm not…"

"Stop. Please, I just need you. I just want you."

"For tonight. What about tomorrow night, or the next? Tonight you struck out, so you come to me for second best."

He shakes his head. "I didn't strike out tonight, or last night for that matter."

"Oh great, because that makes me feel a whole lot better. I don't do sloppy seconds, Kyle."

"Will you shut up and listen to me for a minute? I haven't slept with anyone tonight or last night."

"You looked awfully cozy with that blond chick tonight, I can't imagine she walked away willingly."

He laughs. "No, she drank too much and started throwing herself at Talon then somewhere along the line she passed out on the couch in the bar. I came up here looking for you. But you were gone, no one knew where you were and I panicked. I didn't tell Talon until I came back up after walking through the casino, but then they were…" He doesn't finish his sentence, he doesn't have to.

"I…" I have no clue what to say. He looks so sad standing all the way over there. I want to comfort him, to give him what he wants, but I don't know that I can do that. "I haven't been with anyone since Dan," I say under my breath.

"Jesus, panda. That's a... damn, that's a long time," he stutters his way through his words.

I snort without humor and roll back over. "You're telling me," I mumble.

talon

Don't even think about asking me for their names because I have no fucking clue, nor do I care. All I know is I'm fucking drunk and I need a place to bury my stick. A blond, a brunette and an out of the box black haired chick is exactly what the doctor ordered to cure my itch.

"Did you see that chick?" Blondie says.

"Which one?" says the brunette.

"The one that came running through here all bent because Dex was getting it on with those two chicks."

"Oh yeah, that one, yeah. I'm pretty sure she was crying. I mean, seriously, who wants a fucking drummer when you can have the lead singer?"

"You guys are stupid. She didn't go running until she saw us sitting here. Pay attention next time," the black haired one announces.

"GET OUT!" I growl at the three of them. "Get the fuck out now."

"What the fuck is your problem?" And just like the biggest nightmare imaginable they ignore me, start pawing at me, trying to pull my clothes off.

"I said get out," I growl again but 'they don't move. I manage to disentangle my phone from my pocket. "Mills, get in here and get Dex and his hoard out of here and take these three with you. NOW!"

Despite my phone call, the girls don't leave. They keep going, making out with each other, desperate to undress me, until I finally manage to politely push them back and away. Now that I'm free of them, I go for the bathroom, locking the door behind me.

"This is fucking lame. I knew he wouldn't put out," one of the dumb bitches says and I've about had it. That's when I hear Beck.

"Alright, ladies, party's over. Let's go."

The girls don't give him any lip and after about ten minutes and a shower, Mills pounds on the door. "They're gone."

"Thanks, man." I open the door. "Sorry about that."

"What happened anyway?" Mills asks me.

"They were talking shit. Pissed me off, then when I told them to get out they ignored me. Nothing unusual really."

"What were they talking smack about? You don't usually get agitated without good reason."

This is one of the reasons I keep Mills around. "Addison."

"Oh, shit. She alright?"

I shrug. "No clue, she'd already locked herself in her room when I came back in. I know she got an eyeful of Dex before she made it to her room." I watch Mills flinch. "Yup, pretty much. But I think those three caused more trouble before Addison managed to get out of the room."

Mills gives me a sad smile. "Well, they're gone. Get some sleep."

I nod. "Yeah, you too."

Unfortunately, I'm too drunk and way too fucking horny to talk to her tonight. I'll end up doing something we'll both regret.

Why is this so fucking hard? I've never had a problem getting girls, getting laid. But since her panda wearing ass walked onto my bus, I can't fucking stop thinking about her.

I sit down on the bed, hard as fucking stone and naked, I lean forward with my head down. "Get a grip, dipshit," I tell myself. She's just another fucking chick. Yeah, another chick that while I fucking want her like nobody's business, I can't fuck and throw out. Addison isn't the type of girl you bang and forget. She's the type of girl you fuck and fall in love with.

Chills run through me. Fuck, I need a piece of ass to move past this...but I can't even do that right. Two fucking nights in a row...

addison

"He meant that much to you?" Kyle asks.

"I thought he did, at the time, but now I don't know. I threw myself into work to get through those weeks following his death and I've just stayed there ever since. Being here now is a product of all that hard work."

"Well, you've certainly accomplished a lot."

Over the course of the last few minutes Kyle has made his way closer to the bed, so close he's actually sitting on it looking down at me. His eyes are soft and warm. I want him, I really do, but this is the first time in seven years I've had to face the choice of whether or not I'm actually ready to sleep with someone. "In some areas, yes, I have, in others, not so much."

"What do you mean?" he asks. There is a genuine curiosity in his voice and it's comforting. It doesn't sound strained or forced.

"I mean that because I've been so wrapped up in work that I haven't had much time for other things."

"What about, what are their names? The girls from last night?"

"Sam and Jess?"

"Yeah, you guys seem close."

I shrug and sit up, still holding the pillow tightly to my chest. I push off my hood. "Maybe, but I blow them off so much. Sometimes it's work related and sometimes not. I used the concert in San Diego as an excuse. I wanted to see the show, didn't want to go alone. So I thought I could finally break that barrier and spend a couple of days with my girlfriends on the beach. But as it turns out, I was needed for more important things. I've bailed on them every single time we make plans to do something because I feel bad telling them no. And now I am supposed to make it up to them when the tour is over. I pacified them and I feel bad about it."

"I think last night more than made up for it."

"What do you mean? Wait, do I want to know the answer to that?"

"Probably not. I just know that two of our guys woke up with smiles on their faces."

"Ew, damn it. Wait, two? You mean Jess and Peacock?"

He nods. "I thought you knew?" He cocks his head at me.

I shake mine. "No. I gave Sam a lecture behind the club before I went back to the bus. Tried to talk her out of sleeping with Dex. Dex came out and told her that what I said was true, that he'd have his shit buried in another pussy, or two as is the case, tonight. I told them both I didn't want to hear about it the next day or ever. Sam is the clingy type, sleep with her once and you're screwed. Jess, Jesus, she was always the 'date me, woo me, love me, fuck me' type, I didn't think I needed to...damn it." I throw the pillow down in frustration.

"Well, I wouldn't worry about Jess too much. Peacock didn't pick up a chick tonight, which is probably why he was in the hallway tonight, and Mouse and Dex were otherwise occupied. I think there may be more between Jess and Eric than we realize," he says, and he's absolutely serious about it. "I saw him messing with his phone a lot today, so maybe there is something more between those two. Dex, on the other hand, is being Dex. Wham, bam, thank you, ma'am and all that."

I don't know whether I should feel relieved or not at the information Kyle is telling me right now. I want to believe that it could be something more between Eric, aka Peacock, and Jess. And I warned Sam, so she ultimately gets what's coming to her.

"I'm not ready to sleep with you," I blurt.

Kyle smiles and brings his hand to my cheek. "I know you're not, but it won't stop me from trying to prove it to you."

I smile. "Thank you."

"Now, slide over, I'm snuggling with you."

"Kyle, I…"

"No funny business, I'll be a perfect gentleman, but I'm tired and frankly I don't want to leave you."

"I need to change."

He gestures with his hand for me to go ahead and I do. I slip into my pajama bottoms and a t-shirt, ditch the jeans, bra and other clothes I'm still wearing, before brushing my teeth and climbing into bed.

Kyle wraps his arms around me and I snuggle into his chest. I take a long deep inhale, pulling his scent into me. His scent is all Kyle with a faint hint of cologne. It smells like heaven and I drift off to sleep.

chapter 24

When I wake up the next morning, Kyle is gone. I'm not surprised when I see it's after two in the afternoon. These late nights are going to run me dry. But today is worse. Today dawns with a major migraine. My head is pounding behind my eyes and I refuse to turn on a light. I stumble my way into the bathroom and into the shower without the light on. I don't want to even think about turning it on.

When I stumble out of the shower I go digging blindly in my bag for my migraine medicine. It's too late to take it, but at this point something has got to be better than nothing. I haven't had a migraine in over a year so I guess I was due, but damn it there's a concert tonight and I need to be there.

I find my medicine, down the two pills with a glass of water from the faucet, throw my pjs and hoodie back on and climb back into bed, passing right back out again.

Sometime later there is a knock on the door that wakes me up. "Go away," I moan.

"Red, you alright in there?"

"No," I groan and suddenly the room is flooded with light. "Argh!" I groan, "turn it off. Turn off the light," I shout as I cover my head with the blankets.

"Come on, it's almost show time," Talon says from the foot of my bed, then I feel him pushing down on the bed shaking it.

"No stop." My stomach swirls and I swallow back the bile rising in my throat. "Talon, I'm gonna…"

I bolt out of bed, not thinking about where I am and I stub my toe on the door "Fuck!" I scream as I try and get into the bathroom before I let loose what little contents are in my stomach. Finally, I manage to find the toilet.

"Fuck, Addison, what's wrong with you?" Talon's concern isn't exactly heartwarming as I'm retching into the toilet. He comes to stand near me and pulls my hair off of my face.

"Get out," I manage between heaves. "Don't. Need. To. See. This."

"What's wrong?"

"Migraine," I manage before heaving into the toilet one more time.

"Ah shit, panda, I'm sorry. I didn't… I didn't think. I thought you were hiding in here because you were pissed at me."

What? Oh, the chicks last night. "No, sick." Finally the dry heaves calm down and I'm able to slide myself to the floor, putting my pounding head on the cool tile near the tub.

"What can I do?" he asks, again his concern for me is back and this time it's genuine. I want to cry. He makes me so angry.

"Nothing, show, must go on." I can't even speak it hurts so bad.

"Not the same without you."

"And you can't cancel the show because your PR rep has a headache."

"But I need my good luck kiss."

"Seriously, I just ralphed in the … and you want a good luck kiss?"

He laughs. "After you brush your teeth of course."

"Har Har."

"Here, let's get you off the floor. How's your foot?"

"Hurts," I mumble as I feel his arms come underneath me, lifting me off of the floor.

"Alright, let's get you in bed. I'll get you some orange juice and some medicine. We've still got three hours."

So not gonna happen, but I'm not going to tell him that. At least not right now.

He tucks me into bed, disappears for a few minutes and comes back with some orange juice along with two Tylenol and one horse pill.

"What's this?" I hold up the white pill.

"Eight hundred ibuprofen. The combo works amazing for me." He smiles softly at me and I take them. It's not the first time I've mixed Tylenol with Ibuprofen. "Rest. I'll come back in about an hour to check on you. I'll leave Kyle here as long as I can." He leans over and kisses me on the forehead. "Need anything else?"

My snuggle partner? "No. I'm good."

He kisses me again and leaves the room quietly and I doze off.

I vaguely remember Talon coming in to wake me up an hour later and I shooed him away.

Half an hour later, Kyle comes in. "How you feeling, panda girl?" he says with a soft tug on the ear on my hood.

"Better."

"Want to come down for the show?" I shake my head slightly. "Not even for their kisses."

"Selfish pricks," I mumble and he laughs. "Help me," I tell him.

"With what?"

"Get some clothes so they can have their kisses, then I'm coming back to bed.

"You don't..."

"Shut it and help me." I try and fail at smiling. It still hurts but at least it's not as intense as before.

He sets about his task helping me into jeans and a t-shirt. He manages to find my flip-flops in my mess of a suitcase and slides them on my feet. He goes into the bathroom when I swap one t-shirt for another. It's tighter than I thought it would be, but I'm not going to go through the hassle of a bra and I throw my hoodie back on.

I throw the hood over my messy ass ponytail and find my big dark sunglasses and slip them over my eyes. "Start with the bathroom light," I say. He closes the door and then turns on the light. I flinch and close my eyes, blinking rapidly. Once I adjust, I tell him to open it some more and he obeys what I'm asking him to do until I manage a light on one of the nightstands.

"You good?"

I shrug. I look over at the clock and it's nearly eight. "I need my headphones. I've got to be able to muffle the noise." He nods and finds them in my messenger bag. He gives them to me and I slide them into my ears. He didn't disconnect the iPod so I turn it on. It's the same soft melodies I fell asleep to the other night. The initial noise makes me jump, so I turn it down to a dull, barely there level.

"Ready?" I hear him ask and I nod.

"I'm gonna need food when I come back up."

"I'll take care of it."

"And coffee," I tell him.

He smiles. "On it."

He escorts me slowly down the hall and to the elevator then through the back hallway to the backstage area of our venue. Once we go through the steel door, I can hear Empty Chamber's last song of their set. I lean into Kyle. "Can we get into position without them seeing me?"

He nods and sneaks me quickly to my position next to the stage just as Empty Chamber finishes their song and gives their introduction to 69 Bottles. Thankful for the headphones, I can hear him clearly but the crowd is a dull roar in my ears.

A couple minutes go by as the shuffle of gear happens. Then like out of the fog, the boys, my boys, come walking down the hall toward the stage. Dex is surprised to see me. Peacock is rather indifferent and Talon is looking down at the floor. He looks so sad and I want to run to him and tell him it's okay.

"You look like shit."

"Ever charming, aren't you, Dex?"

"Always," he says wrapping his arms around me, planting a wet and sloppy kiss on my lips and the image of him chain fucking those chicks last night comes unwelcome into my mind and my stomach rolls again. "Thanks, love."

He steps back and I can see Talon has a bright smile on his face as he looks at me. Mouse and Peacock quickly wrap their arms and plant their kisses. "Break a leg, guys."

"Go back to bed," Mouse says with a smile. "Dex is right, you look like shit."

"So much fucking love," I tease. "I crawled out of bed for your happy asses."

He laughs. "I know and I appreciate it." Mouse moves off to the stage behind Peacock.

Kyle takes up his position behind me, wrapping his hands around me and I slouch into him. Exhausted. "We're almost done, panda," he whispers and Talon saddles up to me.

"Thank you," he breathes, taking my cheeks in his hands and bringing his lips to mine. The sensation is overwhelming and I moan into his mouth. I feel Kyle's hands slide along my belly, up towards my chest and my clit throbs, headache forgotten. I feel Talon's erection twitch against Kyle's hand and my stomach.

Talon's tongue slides into my mouth, stroking my tongue and Kyle's hand gently strokes along Talon's erection. Talon's breathing hitches with each gentle pass of Kyle's hand and since my hands are on Talon's biceps, he knows full well who's touching him and it's turning him on more...dear lord, I'm in fucking trouble with these two.

Wrapped in between these two men is my happy place. I bring my hands to Talon's cheeks, holding him to me, not wanting to let him go. He pulls back slightly, pecking me on the lips a couple more times before stepping back. "Kick some ass," I tell him.

"Stay, for a couple minutes."

"Only a couple." He smiles and steps onto the stage.

He does his greeting and the band breaks into 'Your Eyes'. Just for me. Talon is looking at me and Kyle hasn't let me go. I smile at him and take comfort in the man holding me upright. Despite the headache, I stay through the song and into the next one before Kyle makes me leave and takes me back to my room and my bed.

chapter 25

Within minutes of returning back to the suite, I've changed back into my pjs and Kyle has me nestled in bed and he's bringing me food on a tray.

"Thanks."

"I wasn't sure what you wanted so I went with," he opens the dome on the tray.

"Mac n' cheese. It's perfect." I smile at him. "Did you get yourself anything?"

"No, I'm not hungry." I pout at him. "What? I ate earlier," He counters and takes a seat on the bed next to me as I dig into my supper.

I get about halfway through my mac n' cheese and drink down two cups of coffee and then finally two big glasses of apple juice. My head is still throbbing but at least the light sensitivity seems to be disappearing. I settle back against the headrest, my tummy full and my eyes are heavy.

"All done?" he asks me.

"Mmhmm. I am. That was delicious, thank you."

He smirks at me. "I didn't make it, I just ordered it. But you're welcome." He takes the tray from over my legs and back into the hallway for pick up. When he comes back, he stands at the foot of the bed. "Need anything else?"

I smile. "A snuggle buddy?"

He smiles a big smile. "I'd love to, unless of course…" he trails off.

"Of course, what?"

"You'd rather have someone else."

"Nope, you'll do." I grin a cheesy grin at him.

"Oh great, second best." I roll my eyes and it hurts so I can't stop the scowl that marks my brow. He laughs. "I've always said that if you roll your eyes too many times they're gonna get stuck, or in your case hurt like a bitch."

"You're not second best. Now get in here." I pull back the covers and he strips out of his jeans and kicks off his boots and his socks. He keeps his boxers and t-shirt on.

He hesitates before climbing in. "Is this okay?"

I nod and he climbs on in. He wraps his arms around me and I snuggle into him. He rests his cheek against the top of my head and I put my arm around his ribs, pulling him closer to me and I sigh in contentment as I close my eyes and fall asleep too fast to savor my cuddle buddy.

kyle

Lying here with Addison is like pure heaven. She smells so sweet, like vanilla and spices. She's soft to hang on too, not like most of the girls that show up at the concerts, or at least the ones brave enough to throw themselves at us. I like my women to be luscious, a little curvy is always good and Addison is definitely that. Though she is extremely slender, she's soft in all the right spots.

She's got a great ass, a beautiful chest, which from the slip I saw yesterday, she's had some work done in that department, but they still look natural as hell. I shift slightly. Thinking about what I saw makes my already raging erection throb harder. I know she's sick, but she's damn sweet.

The way she asked for a snuggle buddy was quite possibly one of the cutest things I've ever seen. God, I sound like a sap. Or a stupid love struck teenager, but that is something I'm not and I meant what I told her last night.

Since she walked on the bus, I haven't been able to think about anyone but her. No doubt the pain she's endured since Dan's death has been excruciating. My mom really shut down when he died, so I don't doubt that she shut Addison out too. I'd like to find out, but it's not something I'm ready to talk to her about just yet. I need alcohol for that.

I knew about Addison but with Dan up in New York at school, I never went up there. I was dealing with my own demons after my dad was killed. Demons that I haven't faced in nearly a decade. Demons that brought me to Talon and the crew. Demons that I've never dealt with, just buried.

"Hey man." I look over to see Talon standing in Addison's doorway.

"Hey," I say softly. I don't want to wake Addison up. "What time is it?"

"Eleven. The guys went to the bar, I came up here."

"How'd it go?" I ask him.

"Good. I had a hard time keeping my head and I kept looking for her off stage, but other than that, it was good.

We did another encore. So all in all, it was good. How's she doing?" he asks me while looking at her.

"She said she's feeling better, but it still hurts. She ate half of a huge bowl of mac n' cheese, two cups of coffee-" He snorts. "And two large glasses of apple juice then curled up and fell asleep."

"That's good. Glad she's feeling better. I feel so bad because I made her puke earlier. I didn't know she was sick and was messing with her." I watch as he rubs his hand through his hair. I'd be lying if I didn't tell you that his stress makes him sexy as hell. Whoa, where on earth... oh, who am I kidding? I've always thought that Talon is a damn good looking man.

"Mind if I join you guys?" he asks, but I can tell he's unsure of himself. I smile and nod, then watch as he strips down to his t-shirt and boxers and then climbs in on the other side of Addison.

"Does this make you jealous?" I ask him. My voice is calm and I'm honestly curious. I know he likes her, and I don't want to trample on his toes. I really don't want to make him jealous and if he asks me to, I'll stop, after tonight.

He slides closer to Addison and me. "No," Talon answers and I can hear the honesty in his voice. "It makes me horny," he says with a shit ton of nonchalance.

"Care to elaborate?" Before he can answer, Addison shifts slightly in my arms. She hitches her leg up over my hip, and lets my chest go as she shifts onto her back. She's a bit twisted, but her hand comes to rest on Talon's hip. Holding him to her at the same time she's holding me too. Her breathing settles back into a soft steady, sleeping rhythm.

Talon and I both look at each other and smile, but it's not awkward. In fact it's ridiculously comfortable and I realize that I want Addison just a little more, especially since she's now got her pussy very close to my raging hard-on which is starting to grow painful because I can't do anything about it.

"When I think about her, no matter what, it always includes you," I hear Talon whisper.

I look at him quickly, shocked, and he is looking at me with true honesty. It's shocking to see. "Meaning the three of us, together?" I swallow hard.

"Yeah, I guess. I don't know, it's strange. When I see you with her, or when I kiss her before the show and you're there, it's just natural. And I felt you tonight and it... fuck, Kyle, it turned me on that much more."

Holy shit. "So I'm not the only one."

Talon looks at me and it's the same look that he gives Addison when he sings that song but this time it's completely directed at me and I groan. "No, Kyle, it's not just you. But..." he hesitates but I just let him take his time. I won't press him. "I've never... you know."

I smile. "Been with a guy?"

"Yeah, that." He blushes and it's a beautiful sight to see.

"Neither have I," I say back.

His eyes widen. "Never? I always thought you were, well, not gay, but bi at the very least."

I shrug. "I don't know. I've never thought about it. I mean, some guys I think are hot or gorgeous but I've never turned it sexual until she came around. When I see her around you it turns me on like nothing I've ever felt before. I just have to find out why I feel this way."

"That's exactly how I feel too."

"Then stop hurting her," I tell him. He looks at me like I've lost my mind. "The girls, last night."

"That I threw out because they started talking shit about Addison."

I look at him. He shrugs. "Still, they were here and yet you put up this big bad show in the hallway when she wasn't here. Or the chick the night before in San Diego."

"We're not together."

I want to sock his shoulder. "That's not the point," I say a little too loudly and Addison stirs. She never opens her eyes, but it stops Talon and I in our tracks. "Let's talk about this later. The bus leaves at seven tomorrow."

I watch as he nods and then settles in next to Addison. He reaches his arm across her stomach, holding onto her, but I can feel his hand sliding gently along my chest. When I look at him, his smile tells me he knows exactly what he's doing. My cock jumps once again.

chapter 26

addison

It's really warm in here. I'm sweating. Why am I sweating? I move, or rather try to. I remember falling asleep in Kyle's arms then I had this strange dream. Talon and Kyle were talking, they were talking about me. Sort of. God, it's really hot in here.

I finally manage to open my eyes and I'm looking at a white t-shirt. Wait a minute. Kyle was wearing a black t-shirt last night. I pull back slightly and see Talon. Oh my god. How? When? Why? What? I squirm and bright blue eyes meet mine.

"Good morning, Red."

"What are you gonna call me when my red hair fades to pink? Or I change the color?" I ask him and he laughs.

"Red, I think it fits, for now." He winks.

"Good morning to you too. How did you get...?" I squirm again and there is a groan behind me and another set of arms wrap tighter around me. "Oh shit!" I squeal, then lift the covers. "Oh shit." I'm still dressed. Talon is dressed and I turn toward the groan and it's Kyle's black t-shirt. "What the hell happened?" I say looking at Talon.

"I came up after the concert, talked to Kyle some and then climbed in and passed out."

"What time is it?"

Talon lifts his head then groans, "It's four thirty."

"What time's the bus leaving?"

"Seven."

I still have to pack my stuff so I count the time. I have plenty. I look down my body and there are four arms down there. Two belong to me and one each belongs to my bed partners. I smile inwardly. It's like a girl's biggest fantasy come true.

I try and figure out how to untangle my limbs from them, especially Kyle. I don't want to wake him and I don't want Talon to have to get up too early. "Help?" I whine.

I feel his silent chuckle and I can't help but smile too. "With?" he whispers in his sultry voice and my clit explodes with need.

"I have to go to the bathroom and I'm a little trapped."

"Is that all?" I look at him and he wiggles his eyebrows and then ever so slightly and not at all subtly, flicks his hips against my hip and I let out a moan.

I feel Kyle stir and his own erection nails me right between the lips of my pussy and I nearly explode. I can't contain the fireworks of pleasure exploding from my clit. I writhe against him, desperate for him to do it again.

Before I know it, Talon has pulled himself closer to me and I am officially sandwiched between the two of them. My chest is pressed into Kyle's, and Talon's hands are sliding up my body. My hips flick against Kyle's and he groans in response, waking up, eyes wide, but then they soften as I flick my hips again. His eyes meet mine and then he looks over at Talon and back to me. Lust, desperation, and desire are all I can see in his eyes.

The next thing I know, his lips are crushing into mine. Warm and sensual. I am on fire. Moaning into his mouth, giving him an opening, he slides his tongue along mine. I take my free hand and put it back on Talon's hip, holding him to me. With my leg tossed over Kyle's hip, I pull him close to me and I begin grinding against the two men surrounding me. The only two men who've ignited desire in me since Dan. The only two men I've ever really wanted.

The covers fall away from me and both men pull back, disentangling me from them but their hands never leave me. Talon turns my face in his direction and I feel the tickle of his mustache against my lip. I quiver as a thrill runs through me. He quickly replaces Kyle's lips on mine. His lips are very different from Kyle's. They're thicker and maybe a little softer but none the less amazing.

I feel a hand on the zipper of my hoodie pulling it down, exposing my tank top and my nipples to the cooler air causing them to harden instantly. It takes a nanosecond before I feel two separate hands, each one cupping a breast, thumbs stoking over my nipples and my back arches as I moan in pure pleasure.

"Are you ready for this?" Kyle asks in a lust filled whisper.

"Yes," I moan.

"Are you sure?" Talon asks me.

"Yes. I'm yours." Regardless of the consequences. I know now that I have to do this no matter what happens afterward. I don't know if I can walk away from them after just one night, but I feel as though I have to at least try. No I need to do this. I have to see what this means and then deal with what to do next later.

I feel a hand sliding down my stomach, making its way south, past my belly button and into the waistband of my pajama bottoms. My stomach jumps at the tickle of fingers as they slide further south, finding my hairless mound before a finger slides into my wet, slick folds causing Kyle to groan. He captures my mouth. My breathing hitches as his finger twitches against my clit. Kyle releases my mouth and Talon is quick to replace him.

His lips are hard until he realizes how ragged my breathing is. He slows his kisses. Kyle is back, coaxing my lips to part with his tongue and I take him into my mouth. My mouth sucking his tongue, stroking, tasting and devouring him as his hand continues its gentle caress of my clit. My body twitches and my breathing stops altogether as pleasure soars in my veins. I slide a hand into his hair and pull back. He releases my lips with a growl and his cock twitches against my hip.

Talon disappears, pulling my attention from Kyle, I watch as his shirt comes off. His chest is gorgeous, tight muscles and covered in ink, but I can't linger there. My eyes slide south to the tent in his boxers and I can tell that he's huge by the sheer size of the bulge and I shiver with excitement. With my hand still in Kyle's hair, I press his face back to mine. I devour his mouth in a heated kiss with eyes on Talon, burning desire explodes as Kyle's hand increases its pace against my clit. My body jerks with building pleasure and a desperate need to come.

The rest of the covers completely disappear from me and I can feel the bed dip between my legs as Talon makes himself comfortable. Then his hands are on the elastic of my pajama pants pulling them downward. Kyle, realizing what Talon's about to do, pulls back. I look into Talon's pleading eyes and nod. That's enough for him. Faster than I can take a breath, off come my pajama bottoms and panties.

I hear Talon's intake of breath. "So beautiful," he breathes as he draws his lips closer to my dripping pussy that is still being stroked by Kyle's fingers. Talon's hands run along my legs, north towards my sex and his eyes are on fire. That heat I see when he sings to me is now in his eyes as he takes in the sight before him. I spread my legs a little wider.

Kyle is gently tugging on my hoodie, urging me to sit up so he can take it off. His hand comes away from my pussy and it is quickly replaced by Talon's mouth. I shiver as he sucks in my clit. I put my hand on his head, holding him to me, desperate to reach my climax. Grinding my sex against his hot mouth.

Sometime during Talon's assault on my clit, Kyle manages to rid me of my hoodie and I can barely hold myself up anymore so I fall back on the bed. My hand begins sliding up Kyle's leg, climbing higher, seeking out my package. My own toy to play with and when I find it, Kyle groans and Talon's eyes move from mine to Kyle's and I watch as pure pleasure rolls his eyes back into his head as I take Kyle's beautiful heavy length into my hand.

I begin tugging on his boxers and he understands what I want. He slides off of the bed, pulling his t-shirt off. His boxers are fully tented in front of him and my mouth waters, desperate to have him filling it. I lick my lips and bite my lower lip just as I feel my clit harden with its release.

"Ah, Talon, I'm..." I don't finish before my entire body is shaking with a climax unlike anything I've ever felt before. My entire body is trembling and pulsing with each beat of my heart and throb of my clit as Talon's excellent tongue coaxes the rest of my orgasm from my body and my eyes roll back into my head causing me to fall limp on the bed.

chapter 27

My eyes are too heavy while recovering from my orgasm to realize what's going on around me. I feel the bed shift as Talon climbs off. Then someone climbs back on the bed and fingers wrap around my wrists, lifting, pulling me up. "Come here, panda girl." It's Kyle. I do, I sit up and he pulls me up further. "Come to your knees, baby. I want to kiss you." I open my eyes to see the warmest, most genuine smile on his face. "Hi," he breathes and it steals my breath away.

I awkwardly get to my knees and Talon slides up behind me almost immediately. I shiver with excitement. I am sandwiched between two very gorgeous men and when I feel both of their erections pressing against me, I know they're both naked.

Kyle's hands slide to the hem of my tank top, lifting it. I raise my arms and it comes off quickly. "Jesus," they both say and I want to laugh. Then I feel Talon's hands splayed wide, sliding up my back. "So full of surprises you are." I smile. "Fucking gorgeous," Talon says with reverence as his hands continue to glide along my back and along my ink.

"Absolutely beautiful." Kyle's hands slide along my body, up toward my chest. My back arches at their touch and Kyle's hands cup my breasts. He has my nipples between his fingers rolling and twisting. My clit throbs and I moan, pulling his lips to mine as Talon's lips find the hollow of my neck and one of his hands slides around to my front, but instead of stroking me, I feel his hand wrap around Kyle's cock and I moan. Kyle groans out Talon's name against my lips.

But neither one of them stop. With my free hand, the one not holding Kyle's lips to mine, I reach behind me seeking Talon's length. When I find it, I wrap my fingers around it. He is so huge my fingers barely come together. I stroke up his entire length and wonder how on earth he is going to fit anywhere in my body, but I don't care. I need this. I need him.

I stroke. Kyle's lips come away from mine, kissing along my jaw toward the same spot Talon is kissing and licking along my shoulder. Then it happens, something I could only ever imagine in my fantasies. Talon and Kyle bring their lips together in the most beautiful sensual kiss. One that has me in the middle, desperate to join them.

I tug hard on Talon's erection and quickly replace Talon's hand on Kyle's cock. Stroking both men is hotter than I ever could have thought. More than I ever could have imagined and I need this. I need them.

I manage to pull myself from between their bodies with one goal in mind. Their cocks, my mouth. I lay down on my back and scoot so that my head is directly under their erections. Their kissing continues and neither is paying any attention to me.

I bring their heads close together and I take my tongue and lick along the sensitive spots just at the base of their mushrooms and they both jerk. I am rewarded with a double dose of pre-cum sliding slowly from their tips. I lick it up. The combination of sweet and salty is heady, and heavenly. I could get drunk on this.

I open my eyes and they're both staring down at me, watching me, imploring me to continue my assault on their erections. I pull Kyle's into my mouth first, hollowing my cheeks and pulling it down as far as I can bring it. Stroking my tongue on the underside as I do and Kyle's eyes roll back in his head.

I pull his erection from my mouth, letting it go with a pop, opening my mouth to show off the treasure of pre-cum to my audience and they both groan.

Then their hands are on me, rubbing along my stomach and tits. Playing with my dark pink nipples, rolling tugging them between their fingers. I bring my legs back up rubbing them together hoping the friction will help release the orgasm that's threatening me once again.

But Talon stops me. "Oh no you don't. Those are ours," he says, that sultry tone is back and I moan as Talon's hand cups my sex. I take Talon's erection into my mouth. He's much wider than Kyle, but their length is similar. I open my mouth and position him to slide down my throat and I suck him in, swirling my tongue and I watch his eyes turn white and close.

I continue working his cock for a moment and begin stroking Kyle's at the same time. Both men are turning to putty in my hands and I savor it. I soak it up while I can because I have a feeling some major payback is coming my way but I don't care. It's my turn to worship them. Switching cocks in my mouth is heaven and they both seem to be enjoying it just as much as I am.

Then suddenly both cocks are gone. Kyle slides off of the bed and then I can hear him kneeling between my legs and before I can do anything, his arms wrap around my thighs and he pulls me to the end of the bed and he buries his face into my weeping pussy. Within a couple strokes of his tongue my legs begin to tremble. Then without warning he slides a finger deep inside of me and I come. Milking his finger as my hips jerk and grind against his hand.

Kyle continues to stroke his tongue softly along my folds. I reach out for Talon, but I can't feel him on the bed anywhere. I turn, looking for him and he's gone.

"Don't worry," Kyle says from between my legs. "He went to get some condoms."

"Oh." Just then my hair stands on end and I look to the door. Standing in the doorway in all his naked glory is Talon and my mouth starts watering once again. Using my pointer finger, I motion for him to come to me and he does as he hands something to Kyle.

I hear the rip of a wrapper and look to see Kyle wrapping up his cock. He looks at me for reassurance and I smile, nodding slightly. He stands, pushing my knees up toward my head and he kneels on the bed between my legs, and I can feel his erection fall against my sex. I flick my hips. I need this. I need him, but I can't watch.

I look over to Talon and I get an eyeful of 'mister wonderful' between his legs. I look past his cock to his face, but he is watching Kyle. I expect to see jealousy in his expression, but there is none, simply adoration for what's going on between us. I pull Talon's cock into my mouth and he trembles. I stroke his dick with my tongue and Kyle begins to gently probe into me in short bursts, in and back out, opening me to accept him.

Talon's cock gives me a pre-cum treasure that I greedily swallow and it spurs me on to get him off while Kyle assaults my pussy with is slow gentle strokes. I try to flick my hips, encouraging him to go further and faster. It takes several attempts before he gets the hint and Talon begins to slowly thrust in and out of my mouth. He doesn't push far, but it is far enough for me to work his dick with my mouth and I stroke my hand along his shaft. I can see it's working because his face is scrunched up in an attempt to hold back.

Kyle buries himself in my pussy and grunts before he pulls himself back out. The sliding begins. "Jesus, you're. So. Fucking. Tight." Each word said between thrusts. "I, fuck, it's too good. I can't."

His thrusts increase at the same time my own pace on Talon increases. He catches what it is that I'm trying to do and he begins to thrust in and out of my mouth faster.

The orgasm that I really need is building within me. With each stroke of that big mushroom head of Kyle's, I can feel it stroking along my g-spot. I moan around Talon's cock, sending vibrations along his shaft and he groans.

"You're mouth, fuck, Addison, don't stop," he grunts and both their paces become short hard thrusts and I feel both of their heads expand, ready for release and I moan again around Talon's cock, unable to scream, I fight it. Fight the urge to clench my jaw because my orgasm is going to shatter me.

I feel my legs tremble and that white hot desire boiling in my blood. My limbs go stiff, and I explode into a powerful orgasm that sends a hot rush of fluid around Kyle's cock. Talon explodes into my mouth and I greedily swallow it back, fighting to keep it down, desperate to take his entire load.

My pussy contracts again and again as Kyle's thrusts slow. Damn it, I hate condoms. That's the last coherent thought I have.

chapter 28

Both men are still hard as they extract themselves from my body, but there is no cuddling going on. Kyle disappears into the bathroom, attempting to pull off his condom and Talon slides off the bed. "Roll over beautiful." He looks into my eyes with all the passion and lust I've seen before and I shiver.

Finding the strength to roll over is nearly impossible but the anticipation of having him buried inside me is so much that I can't even begin to think twice about it. I roll over and bring my knees up so that my ass is in the air. I can't see it, but I can hear the wrapper of the condom being ripped and the crackling of the condom as he stretches it down his length.

He comes onto the bed between my legs. His hands glide along my back once again. He's soaking up the tattoo on my back. In all its black and grey glory. His hands slide south to my hips where he encourages me to raise up just a little higher and I do. Then I can feel it, the wide bulbous crown of his erection is probing, seeking entrance in my depths and I shiver again. I want this, I need this. I slide back toward him. "Easy," he groans in desperation.

It doesn't take me long to understand why taking it easy is necessary. He's absolutely huge. I feel the walls of my pussy stretch to accommodate his girth, but it isn't painful, in fact it has my orgasm building again. I arch my back further, inviting him in, silently begging him to go faster, but he doesn't. He takes his time and the anticipation is killing me.

Kyle joins us. He is standing at the bed, opposite Talon. I peer up at him and he's still rock hard. My mouth waters and I lick my lips as he takes his cock in his hand. I moan as he strokes himself and Talon becomes sheathed in my warmth. It feels like he's reached my belly button he's so long, but I can feel only the slightest tickle of his balls against my folds and I know that I cannot take him all. He's so big and I am stuffed. He doesn't move, giving me a moment to adjust to his length and width.

Finally I can't take it anymore and I rock forward and back. He takes the hint and begins to move. I stare up into Kyle's eyes and my own roll up in intense pleasure. "Feel good, baby girl?"

"Yesss," I moan. Kyle lets go of his cock and climbs onto the bed but he doesn't come in front of me. He lies down close to me, and I feel Talon wrap his arms around my chest, steadying me, and he pulls up.

"Make room for him," Talon whispers and I help him lift me. Kyle slides in under me. I settle back down, holding myself up with hands on either side of his hips and his cock is right there, ready to be taken by my mouth.

The next thing I feel is Kyle's fat wet tongue slide along my clit and I nearly explode. "More," I moan when I don't feel him lick me again. Talon begins to move again and I let out a scream of pure pleasure as I pull Kyle's cock into my mouth.

"Ahh." So much pleasure. So much... "Fuck!" I scream as I let Kyle fall from my mouth and an orgasm takes me hard. My pussy is squeezing and milking Talon's cock and Kyle's tongue doesn't let up.

As soon as I am back in control of my body enough to remember the beautiful cock in my face, I begin licking and sucking it, stroking it with my hand.

Filled with Talon's cock, sliding in and out of my sex and a mouth full of Kyle with his wet tongue lapping at my pussy like he's starved for me, has another impending orgasm building quickly. That is until I feel Talon's finger stroking along the tight bud of my back door. The pleasure is so intense I moan again, sucking Kyle deeper into my mouth.

"Ahh!" I moan. "Too. Much. Fuuuuuccckkkkk," I scream as Talon pounds his cock inside of me. It's too much, fuck me, I can't...my body locks down, my orgasm sending sparks through my veins, my body convulsing with each thrust. I wrap my lips around Kyle and I suck him like my life depends on it. Sucking and fucking and feeling.

Then I explode. I'm flying high above the clouds as I shatter into thousands of pieces.

My body is shaking, convulsing and utterly spent as I feel both men explode. Kyle's sweet and salty gift is sliding down my throat and Talon slams into me one final time with a carnal groan as he explodes.

My body relaxes onto Kyle, his hips thrusting slightly against my mouth as he milks the rest of his orgasm. Talon's short thrusts and grunts are nearly enough to build another orgasm, but I force myself to settle. I can't take another one.

Somehow, though I'm not entirely certain how, I end up in the shower, but believe me it is not unpleasant by any means. I am sandwiched between two of the most gorgeous men I've ever met. My heart bursts with pride and I can't help but be excited to do that again.

Both Kyle and Talon take their time, but I am not allowed to lift a finger as they wash me. The scent of my vanilla body wash is strong in the air and I am covered not only with them, but with the gentle strokes of their hands along my entire body. It's enough to send pulses to my clit. My desire to have them again explodes.

As they wash, they play. Licking and sucking on my nipples and their hands gliding gently along my sex, and over every inch of my body. When I try to return the favor, my hands are swatted away.

"Let us do this. Let us take care of you," Talon whispers in my ear and my head falls back to his shoulder as the pleasure rocks through me. "This is not about us. This is about us taking care of our girl."

My eyes roll up into my head as I feel Kyle's hands sliding along my pussy in the softest of touches. My whole body shakes with orgasm and anticipation.

Two orgasms later and one seriously clean female, the boys turn off the water and wrap me in a towel. They both set out to drying my hair, my arms and my legs as I stand there in the shower. Once I'm dry and they're both shivering from the chill in the air, they begin to dry themselves individually. I watch as they both move with grace and their cocks bounce with their hardness. I want to take them both in my hands but my attempts are thwarted by both of them each time. Kyle shakes his head slowly at me.

"There will be time for that later," he says huskily, then smiles and winks at me. "We have to get moving."

Oh shit, the bus. I'd forgotten completely. "I think we need to talk," I say softly.

"Yes, we do," Talon says behind me. "Once we're settled on the bus."

A couple of minutes later they leave me to get dressed and get my things packed. Though they're only gone for twenty minutes, I miss them both terribly. How could I become so attached so quickly? It's disarming and I'm not sure how I feel about all this right now. I get dressed quickly, I had a feeling that they'd return once they were done with their own stuff and I was right. Talon is first and he comes straight to me when he enters the room. There is something in his eyes, something I don't quite understand. It isn't love, but something close to desperation.

"Hi," I breathe and he smiles. He brings his lips to mine and I melt against his body. Going limp, remembering what his mouth was doing not long ago, feeling every emotion he's feeling in this moment through our connection and I can't breathe.

"Hi," he says when he pulls back and I'm sucking air into my lungs like nobody's business. The back of his hand strokes along my cheek and I lean into the feeling.

He pulls back from me and takes whatever it is I have in my hands and puts it gently into my suitcase. "What else?" he asks and I can't think because Kyle has just walked into the room. He repeats the steps that Talon took. Taking me in his arms and kissing me, hard and needy. I melt into him. Though his kiss is different and distinguishable, it's no less passionate.

"Hi, panda girl," he says as he backs away.

"Hi," I breathe like a horny teenager who has her first crush. He smirks.

Both of the men go about finding all my stuff and packing it for me into my suitcase. I feel completely helpless, but they both insist on doing it and I'm packed in record time.

Before they leave with my stuff, they tell me to take a walk through and I do, double checking to make sure nothing is left behind and I find nothing left. I really need some time to think about this, but I have a feeling that neither of them are going to let me think for very long and that bothers me. This is a lot to handle. They are a lot to take in and I need to know where we stand before I can even begin to decide what to do next. Thank god, we're supposed to talk on the bus.

chapter 29

It doesn't take us very long to get back on the bus and no surprise to anyone, we're the first to get there, but we only have about twenty minutes to spare. Kyle and Talon set to work on making sure everyone is at least awake and moving and then getting them to hustle their asses.

The problem is that the bus won't leave without three very important members of the band and the downside to that is the fact that they know it. I'm tempted to leave and teach them a lesson. I mean shit, it's Vegas, they can be on a plane to Phoenix in two hours. Rusty and Beck stay with us while the other bus takes off. Mills goes with the other bus, which is surprising, but I'm pretty sure he's exhausted.

That other bus is almost more important to get to our destination than this one. It's got equipment on it. We can get the band there but they're useless without equipment. There are two semi-trucks that alternate locations so they're always there at least twenty-four hours before the show. The semi-trucks carry the band's stage gear. Following those trucks are the roadies who set up gear and make no money doing it. They usually sleep in their campers or their tents. It's strange and not something I could have ever done.

Okay, now that I can no longer distract myself from Beck and Kyle's conversation, I gather that last night was overly wild. I fight a snicker. No wonder Mills and Leroy took off with the other bus. I think they really needed sleep. Beck and Rusty are showing the wear and tear from last night as well.

Kyle, Talon, Beck, and Rusty set out to round up Mouse, Dex and Peacock. I go to work with my laptop. Checking my email, the Google alerts, and posting a couple tweets for the band, "thx #Vegas for a kick a$$ time, packing the bus for PHX." It is immediately retweeted like a hundred times. It gives me encouragement to continue this tweeting thing for them.

In the midst of rather mild headline emails I have an email from Cami regarding our dinner plans. She has some friends coming into town, from North Carolina, that were going to be there Monday but they're postponing to Tuesday. She's going to turn it into a dinner party with Talon, the rest of the band, Kyle and myself on Tuesday evening. She's arranged for limo service to pick us up at our hotel around seven. I make a mental note to tell Kyle and of course Talon, which after this morning, I will be telling both at once.

The relationship between the three of us has shifted, or at least I think it has, and I no longer feel intimidated about talking to Talon about 'business' related items. Kyle was easy because he's their manager. He handles nearly everything pertaining to their road related needs, and everything else too. I've also noticed that he is the one who handles certain payments and other financial aspects.

Regardless, the dynamic of our relationship has changed, at least in my mind. I can only hope it has in theirs too.

Seven comes and goes and we're still missing Dex and Mouse. Peacock stumbled onto the bus with about two minutes to spare.

It's now twenty after and Rusty has gone back up to help Talon, Kyle, and Beck drag out Mouse and Dex. At this point I think they'll be dragging them out by their toes.

The seven o'clock departure is a soft deadline. They're set all over the tour, though we don't tell them that, and they're usually an hour before, especially when leaving a hotel early in the morning. Looking at my watch it's creeping closer to seven thirty and eight is the deadline, whether they're on the bus or not, the bus is leaving. Since today is Sunday, our show starts at six instead of eight and sound needs to be done by five at the absolute latest.

I start going through the rest of the tour, making notes on tour stops that have hotels. We need to make adjustments to our stays because going forward, the men need to stay on the bus the night before we're scheduled to leave or be rounded up after their nights out, before they pass out in the hotel room. When I'm done, I email Kyle because he's helping corral the delinquents back onto the bus and taking care of the hotel.

I get a reply back that says…

Thank you for this, I was going to do this later. This is bullshit, and to top it off, this is something my assistant should be doing, not you. But thank you.

I smile at his reply and reply back to him.

Your assistant is an idiot who's petrified by her job. Namely the band. Or she's jealous because she's the only other female and not receiving any attention. LOL. I'd be happy to talk to her, but I think, since she's not doing the things that she should be doing, that maybe her position should be evaluated. Where did you find her anyway?

It doesn't take him long to reply back and I nearly blow coffee through my nose.

Honestly, I have no idea where I found her, in fact, I didn't. The label sent her. I knew when she showed up that she was going to be an issue, but the label said she was experienced. Which she is, but she is either getting drunk out of her mind or hiding in the corner. Case in point, she isn't here. She's on the other bus, oblivious to the fact that her band isn't behind her. She's not much of an asset to me or the band, maybe you could whip her into shape.

talon

"Fuck you, Dex, get your ass moving." Beck, Kyle and I just threw out four chicks, who all went from passed out, to half ass covered in a damn nanosecond and out the door. I guess when you're surrounded by three big ass guys, you move your ass. Two of them couldn't keep their eyes off of me and Kyle. Eye fucking both of us, but for the first time in my life, I cringed at the idea. Don't get me wrong, they weren't unattractive, but Jesus, they'd just spent the night screwing Dex. "Damn it, Dex!"

"Get off my nuts." His words are slurred and have very little effect on me, frankly I don't give a shit.

"Fuck you again, Dex, you're late, you've missed bus call, we've got a tight ass fucking schedule today, fucking move it."

"Bite me, dick. Just because you didn't fucking get laid last night doesn't mean you have to be a cocksucker."

I pull my arm back to fucking clock him one and Kyle stops me. "Leave it. Punching him ain't gonna get his drunk ass out of here any faster."

"You gonna let your little bitch stop you like that?"

"God damn it, Dex!" Beck barks and grabs Dex by his t-shirt, slamming him up against the wall. "You're fucking late, grab your shit and get the fuck out of here."

"I'm going to get Peacock and Mouse out of here. Come on, Talon, come with me?"

I'm so fucking pissed I want to beat the shit out of him, oddly enough Kyle knows that, and he knows to pull me out of here. Fuck him, fuck his bullshit. We've been on the road for all of three days and he's right back to his bullshit again. "Put a fucking collar on him," I snap as Kyle pushes me out the door.

addison

I don't get to reply back to his message because he climbs onto the bus behind a very hungover or still drunk, I can't tell, Dex. He stumbles toward his rack and climbs up and I can hear him snoring before his head even hits his pillow. I roll my eyes. I look at Kyle and we both bust out laughing. Between Dex and our email conversation, it's almost too much to look at him. But he comes over and kisses me on the cheek then takes a seat.

"I think you should be promoted," he says deadpan.

"Is this because I slept with you or because of my mad skills?" I say lightheartedly and he looks at me, dead serious.

"Both. Because business isn't your only mad skill." He wiggles his eyebrows at me and I bump shoulders with him laughing. "I feel awful," he says with a sad look in his eyes.

I scowl at him. "Why?"

"Because we completely assaulted you and never even bothered to ask how you're feeling after yesterday."

I snort a laugh. "I feel amazing." I smile and I know I'm glowing.

He smiles at me. "Good."

"Besides you took very good care of me afterward, so believe me, I feel better than I've felt in a long time."

"Good."

"Have you and Talon talked?"

He shrugs. "A little."

"And?" I prompt him.

"And we're both a little shell shocked about what happened, not because it happened but because of the fact that it all happened so fast and that we both fell into it so easily. Believe me, panda girl, it's not a bad thing." He winks at me. "But we promised we'd talk, just as soon as we're settled on the road."

Just then Rusty comes onto the bus. He's carrying a box full of something, pastries maybe and a jug of, I smile. Orange juice. "I got some bagels, cream cheese and OJ." He sets them on the table. "Talon, Mouse, and Beck are on their way down now."

"Good," Kyle says, standing up and going to the cupboard and grabbing some paper plates, a stack of red solo cups and then to the drawer for a knife.

He sits back down and dives into the box of bagels. He pulls out one then looks at me. "What kind would you like?"

"Plain."

"You're boring," he teases me and digs out a plain bagel and the strawberry cream cheese. I watch as he cuts my bagel and covers it in spread. Then he serves it to me without a second thought for himself. Then he pours me some orange juice. "Bon appètit." He smiles as he gestures towards my feast. Then he sets about making his own bagel as Rusty makes his.

About the time they finish dressing up their goodies, the guys are coming onto the bus. Mouse looks like death warmed over, but at least he doesn't seem to still be drunk. He, like Dex, makes a beeline for his bunk and literally falls down into it. Beck turns to the driver. "Let's roll."

I look down at my watch. Forty minutes late, praying there is little to no traffic so we can make our arrival on time. Hopefully.

chapter 30

Kyle and I hang at the table in the galley after Talon grabs himself a bagel and disappears into his bunk, shutting the door. Both Kyle and I look at each other and shrug. "Dex pissed him off pretty bad," Kyle whispers. "Just give him a minute." I nod and we go back to discussing our travel schedule changes.

"Phoenix is a short distance, but Atlanta to Orlando is a bit farther, especially after we've been there for a while, there needs to be a curfew in place for that night."

"I agree," Kyle says.

"We've added seven new shows to this tour because of their performance; I do not want to ruin that reputation by showing up late, which we're coming close to doing today."

"Right, but we also have a two hour earlier show, so it wouldn't have been as dire and likely won't be in the future."

The conversation continues for some time until finally Talon emerges from his room wearing a pair of flannel pajama pants, flip flops and a t-shirt. He shuffles to the fridge for a bottle of Gatorade and turns to us. We're both watching him and he smirks. "What?"

"You're just so..." I lose the words when his eyes narrow and he starts to seduce me with his gorgeous vibrant green eyes.

"That's what I thought," he smirks. "What are you two talking about?"

Kyle launches into my idea, giving me full credit for it, which I admire. He and Talon slip into discussion about what happened this morning with the guys, not with us, thank god. No need to air dirty laundry for the whole bus to hear, especially considering Rusty and Beck are dozing on the couch next to us.

Talon grabs for my hand. "Come on, we need to talk." He looks at Kyle. "You too." I smile and I'm impressed that Talon is leading this charge. Impressed because he is the one I expected to run from this. In fact he kind of did when he disappeared into his room shortly after boarding the bus, but he's owning up to it now as he leads me back to his room. Once we're all inside, he closes the door.

He turns to me, wrapping me in his arms and planting a beautiful kiss on my lips. There is no tongue involved, but the kiss is soft and sweet, and my pussy heats. Jesus, after this morning you'd think I'd be worn out, then again, I have nearly eight sexless years to make up for and who better to do it with than these two.

With Talon's lips still on mine, Kyle comes up behind me, wrapping me in his arms, holding me to him and pressing me into Talon's hard chest. Passion ignites once again and I moan. This, right here, between these two men, is exactly where I need to be. Their loving embrace is heartwarming beyond anything I could have ever thought. But I can't let this continue until I know where this is going. Yes, the sex is amazing, fucking A! I want to do it again and again, but I think some ground rules need to be set.

"We need to talk," I whisper between kisses and both men gradually pull back and I shiver at the cool air radiating around me at their loss.

"Where to start?" Talon says looking into my eyes.

"How about with how you two are feeling?"

"And she successfully defers to us first," Kyle teases. "Well, bottom line, this is new to me and I know it's new to Talon."

I turn to look at him. "How do you know that?"

He smiles. "Because, when Talon climbed into your bed last night, we talked about it."

"So I wasn't dreaming, you guys really were talking?" They both stiffen. "Relax, I don't know or remember what was said, it just seemed like it had a lot to do with me."

"It did," Talon says and I turn toward him.

"I'm gonna get whiplash if I keep turning between the two of you." I grab their hands and pull them in the direction of the bed. As I climb up, I drop their hands and go up near the pillows and lean against the headboard. They follow my lead but sitting in front of me, cross-legged like little boys on a carpet waiting for the teacher to read a story. It makes me smile.

"What was the conversation about?" I prompt.

Kyle speaks first. "Us, trying to decide where we stood with each other. Before the show last night, while he was kissing you, I rubbed my hand along his, well, you know, anyway. I was concerned that I'd crossed a line or that he thought it was you. I quickly realized that he knew it was me and that he enjoyed it, but that neither one of us have ever done anything like this."

"You could have fooled me," I say seriously. "You've never had a threesome before?" I'm honestly curious.

"We have separately and together. But there has never been an attraction between us. Until you." Talon is very serious when he talks. "I'm not sure what it means, and I certainly don't know where it will lead between Kyle and me; but I know my attraction to him comes from being around you. There is nothing sexier in the world than seeing him kiss you and hold you."

His words strike me deep. When I first met Talon, I expected a complete hard ass, someone who didn't give a shit about anyone or anything, and maybe that's the case, outside of this room, but something has changed in him, with him, and it makes me want him that much more. "So in other words, you both want to 'try' to be with one another, with me?"

Kyle and Talon both look at each other and then back at me. The answer is clear in their eyes and the answer is yes.

"You both realize that I've never done anything like this before, right?" There is no shock, no malice, no nothing that crosses their features. "Kyle knows some of my story, but it's been over seven years since I've been with someone, until this morning." That gets Talon's attention.

"How is that possible, Addie?" That's the first time Talon has used my nickname and my heart swells a little more. "You're fucking gorgeous. You could have anyone you want. In fact, you should have anyone you want."

I smile sadly at him. "Talon, I think it's time I tell you my story."

chapter 31

"Jesus, Addie," he says when I finish telling him about Dan and what happened. Then launching into why I threw myself into work and then finally my difficulty with friendships and relationships in general.

"The worst part of it all is that after the funeral, no one, besides my mother, cared about me. No one called to check on me, to see how I was holding up. It's like I was lost in the wind."

"Damn it, Addison, I'm sorry," Kyle cuts in. "I had no idea they'd done that."

"Kyle, it's not your fault."

"Wait, why would it be Kyle's fault?" Talon asks. I left out that part of the story, unsure of how to tell Talon.

"Because Dan was my brother." Kyle handles it for me.

Talon is visibly shaken by Kyle's admission. "I didn't know, not until it hit me before the San Diego show. It hit me. I'd been trying to place Kyle, figure out how I knew him and it turns out that I didn't know him, but he was familiar somehow."

"I was dealing with so much shit at the time when Dan died. I didn't care about anyone but myself. Which is how I ended up in rehab and then finally at Penn State. I got my shit together and found myself in college, which is where I met Talon and this is where I've been ever since."

"So it comes full circle," I say quietly. Talking about Dan to Talon has actually been a relief. Almost as if a weight has lifted from my shoulders. "By the time I realized what I was missing out on, I was so engrossed in work that I didn't have time for anything or anyone and a part of me regrets it. Regrets that I let a dead man rule my life for so many years. But it all happened so fast, I never really gave myself time to forgive, to deal with it." The tears streak down my cheeks. "And now I've gone from nothing to you and this and I'm so confused."

"Stop, Addie, please. We will figure this out. Some way, somehow. I don't know where to begin with all of this either. I just know one thing. I want to be with you and oddly enough, I really want to be with Talon too."

I watch as gentle smiles spread across their faces. "I, damn it you guys, I don't know what to say," I mutter.

"Don't say anything, just let us hold you," Talon says as he slides closer to me. I wrap my arms around his neck and hold him to me. Kyle joins us and in an awkward shift we all manage to lie down. Me in the middle. Kyle spooning me and me spooning Talon.

We don't say anything for a long time. We all just lie there, soaking up each other. Kyle's hand goes from my hip to Talon's hip. Talon shifts, pushing back into me. I can feel Kyle's erection pressing against my back and just like the strike of a match, I'm on fire. Burning for them, needing them as much as they seem to need me.

"I have one request," I whisper.

"Anything," they both say in unison.

I smile. "Me and only me. No one else besides the three of us." Talon turns in my arms so he can look at me.

"This is new to me. I've never wanted a commitment, I've never longed for anything outside of the bedroom and more than anything, I've never had the same woman in my bed twice. I won't lie. I am going to fuck this up. I just know I will." His eyes are radiating sadness, I know how he feels and I want to cry.

"Am I enough for you?"

"I hope so, I think so. I just need time to know so."

"Talon, you've already started to prove that to yourself. Don't put so much doubt in your own head," Kyle says over my shoulder. "The woman Friday night? The fact that you came up to the suite instead of partying with the guys. Don't be so hard on yourself. No one is asking for a commitment from you, but if she is really what you want, you won't hesitate. It will be easier than you think."

"What happened Friday night?" I ask, honestly curious. He had a buffet lined up on the couch when I came back to the room.

"I tried to kick them out and they refused. I had to call Mills in to get them out of my room. But the truth is, I wouldn't have kicked them out if they hadn't started talking about you."

"But you had the willpower to recognize that, and that Talon, is a step in the right direction," I tell him, stroking his cheek. "This is going to take some getting used to for all of us. Believe me. I am a ridiculously independent woman and if the way you two took care of me this morning is any indication of how this is going to go moving forward, it is going to be a major adjustment for me too. So patience is a given. It has to be. But you also need to understand that if I leave a party, or backstage or anywhere that you are, it's not always going to be because I'm pissed off or jealous, like Friday night, but sometimes I just need my alone time."

"We all do," Kyle says. "It needs to be an unspoken term of this arrangement."

We all snuggle back into each other again. This time Talon stays facing me and they're both stroking my hair softly. Comforting me, enveloping me in their warmth. A sensation I know will never get old. It will never fade away, at least not when it comes to these two. I've never felt safer than I do right now.

My eyelids grow heavy and I fall asleep in their arms.

When I wake up sometime later, I can tell that the bus has stopped, but I find that I'm all alone. My heart breaks just a little bit. I feel like I've inadvertently given them their chance to run. Until I look at the clock and see that it's 4:30. I sit up quickly. Jesus, I have an hour and a half to get ready. Shit. I wanted some more time because, well, I have a plan for tonight.

chapter 32

talon

"Are you sure you're okay with this?" Kyle asks me.

"What choice do I have?"

"A lot," he says back.

"No, I really don't. From the moment she walked onto that bus, I knew there was something special about her. Something beyond anything I've ever known and felt." God, I sound like a fucking sap. "But the point is that I knew I had to have her. Except at the time I thought I was content to stick it in her and be done, get it out of my system, but over the last couple of days I feel so much happiness when I'm around her. She makes it all go away. She makes the years of pain just disappear and it's addicting and it makes me want to be a better person."

"Yeah, I know. Believe me, I feel it too."

"I can't make her choose, Kyle. I can't make her choose which one of us she wants to be with."

"Why not? It would be easier," he says, and he's dead serious, but in the same token, he doubts his words.

"No, it wouldn't. The way I see it is like this. If you get her, I'm left to be envious and jealous and perpetually horny because any woman I would try to hook up with wouldn't be her. Instead I'll have to watch my best friend with her. If she chooses me, I'll feel bad for leaving you out, feel like I've stolen something from her and I will fuck it up. I know I will. I always do, Kyle. If we both have her, I don't have to feel jealous because I'll have her too and as a bonus, I get you."

He smirks. "Are you getting soft on me?"

I roll my eyes. "No. But I meant what I said. I've seen your shit before, we've shared women in the past, but never have I ever been so turned on by seeing you two together. It's strange and it's fucking hot."

"I have to agree with that. But I'm not sure how far I'm willing to take it between you and me." He gestures between us.

"I'm not going to go kissing you, publicly, if that's what you're worried about. What happens behind closed doors is another story. I've always found other men attractive, but like you, I just never acted on it. I know that there are a couple of things that after this morning I'm itching to try," I tell him. No need to go into detail about how I enjoyed his little tongue trick on my nuts this morning and how I have a deep craving to have his mouth wrapped around my tool. Those are fantasies that I'm desperate to turn into a reality, but I don't want to push him too far, too fast.

"I'm worried about our friendship," Kyle says extremely serious.

"How so?"

"Well, you know what they say; sex between friends is usually the death of a friendship."

I try not to laugh because he has a point. "Look, I won't let it come between us if you won't. If we keep it the way it's always been out of the bedroom, then there is nothing to worry about." He nods.

We hear a whistle and our heads whip around the second Dex spouts his shit. "Hot fucking momma, come here, let daddy show you a thing or two." I look straight at Addison walking through the back door. Then I watch her shudder at Dex's words and not in a good way. It makes me smile, but her outfit makes me hard.

She's wearing a corset tonight, a strapless black and purple number. Her tattoos on her shoulders pop with their bright colors and I realize now that this is the first time the fairy on her back has ever been exposed, except of course this morning when we stripped her. Her corset is matched with a very short leather skirt, fishnet stockings, a fucking garter belt holding them up and boots that go all the way to her knees and are at least four inches high.

"Fuck," Kyle growls next to me.

"You took the words right out of my mouth."

"Dude, she's fucking ours. You know that?"

Kyle's words hit me like a fucking freight train. She's ours. She's mine, she's his. There is no jealousy, no envy, simply contentment and desire as she walks in perfectly measured strides toward us.

Her hair is up, but it's high on her head. Like they used to wear it back in the fifties or sixties and it folds nicely into the pony tail at the back of her head. Her make-up is dark, but bright red lipstick accents her features perfectly.

"Hello, boys," she says as she comes to stand in front of us.

"Rusty's on you tonight," I growl.

"No, he's not. He was falling asleep on the bus, so I sent him to bed. Besides, I have you two to protect me now, don't I?" She raises her eyebrows, but beneath the mask she's wearing, I can tell she needs the reassurance.

"Damn straight," Kyle says sternly and her face lights up into a bright smile.

"I need to kiss you," I groan.

"Then kiss me." Those three little words were all I needed to hear and I charge at her, hard and desperate, wrapping my arms around her, holding her to me while my lips crush into hers. Lightning ignites in my veins and I need her, right now.

I push her backwards into an open door of a dressing room, the one I was given, not that I need it. As soon as we're inside, I spin her around, pinning her to the wall next to the door. I take her hands and pin them over her head. "Fucking gorgeous," I growl and look over at Kyle standing in the doorway. "Get in here," I say and he obeys me, stepping into the room and shutting the door. His obedience sends a shock wave of desire through me. Dominant? No, but I love control, and I love it rough and right now, she's giving me exactly what I need.

My lips are hammering hers with hard kisses. I push off of her. "Kyle, take her," I command and he takes her. Keeping her arms pressed above her head he grinds himself into her pelvis and she moans. "Fuck me," I groan as I press into Kyle's backside, my hands sliding along his shirt, pushing it up.

He pulls back from kissing her long enough for me to pull his shirt over his head. His muscles are tight and I rub my hands down his back. He hisses a breath through his teeth when my nails scrape down his back and I slam into him with my body, holding both of them to the wall.

Hot, passionate and rough. Addison moans as Kyle dips his head lower, along her shoulder, down her breasts. I feel him tug her corset down, freeing her breasts and she cries out in pleasure as he sucks a beautiful nipple into his mouth. I sink my teeth into Kyle's shoulder, wrapping my arms around him, reaching for his fly. I pop the button and rip the zipper down.

I slide my hands into the waistband of his pants and push them down to his thighs. I feel his cock bounce as I free it and I grip it in my hands. "Talon," he moans against Addison's chest. "Fuck, don't stop." And I can't. I grip his cock and begin stroking it. He pulls back from holding Addison against the wall to push himself against me.

I look at Addison over my shoulder, conveying my own need and she slides down the wall. I feel her hands against Kyle's thighs and then stroking along his shaft right along with me. Then I feel her wet lips against his erection and hear her swallowing.

She slides back up the wall, grabbing the back of my neck as she pulls me around Kyle and into a deep, open mouth kiss. It's hot and firm and tastes divine. She's brought me a sampling of Kyle and my cock throbs. We only kiss for a moment before she's sliding back down the wall and I resume stroking Kyle. I expect her to help me get Kyle off, but instead her hands are on my thighs, sliding up to my belt.

Kyle widens his stance as I continue stroking his length. Fuck, he's got a big cock.

The next thing I know Addison's mouth is on me, sucking my cock into her mouth, pulling it in deep. She sucks me with vigor. I loosen my grip on Kyle and she grabs my shaft, stroking it in time with my strokes on Kyle. We're both groaning and I can tell Kyle is getting close, so close.

"I want you both. In my mouth," Addison says before sucking my cock into her mouth and stroking it with her hands.

I lean into Kyle's ear. "Are you ready?"

"Yes," he breathes.

"Let's give our lady what she wants."

I feel him turn slightly so I back off, releasing my hold, and his hand takes my place. I look down and Addison is looking up at us, watching both of us stroke our hard-ons right above her. Her breasts are being pushed up by her corset and her beautiful puffy nipples are hard. Looking past her tits, I can see she's buried her hand in the waistband of her skirt. I smile as I watch them bounce with each stroke to her pussy.

She throws her head back, letting her tongue slide along her bottom lip as she opens her mouth wide. I stroke my head against her mouth and that's all it takes. The fire burns from within and I explode, careful to get as much, if not all, in her mouth. Kyle is quick to join me, taking his cue from me as we both let loose our orgasms right into her hot, waiting mouth. She groans, swallowing it down, wiping her lips with her tongue and shuddering in her own release.

The fire has dulled within, but I am rock hard once again just looking at her on her knees staring up at us. Fuck, what have I ever done to deserve them?

chapter 33
addison

There is a pounding knock on the door. "Fifteen minutes," someone shouts.

"Got it," Talon hollers back. It brings me out of my post orgasmic high. Talon was turned on by me and then the hottest thing I've ever seen in my entire life was when he took it out on Kyle. He didn't race to fuck me, he didn't race to do anything hardcore with me. He stepped back and traded places with Kyle. Allowing Kyle to pleasure me while he took comfort in Kyle's erection. It took everything I had not to come the moment my finger grazed my clit. Watching them, stroking their shafts above me was probably the hottest thing I've ever seen or could ever imagine happening.

I'd always thought of facials as degrading to the woman receiving them, but holy fuck, I can't wait to do that again. I think it helped that there was nothing empowering in it for the guys. They were revved up and I was the cause of that. I knew my outfit would turn heads, but I never imagined it would elicit such a no holds barred passion between the three of us. Hell, even between Talon and Kyle.

Then when Talon took the wad of Kyle's cum from my mouth, I was done for. I knew then that this is really something Talon wants and Kyle's reaction was electric. Though I think we might still be a long way away from them working each other over without my help, it's an amazing sight to see none the less.

"Addison."

"Wha, huh?"

"You checked out on us, where'd you go?" Kyle asks and I smile.

"To about five minutes ago. Fuck me, that was..." I trail off as I watch the lustful glean shine in their eyes as they look at each other. "Yup, that covers it."

They both laugh and pull me off of the floor, wrapping their arms around me. They hold me tight and close. "You're so fucking beautiful," Talon murmurs and I can hear Kyle's silent agreement.

We stay like that for more than a few minutes. Me just being held tightly against both of them. Then Talon pulls back. "I need to go talk to the guys. Will you wait for us in your spot?" He smirks at me.

"I wouldn't miss it for the world."

"I know." He gives me a shy smile. "You proved that yesterday." Then he kisses me, short and chaste, but no less breathtaking. He leaves the room, closing the door behind him.

"You okay?" Kyle asks me.

"I'm great, why?"

He shrugs and pulls back, looking at me. "I feel like we used you."

I shake my head softly and close my eyes. "Not in the slightest. Everything that happened, happened because I wanted it to. I got off too."

He gives me a sad half smile. "I know but by your own hands."

I bring my hand to his cheek and he tilts his head into my hand. "So did you," I say with sincerity.

"We both had help."

I snort a laugh. "Yeah, and so did I. Believe me, Kyle, watching you two do what you did, not only what Talon was doing to you, but you both standing over me, was by far the sexiest thing I've ever seen in my life. Though it may not have been the touching kind of help, it was better than watching porn. It was amazing knowing that with a few simple words, you would both stop, or do anything I asked. That was empowering. Now, a more important question. He was pretty rough with you. How do you feel?"

There is a slow satisfactory smile that spreads across Kyle's lips giving me all the answers I need to that question and I smile.

"You like it, didn't you?" I ask.

He nods. "I was lost in everything- you, him, the whole thing. I would have, easily could have taken that a lot further than just a hand job and I wouldn't have thought twice about it."

"Good. I'm happy to hear it."

"Are you trying to tell me that you wouldn't want us if we weren't so into each other?" The question is serious but there is a glint in his eye that tells me otherwise.

"No, I'm not. But believe me when I tell you that your attraction to each other turns me on almost as much as you both do when you're near me, touching or kissing me. I never, not in a million years, expected that I would enjoy sex with another man, let alone two, let alone two very sexy rock gods who are into each other. It's heady and it's very confusing, but if there is anything I've learned in the last fifteen hours, it's to follow my heart."

With that he kisses me. Soft and sensual, holding me to him and I melt into his touch. Talon and Kyle are like polar opposites. Kyle is soft and sensual, a teddy bear. While Talon is rough and a little crass with his words and his actions. Both, while great separate; are beyond comprehension together.

There's another knock at the door. Kyle pulls back and steps away. "Come in."

Talon opens the door with a wide smile on his face. "We still good?"

I look at Kyle and back to Talon. "We're great," I answer just as Empty Chamber kicks up the strings to their second to last song. "Show time," I say and walk toward Talon, who hasn't moved, so I lift up on my toes and kiss his cheek. "No more for you until you go on stage. There isn't enough time to attack me again."

"Wanna bet," he growls but I can tell he's playing. "Go on, get your butts out there. Oh, and Kyle?"

"Yeah?"

"We need to do something about your assistant," Talon says solemnly. I, on the other hand, start laughing. "What's so funny?"

I settle down enough to tell him that Kyle and I had the same discussion this morning. "We're gonna figure something out, let's talk later about it," I encourage and Talon nods. His hand slides off of the door and up to the top of my corset. He tugs on it slightly, adjusting it and then I feel his knuckle graze across my nipple and I shiver. "Not fair!" I moan.

"I never said I would play fair. This is payback for the raging hard on you're about to give me. Now get out there before I drag you out." He smirks at me and I take Kyle's hand. Talon steps back then turns back to where the band is hanging out getting warmed up and I take my spot next to the stage. Kyle disappears, wherever it is that he goes because he always seems to come out of nowhere when he embraces me and I listen to Empty Chamber's last song. Momentarily realizing that if they decide to change it up, I'm totally screwed.

I was worried about Talon's assault on Kyle, though he gave Kyle every opportunity to say no, I'm worried that they're both being pushed too far, too fast. I don't want that because that's only going to drive a wedge between the three of us, if at any time either one of them go somewhere the other isn't ready for yet. I think we need to discuss a safeword. Something that will stop everything, so we can talk about it, discuss it. Not that 'stop' wouldn't be enough, but stopping completely as a threesome.

I am all for pushing boundaries, I'm all for trying new things, but I am not at all about pushing someone to do something they can't handle and I can see where this sexual adventure could push those limits.

chapter 34

Tonight's walk is no different than any other night, but yet it feels so much different. First of all, I know what to expect, but I am unprepared for the firework frenzy that Talon and Kyle ignite within me when they take me in their arms. This time they both kiss me at the same time. Kyle takes my neck and Talon devours my lips and tongue. Both hard, both wanting, and neither one willing to pull away from me. It's Talon who pulls back first. "Kick some ass, big man."

"Can I lick yours later?" he says back.

I blush. "Yes."

A wicked smile spreads across his lips and he backs away for the stage. "Hello, Phoenix," he growls into the microphone and the crowd goes wild as Dex starts pounding on his drums and Mouse brings the crowd to a higher level of excitement when he starts playing the chords of 'Walk Away'. One of their monster hits. Kyle hasn't moved from having his arms wrapped around me and we start to dance as Talon entertains the masses. For the first time, I stand there, with Kyle's arms wrapped around me throughout the entire concert.

I watch as Talon frequently looks over at us, smiles and then goes back to singing. Sometimes there is so much heat in his eyes, both Kyle and I shiver and I can't help but notice the bulge in Talon's pants that just never seems to go away, it makes me smile to know that it's for me and Kyle.

Finally they start to play 'Your Eyes' and Kyle spins me around, pulling me into his arms so we can dance together. The song is soft, but still has a great alternative beat to it. But the band plays longer than normal and I feel Talon's hand on my arm. "I'm not stealing her," he says to Kyle and understanding crosses his features and he nods. "Come here, panda," Talon says.

Goosebumps radiate from my heart and my nipples harden beneath my corset as Talon drags me on stage. "No, no, no," I protest.

Talon pleads with me silently and the rest of the band is encouraging him to do this and I blush. "Ladies and gentlemen," Talon says into the microphone as he spins me around to face the crowd. "I'd like to introduce you to a very special angel in my life and tonight, I dedicate her favorite song, to her." Oh god. I put my head in my hands and the guys pick up the pace, bringing the song back around to the beginning. The crowd completely disappears. It's only Talon, and I can feel Kyle's presence and nothing else.

Talon starts to sing. Staring straight into my eyes. Without thinking about it, I start to sing along with him. His eyes widen and he steps a little closer to me, putting the microphone between us. I stop singing.

During a musical interlude in the song he mouths, "Don't you dare stop singing." Oh shit. He kicks back into the song and I sing along with him. A few lines into it and with some major encouragement, I really get into the song. I'm singing along but when the crowd starts screaming with excitement I realize that Talon isn't singing anymore, he's watching and listening to me sing his song. I blush as red as a cherry and stutter. He catches onto my distress and picks up for me. We finish out the song together.

The crowd goes crazy, chanting and cheering for our impromptu duet and I'm floored. I've always known I could sing, but I've never made a point of doing it. Talon takes my face in his hands and he kisses me so sweet and tender that the world melts away. He pulls back and smiles. Then he ushers over to Kyle for him to join us on stage.

What the hell is he doing? Kyle comes to stand next to me. "Ladies and gentlemen, if it weren't for these two amazing people, we would not be standing here tonight performing for you. If it wasn't for your love of our music, we wouldn't have a reason to be standing here. So join me in a round of applause for these wonderful amazing people and our crew back stage."

Talon pulls me in for a sideways hug and then he pulls Kyle into our hugging circle too. It's odd but yet so natural, despite the seventeen thousand people watching us. Talon pulls back, winks at both of us and we take our leave of the stage. Kyle's hand is on the small of my back and Talon doesn't take his eyes off of me. I blow him a kiss. He smirks and goes back to being himself on stage.

There are only two more songs left in their set and Talon does what he does best, playing with the crowd and singing like nobody's business. For the last song he picks up his own guitar and starts to play. Talon with a guitar is something else. Short of him being naked, this is the next best thing to watch on the planet. Kyle still doesn't leave me. He wraps his arms around me once again.

"You never told us you could sing."

"Oh please, I can't hold a candle to half the people out there today."

"Bullshit. You should be out there."

I roll my eyes. "Yeah, right."

"Addison." Shit, I know that voice, panic races in my veins and I turn to see Cami and Tristan standing just off stage. I disentangle myself from Kyle's hold and go to them.

"I didn't know you guys were coming."

"We had a blast in San Diego we thought we'd come again. Can we talk?" I try to decide if she's pissed or not and I can't quite tell.

"Sure." I turn to Kyle. "We're gonna take Talon's dressing room."

He nods and I turn back to Cami and Tristan, leading them toward the room that Kyle, Talon and I shared a couple of hours ago. That was probably a bad idea. My nerves are shot and I'm not thinking clearly. God, I hope she's not pissed about the singing, plus his angel comment. Jeez, of all the shows he could have done that, he had to do it here. Dammit, dammit.

I open the door for them, they step inside, and I follow them in. "What can I do for you?" I say, trying to stay cool.

"I'm a little shocked at what I just saw."

Oh shit. "Which part?"

"Well, I'm not concerned about whatever relationship you're building with these guys if that's what you're so worried about. I am by far the last person on this planet that can stand here and criticize you for that." Her head bobs pointedly in Tristan's direction. He snorts a laugh. "No, Addison, I want to sign you."

chapter 35

I fall back into the couch that's behind me. "You, what?"

Both Cami and Tristan laugh. "I want to sign you, to Bold, as a client, Addison. Have you ever done that before?"

"What, sing? All the time, in my shower."

She laughs. "You've never performed before?" I shake my head. "You could have fooled me. You were amazing up there. So natural."

I clear my throat. "I think Talon had a little to do with that. He's comforting."

She smiles. "I could see that. But seriously, I'd like for you to consider it."

"Is that even possible? I mean, I work for Bold."

"True, you do, but there are always ways around that. Look, we can discuss the details after the tour. I want you to really think about it. If you enter into a life like Talon and his guys live, there is very little chance of going back. I wouldn't be surprised if your celebrity increases just from tonight. Watch yourself with that. It's a hard thing to get used to. I know, it's been three years and I'm still getting used to it, though they leave me alone now. But, well, you know how it goes. You're no stranger to this industry. So at least you have some inside information. But you can't decide one day you want to do it and then the next day take it all back."

I nod. I'm barely hearing her; I'm so taken aback by her offer to sign me. Why me? That is a question I will be asking for a very long time.

"I promise I will think about it, but can I email you with any questions?"

"Absolutely. There's no pressure, if you decide you don't want to you don't have to. But a piece of advice, stay away from the labels. If they come after you, you better come to me," she says seriously. Tristan, standing quietly behind his wife nods in agreement.

"They're animals, Addison. Watch yourself," Tristan says with a smile.

"I will, and I will keep you guys posted if anything comes up." I smile. "So, did you guys enjoy the show?" Just then the noise level picks up as the door opens. Talon is standing there.

"Sorry, Cami and Tristan," he says to them then turns to me. "You okay?"

I smile. "I'm great." I can hear the crowd is shouting encore repeatedly through the door. "You guys going back out?" He nods with a shit eating grin on his face that's infectious. "Go get 'em, big guy." He laughs and shuts the door as he leaves.

I turn back to Cami and Tristan who are both smiling from ear to ear. "Where were we? Oh, the show, did you enjoy yourselves?"

Cami nods with enthusiasm. "It was almost better than San Diego. Though I'm not sure how," she laughs.

"I really like them. I'm supposed to be in New York when they're in town, I just might have to sneak in again," Tristan says. "It's been a while since I've been excited about a band like these guys." His smile is bright. Tristan is surprisingly shy, but when he lets his guard down he's super sweet.

"Well, we'll be over on Tuesday for dinner."

"Oh yeah, about that. I wanted to give you a heads up. This is turning into an all-out shindig. Some of my friends and their boyfriends, girlfriends and husbands are coming. I don't expect any crazy fangirl moments, but I wanted you to warn the guys. Oh, and bring Kyle." She winks.

"Jeez, nothing gets past you does it?"

She laughs. "No, it doesn't. I know a love-struck teenager when I see it and you've got two of them."

I sigh. "Yeah."

She laughs. "Well, apparently we need to have coffee while you're here. You know, girl talk." She winks.

"Oh no, I couldn't, you're so busy…"

"You have my number. If you need to get away, call me." She winks again and I nod. "We're gonna duck out of here before the hoard crawls their way back here."

"You don't want to say hi to the guys?"

She shakes her head. "We'll see them Tuesday." I nod and she comes over. I stand up and she gives me a hug. "Keep up the good work."

She moves to the side, making room for Tristan to come in too. "You're doing great. We'll see you Tuesday."

"Thanks, guys," I say and walk them out of the dressing room. Kyle is standing only a few feet away while 69 Bottles is playing to the crowd. Cami and Tristan slide out of the back door and out of sight.

"What on earth was that all about?" Kyle says into my ear as the back door closes.

I laugh, "I thought I was getting fired."

"Me too." Kyle snorts. "So are you going to tell me?"

I shrug. "Maybe." He spins me around.

"Don't make me kiss it out of you." I laugh at his words and his tone. He's serious.

"I don't think that's possible, but I don't mind if you try."

"Oh really?"

"Really." Our mouths draw closer together. I feel like I'm in a movie, drawing out that slow sensual kiss that you know is coming.

"I know I could kiss it from you."

"If you're so sure, do it," I mock and his lips crash against mine. I moan.

"Tell me," he whispers.

"Nope."

His lips are back on mine. His tongue teasing my lips, sending shivers through me. My nipples are hardening against my corset and I quiver.

"Tell me, baby girl." I melt against him and his lips find my jaw.

"Mmm, that feels so good. Don't stop."

"Hmm," he whispers against my neck. "Maybe you'll tell me if I stop kissing you." I can feel his lips tickle along my neck with the slightest touch. His tightly trimmed goatee adding extra sensations. Then I hear his tongue as it licks his lips and he nips my skin. I shiver.

"Kiss me," I beg.

"Tell me," he counters.

"You're killing me."

"Tell me."

"Kiss me."

"Tell me."

"Take me." As I suspected, he can't resist my need and his mouth is back on mine and he's pushing me against the wall, holding me there, pressing into me. I vaguely notice that the crowd is still cheering but the band has stopped. Talon will be here momentarily. But Kyle's lips are keeping mine too busy to speak. I moan into his mouth.

"You better be saving some for me," Talon growls with anticipation as he enters the room. Kyle kisses me for another few seconds and then pulls back. Both of us are equally breathless, I feel like I need to bend over and hold my knees.

"She won't tell me what Cami and Tristan wanted. So I thought I'd kiss it out of her."

Talon snorts. "How's that working for you?"

Kyle pouts. "It's not."

They both laugh. "I figured as much," Talon says. "Come on, I want my panda with me in the greenroom. You too." He looks to Kyle. "I just haven't come up with a nickname for you yet." Kyle actually blushes. "Come on."

Talon pulls me into a quick kiss before pulling me and Kyle off to the greenroom. When we get in there, we're the only ones there and Kyle closes the door behind him. I take a seat on the couch and Talon comes up behind me, standing behind the couch. His hands are on my shoulders, before sliding down and into the thin top of my corset, quickly finding and pulling my nipples between his fingers. I writhe underneath him. "Will you tell Kyle now?" he asks.

I moan. "No," I breathe.

Talon's fingers tug a little harder and roll my nipples between them. "Ahh," I groan.

"How about now, angel?"

"Harder," I demand and he complies, tugging and pulling, twisting and rolling. The spark ignites in my clit and I want to explode. I've never come from nipple stimulation but I'm so wound up, I just might. I flick my hips against the couch.

"You hussy," Kyle admonishes. "Maybe we're going to have to fuck it out of her."

"Yes!" I groan.

There is a rush of noise outside the door and Talon pulls his hands from my corset just as I'm about to come. I pout prettily and whine at the loss of touch. "Maybe we should deny you all the things you want, like that orgasm playing with your pussy right now. Make you sit on it for a while," Talon says, there is a bit of snark in his voice so I know he's teasing, sort of.

It doesn't stop me from saying a whiney, "no." They both laugh just as the door opens. I cross my arms over my chest and make a show of pouting just as Dex, Mouse and Peacock come walking into the room.

"What's her problem?" Dex asks catching the look on my face.

"Punishment," Talon says and Dex busts out laughing.

"What she do?"

Talon takes a seat next to me, pulling me into him. "Nothing actually."

"Oh, ouch. Sucks to be you, sweetheart."

"You have no idea," I whine, which of course makes Talon and Kyle laugh. I huff. "So not fair."

Talon picks me up and sets me on his lap. I can feel his erection pressing right into my sex and I decide that it's time for payback. I grind my butt against his crotch. I hear him hiss through his teeth just as the room fills with crazy women and fans buzzing with excitement.

I squirm and I feel his hand on my side, he pinches me and I bounce. He hisses again. Ha! That backfired. I smirk.

He leans up and whispers in my ear. "You're being a bad girl." I squirm again at his words.

"You make me bad," I whisper in his ear.

"Don't make me get Kyle."

"Mmm," I whisper a moan into his ear.

"Fuck!" he growls harshly but softly into my ear.

chapter 36

"We have to attend this party," Kyle argues with Talon. I can't help but smile. "We agreed we'd be there. We don't have to stay all night, but we have to go."

"Yeah, I know," Talon whines then kisses my shoulder. "What about the rooms?"

"One of the guys took care of it already. They have keys and our luggage has been taken up." Kyle looks at me, "I just had them take everything up. I hope that's alright?" I nod.

"I just think we've made her suffer long enough."

"Her?" Kyle says. "She still hasn't told us about her meeting with Cami and Tristan, and because she didn't pull the confidential, none of your business card, whatever it was, we need to know. So I say she can suffer a little longer."

I groan. "Fine."

They both laugh. "Too late now, panda. We will get it out of you, but not right now," Talon says with a smirk as he starts to stand up with me in his lap. I squeal.

"Oh my god, you're gonna hurt yourself. Let me get up." I scramble trying to stand up and Talon wraps his arms around me and nestles his face into my neck. "I know you don't want to go, baby, but we have to. Just for a little while. Then you can take me back to the hotel and have your evil way with me."

"Promise?"

"Aw, of course I do."

"Okay," He pouts and it's kinda cute. I look at Kyle and he doesn't look any happier to be going to this party either. I try and stand up but Talon won't let me go.

"You know, the sooner we go, the sooner we can get back to the hotel," I tell him.

"Fine," he grumbles and releases me. I climb off of his lap where I've been for the last forty-five minutes and I've managed more than a few nasty looks from the chicks who were determined to try and get in Talon's pants tonight.

I was even more surprised when Kyle turned them away. The other guys weren't complaining at all the extra attention. Considering we don't have anywhere to go until Wednesday, I have a feeling it's going to be a very long night for all of us. I turn around to help Talon up off of the couch and he takes my hand, pulls me down and plants a kiss on my lips.

"You're bad," I whisper. "Now, let's go."

He stands begrudgingly and finally the three of us are out the door, down the hall and crashing through the back door. The buses are gone from the back of the lot, which helps because the fans will follow the buses wherever they go. So there are only a few mingling fans out back behind the fences.

Rusty and Mills are standing next to a town car and the driver opens the door for us to climb in. Kyle goes first, and he slides all the way over. Then Talon ushers me in. I slide in. "Scoot," he says and I slide into the middle as he folds his massive body in next to me. Mills climbs into the front seat and I haven't a clue where Rusty goes.

Kyle looks at me, I look at him and he brings his finger to his mouth, puckering his lips in a silent "Shh." I nod and his other hand comes to rest on my knee. I lock my legs together. No, no, not here. Not in the car, not with Mills and some random stranger. His hand slides up my thigh and that burning need to come explodes as my legs fall slack to the side as his hand slides up higher, seeking my core.

It only takes a second for Talon to catch on to what Kyle is doing and a wolfish smile spreads across his face as his hand comes across his body to mine. His fingers brush across my nipple and my head falls back and my mouth goes slack. My breathing hitches. Kyle leans into my ear. "Be a good girl, don't make a sound and I'll let you come."

Fuck me. I can't, there is no way. Just then his fingers brush against my clit and Talon's fingers pinch my nipple. I stop breathing and bite my lip. With blood rushing in my ears, I can hear nothing around me. I pray to god I'm not making any noise. If I am, I pray that Mills and the driver are professional enough to not make a big deal out of it.

Kyle's ministrations pick up and my hips flick. Talon's hand moves from one breast to the other, giving that nipple some much needed attention and I'm close. So fucking close.

Kyle turns slightly and I feel his hand shift with a finger pressed against my clit, I feel him looking for my entrance with another finger. He doesn't slide in once he finds it. He doesn't have to. I tremble. The orgasm is right there, right on the tip. Talon leans into me ear and whispers, "Come for him, angel. Coat his finger with your slick heat."

I turn my face to find his lips. I kiss him hard and fast, giving him everything I have and letting my cries of pleasure melt into his mouth. My body shakes, my clit radiates more pleasure with each milking flick of Kyle's finger. My body twitches each time he passes that hypersensitive spot, and gradually his motions slow.

Unable to breath with Talon's tongue on mine, I pull in a long shaky breath as I desperately try to calm myself down.

Kyle extracts his fingers from within me. I want to grab his hand and suck off my juices but Talon beats me to it. He takes Kyle's hand and sucks his fingers into his mouth, then moves onto his thumb, licking and sucking on it. My mouth falls open and the fire is back as I watch Talon's magical tongue on Kyle's hand and Kyle has so much lust in his eyes as he watches Talon.

Fuck me! How in the hell did I get myself sucked (no pun intended) into a manly sandwich such as this? I certainly have done nothing to deserve it.

A couple more minutes and Talon releases Kyle's hand and I pout because all my essence is gone from him and I wanted a taste.

"What's the matter, baby girl?" Kyle asks

"I wanted a taste."

"Oh fuck, that's...shit, that's hot," he whispers in my ear and I smile. "Later," he says just as the car pulls in front of the club.

"We'll go around back," I say without thinking.

Talon is actually upset. "You most certainly will not. You're going in with me."

"I'm sorry, Talon, I just. Crap, I'm sorry."

He kisses me on the cheek. "I know, it's okay. Remember, smile."

"That's my line," I say with a smile.

"Maybe, but this is your first press gauntlet."

"No argument here," I laugh and I take Kyle's hand in mine as Mills opens the door and I am assaulted with screams, camera flashes and a desperate desire to run away. When I signed on for this gig, I never imagined sharing a bed with any of them, let alone walking a press gauntlet, as Talon's girlfriend I guess, since he refuses to let my hand go as I slide across the seat. Kyle, on my other hand, is my grounding force and it's a heady balance and it is certainly one that can get me through anything.

When I stand from the car, the flashbulbs are blinding, the cheers grow louder and the reporters start shouting. "Mr. Carter, is this your girlfriend? Is this your woman? Why did you duet with her tonight?" Wonderful! I scream in my head, but Talon does what I've told him.

He moves forward so that Kyle can climb out. I refuse to let him go and Talon doesn't seem to mind as the three of us slide inside the downtown Phoenix nightclub.

chapter 37

The club is packed and we enter to a roar from the crowd. There are signs everywhere for the record, the album and the label. Now I see why it was so important that we come to this party. It's sponsored by the label itself. It has to be. Now, I'm even more nervous. I hope they're not here and just sent the banners and such to be set up. Though it may be sponsored by the label, doesn't mean the drinks are free. Usually they slap their posters up and that's about it.

Talon ushers Kyle and me over to where the rest of the band is. For the first time since San Diego, Peacock has a chick on his lap and I wonder what happened with Jess, but shrug it off. Peacock is a good looking guy and the bass player of a very popular band; he deserves to have all the girls he wants. It is with that thought I think back to what Talon said earlier about him screwing up and how it will likely happen and there is a thought that passes through my head. *How can I hold him back from being the rock star that he is?* That was maybe the wrong question. I don't want to hold him back from being a rock star; I want to hold him back from being a rock star sex god. Granted being a rock star doesn't mean you fuck anything with legs and a pussy, but should I be tying him down to me? I pray to god I'm not. I know I am not ready for that level of full on commitment. When my gut wrenches at the idea of him with another woman, I have my answer. Mentally, I'm so not ready, however my gut instincts are obviously taking over.

Dex and Mouse are working their usual hoard of women. I roll my eyes. These girls could do so much better. God, they're not the only ones. Wait, what? God, I need to stop doubting myself, doubting who I am. Out of all these women, Talon is choosing me. Kyle is choosing me and this whole thing isn't even twenty-four hours old. I'm beating myself up for nothing.

"What do you want to drink?" Talon asks me.

"An Irish Bulldog."

He raises an eyebrow at me in question. "It's a Colorado bulldog, add Bailey's."

"Ah, okay, what else?"

"Mr. Carver, if I didn't know better I'd think you were trying to get me drunk."

He shrugs. "Maybe."

"You don't need me drunk to get me into bed."

"Mmm and don't I know it, but I want you to relax a little," he says with a smile.

"I'll start with one." I smile and he nods.

"Kyle, what would you like?"

"I can get 'em," Kyle says.

"No, I want to. What do you want? The usual?" Kyle nods. "I'll be right back." Talon kisses me on the cheek but I see him take Kyle's hand in his and give it a squeeze. Talon's way of kissing Kyle.

I really hope he does that because he doesn't quite know how to show affection to Kyle and not because he's trying to hide himself or his feelings from everyone else. I let it go and remind myself that this is so new, there are too many questions and nowhere near enough answers from any of us right now.

Talon did say, when we talked this afternoon, that he wasn't going to go kissing Kyle in public, and that what happened behind closed doors was our business, but I have a feeling that it's going to mean more to both of them if it isn't just about the sex between the two.

The party is in full swing and I'm working on my fourth Bulldog. Kyle about flips his lid when some random guy shows up with a drink for me. I respectfully decline it and Kyle steps up to push him off. I'm glad Kyle handled it because Talon radiates with anxiety until the guy walks away. Luckily Rusty and Mills are on it. Taking the drink from the guy and taking it back to the bar before he tries to pass it off on someone else. Usually if a guy is going to buy a drink for a woman, it's through the bartender or the server. Not a guarantee, but certainly a little safer than what he was trying to do.

"Was it drugged?" I ask randomly.

Talon shrugs. "No way to know and because no one saw it, we can't do anything about it. Never, ever take a drink from anyone, please?"

"I won't." I kiss him on the cheek. "Relax, Kyle got it and I wouldn't have taken it anyway." I look at Kyle and mouth a thank you and he blows me a kiss. "Besides, I'm draped all over you and he had the balls to bring a drink over here in the first place. He deserves whatever happens to him," I snicker. I watch as Talon's lips twitch because he's fighting a smile.

I've been sitting on Talon's lap for some time. He was getting mobbed by girls and all but begged me to sit on his lap so that they'd stop. I can't say no to that, but now Kyle is having to deal with it. Mouse finally vacates the couch with his chick, no doubt headed for the bathroom in the back to bang her senseless. As soon as she's gone I motion for Kyle to take his seat. He gladly comes over quickly and sits right next to Talon. I smile and stretch my legs out onto his.

"Now this is what I'm talking about," I say quietly and both guys laugh. I nestle into Talon's lap and rest my head on his shoulder while he gently strokes my back and Kyle's fingers caress my legs. All the contact points are enough to send me into overdrive. I shiver. "I need you," I say against Talon's neck.

"Then let's go." He looks at Kyle. "She needs us."

Kyle moves quickly to stand up and I laugh. These two are too much and I don't care, I will figure out a way to do this with them, I need them both. I'd take them in the bathroom but I don't think I can handle that. Not yet anyway. I need a bed.

Talon leads both of us to the back. Mills and Beck are quick to step in front of us, leading us out the back door. It amazes me just how much they know about their surroundings and how easily they read the guy's intentions before the guys even have a clue what they are.

When we hit the back door, there are a couple of town cars parked out here waiting for the band and we climb in the same as before. "The hotel is across the street," Mills says as we climb in. "But the car will take you to a private entrance." He reaches into his pocket. "Here are your room keys and Beck will escort you. I'm going to keep an eye on things here."

"Thank, Mills," Talon says as he climbs in. Mills closes the door and we're off in no time flat. The driver goes a block, turns right at the light, then another right then through an intersection and finally into a parking garage.

Once underneath, all is quiet and Talon hands us each our keys to the suite. "Room seven oh one."

Beck turns to face us. "The elevator will take us straight to the seventh floor."

"Perfect. Thanks, Beck," Kyle says as we pull up to the elevator.

"Wait until the elevator arrives." Beck climbs out, shuts the door and pushes the elevator button. It opens immediately and he holds it with his hand. Talon opens his door and climbs out. He waits for me.

"No, get in there." I tell him and he hesitates then goes and slides into the elevator. Kyle and I quickly climb out and we're able to join him without incident and we're quickly whisked up to our floor. Beck blocks our exit to make sure the hallway is clear and when it is, he lets us pass. Kyle leads the way, Talon rests his hand on my lower back. The contact sends a shiver of excitement though me as he pushes me along. Beck is bringing up the rear.

It feels a bit dramatic, considering nothing actually happened tonight to warrant their concern. However the flip side of that is if they become too complacent, something is likely to happen and no one is prepared.

We slide into the room and Beck takes his post outside. I wonder if they really stay there all night. Seems a little unfair, and likely ridiculous considering it brings more attention to the room.

No sooner does the door close behind us and I am being pushed against the wall by both Talon and Kyle. One on each hip. "Did you miss me, boys?"

"Yes," they say in unison and their mouths are quickly all over me. Then, out of nowhere, Kyle wraps his fingers around the back of Talon's neck, pulling him toward him. Without hesitation from either man, Kyle's lips land on Talon's and I melt into a pool against the wall. The kiss is soft, but yet very masculine if there is such a thing. There's no tongue, but there doesn't need to be. Their lips are moving in sync with one another and I'm speechless as my pussy weeps down the inside of my thigh.

chapter 38

I could almost be jealous of their kissing, mainly because their arms are holding each other and I'm just an innocent, very turned on bystander. Fuck, it's hot. I can't even find the words to describe the beauty of these two men kissing each other, but there just are no words.

I watch as Kyle's hands begin to work at the buttons on the leather vest Talon is wearing over his t-shirt. If I wasn't so horny and unable to move, I would take a seat and watch the show, but I can't because I'm mesmerized to the point of it being hypnotizing. Once Kyle has the vest undone, he slides it from his shoulders. As soon as Talon is free, he goes for Kyle's shirt. Pulling it free and lifting it over his head.

Kyle doesn't hesitate in lifting his arms and Talon quickly tosses the shirt to the floor. Now bare chested and exposed a couple feet in front of me, I can truly appreciate the tattooed beauty that is Kyle Black. His pecs are well defined, his skin pulled tight against the muscle below the surface. He has beautiful brown nipples in contrast to the light chest hair along his breastbone. He has a dragon over his left pec, right near his heart.

He's sleeved from shoulder to wrist with various objects, symbols that one day I hope to ask him about. On his left shoulder, something catches my eye. Mixed in with the mosaic of colors and designs is a name. One name. Daniel. Whether for his father or his brother, either way, it's beautiful. I bat back tears.

Kyle goes for the hem of Talon's shirt, pulling it up and he breaks the kiss to remove his shirt. Talon is equally beautiful in a different kind of way. He's very muscular. Including a beautiful six pack and that gorgeous V that I just want to lick and kiss. My mouth is watering but I'm too entranced to move.

Talon's hands are rubbing along Kyle's chest and down to his stomach and I whimper. My pussy is ready to be touched and I am so close to doing it myself. Just watching these two strip each other is the hugest turn on. Watching them touch and caress each other. Shivers run through me and I shake in anticipation of what they're going to do next.

"You think we might want to pay attention to our girl?" Talon breathes against Kyle's lips.

Kyle smiles. "I think she's enjoying herself watching us. My guess is that she's about ten seconds away from sliding her hand under her panties."

Talon laughs and I snort, "Eleven seconds at least."

They both look at me. "You're so full of shit. I saw you shiver," Talon says. "Were you hoping we'd forgotten about you so you could watch?"

I moan and nod. They both grab one of my hands and start to lead me toward the bedroom. I am so wrapped up in their shirtless bodies that I don't bother looking around the suite. "We will never forget about you. But it was one hell of a show, wasn't it?" Kyle teases me with a grin.

"Umm, yeah," I breathe. "And I was about four seconds away from stuffing my hand down my pants." I laugh and the dirty looks in their eyes tells me that I'm in real trouble.

We cross the threshold into one of the bedrooms. It's obviously the master of the suite because it's huge. A king size bed dominates the room, but there is plenty of room surrounding the bed. They lead me to the end of the bed and before I can even consider doing anything to them, I am sandwiched between them. My back to Kyle and my front pressed tight against Talon's chest.

"I think it's time we put you out of your misery," Talon says as he takes my head in his hands, bringing his lips to mine and I melt. His lips are soft and warm. I can taste a little of Kyle on his lips and it's an amazing combination. My mind goes blank of all coherent thought.

I can feel Kyle's hands wrap around my waist, finding the button on my skirt and undoing it. Then he gently pushes it down my legs and as soon as it gets past my thighs it falls to the floor and Kyle disappears from behind me.

"Fuck me," He breathes and Talon pulls back, looking over my shoulder at Kyle. Then just like that, I'm standing alone at the end of the bed. On the verge of exploding as they're both ogling me. "Turn around, baby girl." Kyle commands and I obey, turning slowly.

I'm left in my fishnets, my garter, my pointless thong panties and my corset. With the tops of my fairy's wings and my sleeves exposed I can picture their visual. I keep turning until I am facing Kyle and without warning I am ensconced once again in a tangle arms and bodies and Kyle's lips are slamming into mine. Hard and hot. Heavy and desperate.

Talon's hands slide up my corset, cupping my breasts and sliding his fingers along my nipples and I shudder. God, I need them. I need this. Kyle's tongue begins an erotic dance with mine and Talon's lips are kissing along my collarbone. My nipples harden further into tight painful pebbles.

I begin unbuttoning Kyle's pants, pushing them down and freeing his cock. I kiss him deeper for a moment then try to turn around to face Talon. They realize what I'm doing and give me a little space to move around.

As soon as I'm facing Talon, his lips are on mine. His tongue slides quickly into my mouth and my hands go to his belt and undo it. Then the button and his fly, before sliding both his boxers and his jeans down his thighs. I can feel his cock bounce between us and then hear the slap against his stomach at the force of being freed. He hisses.

I turn again with my back to the bed and I push them both on their chests so that they back away a step or two. When I'm free of their bodies, I sit down and slide onto the bed, crossing my legs at the ankles. My boots are still on, and I'll get around to undoing them shortly. Right now, I want them to continue my show.

It doesn't take them very long to take in my composure and then look at each other. I watch as they take in each other's nakedness and then Kyle starts toeing off his shoes and pushing out of his pants and his socks. He's completely naked and Talon quickly follows suit and before I know it, they're back in each other's arms, right where they left off. Kissing each other. Kyle's hands are on Talon's cheeks and Talon's hands are sliding along Kyle's naked torso, but rather than going north, he's working his way south. Working toward his erection.

Kyle's kisses grow more urgent with each soft pass of Talon's fingers and the closer he gets to reaching his goal. I set about untying my boots, but I do it without removing my eyes from them. The moment Talon's hands reach Kyle's erection, he releases Talon's lips and throws his head back, groaning.

chapter 39

Talon doesn't stop what he's doing to Kyle. I watch as he continues stroking Kyle's erection and gradually the first touch wears off, bringing his head back toward Talon. I watch as Kyle's hands begin roaming across Talon's chest, heading south, ready to engage just as Talon is doing to him. Talon thrusts his hips forward in encouragement. Kyle takes the hint and grabs a hold of Talon's hard cock, pushing and pulling his hand along Talon's shaft. "Fuck," Talon groans and I shed my boots.

I continue watching. I want to shed my panties and leave the outfit on. It has driven them to this point and the least I can do is honor them by keeping it on.

Kyle falls to his knees in front of Talon. His eyes plead for permission just as I lift my butt to remove the scrap of material keeping me from plunging my fingers in and out of my pussy.

Talon nods and Kyle slides forward, ready to take Talon into his mouth. "I've never done this," Kyle whispers. I can hear the fear and the concern in his voice.

"Neither have I," Talon says softly, "but I don't want you to stop."

Kyle nods and braces himself. He wraps his fingers around Talon's length and brings his mouth slowly to the swollen crown. He sticks his tongue out, licking.

His hesitation is palpable and visible in his shaky movements, watching his distress sends a wave of calm through me. "Kyle?" I ask.

"Hmm?" His eyes meet mine and they're wary. Scared, but he's still hard, so this is not a turn off to him.

I don't ask him what I'd intended to, it's time to try and help my boys. I slide down off the bed at the same time I pull one breast free of my corset. Talon is looking down at Kyle, while Kyle is watching me, I pull my other breast free, exposing a part of my body I know they love. Helping them, showing them that this is all okay. My nipples grow diamond hard as they're exposed to the coolness of the room.

I settle myself next to Kyle, who blindly reaches for my hand, intertwining our fingers. He's taking strength and comfort from my presence. I can also see the muscles in Talon's legs relax a little as I scoot closer to Kyle. "Stop if you don't want to do this," I say to Kyle.

"I want to do this," he says determined. I smile at him. With my free hand, I gently stroke along his hard shaft, letting him know that this isn't just about Talon. His hand squeezes tighter around my fingers and he looks back up at Talon.

I hear Talon's rush of air leaving his lungs and I see the lust and desire fill Kyle's eyes. Again Talon nods, letting him know it's okay, and that he wants him to continue. With a little squeeze on my hand, Kyle gently licks Talon's cock. Once, twice, a third time. Talon's legs begin to shake and his breathing hitches with the pleasure Kyle is providing him.

Deciding that I need to help keep them going, I take my hand away from Kyle's erection and run it along Talon's leg, pushing all my strength into him so that he too knows I'm here for him. After a moment I begin sliding my hand up Talon's leg, toward his erection.

I stop when my fingers tickle along his balls and he shudders violently, I can hear his teeth grind together before the hiss of air sucks through his teeth. The action is immediately followed up with a moan around Talon's cock. I know that Kyle is getting his first real taste of pre-cum.

Kyle pulls back, looking at me with the same lust he had for Talon. I release his hand, cup his neck and crush him to my lips with greedy hunger. I can taste both of them on Kyle's tongue and it sends my clit pulsing once again.

"Fuck, that's so fucking hot." Talon's hand strokes my hair and finds my hair tie. He makes quick work of removing it so he can run his fingers through my hair. I love having his hand on my head and having Kyle at my lips is even better.

I pull back and quickly take Talon's erection into my mouth, licking and sucking as Kyle watches me closely. I let my hand fall down Kyle's neck then his chest, straight down to his cock. I gently tease it and stroke it at the same time as I grip Talon in my other hand. Stroking in time with my mouth. "Fuck," he groans and his legs start to tremble. "I've got to... Dammit!" I smile and am encouraged by Kyle's lack of hesitation when he wraps his own hand around Talon. I let Talon fall free and Kyle doesn't hesitate sucking him into his mouth. Kyle broke that barrier of uncomfortable and drove straight into 'I need more.'

Sometimes, all it takes is one time to hook you into enjoying something forever.

"Talon. Lay down," I say and Kyle releases him. Talon stumbles the couple of steps to the bed and plops down. I giggle. He's in a lust coma, and fuck, it's hot. Kyle needs no further direction from me. He climbs up onto the bed, pushing Talon to slide backward a little bit and he does. I can tell the moment Kyle takes hold of him because I watch as Talon's muscles tighten and contract, followed by a pleasure filled groan.

Talon is watching Kyle, but he has one eye on me. Curiosity and pleasure dance behind his eyelids. I stand up behind Kyle and gently place my hands on his ass. He jumps at my contact. "All you have to do is say stop, and I won't hesitate." I watch as he moans and nods around Talon's hard-on.

Talon gives me a questioning look. My answer is to slip my middle finger between my lips and suck. His eyes widen, a little in fear but also in excitement. I suck for a few more seconds and then lean down and kiss Kyle on one of his ass cheeks. He flinches again. "Relax, baby. I promise I'm not going to hurt you." I stroke my dry hand along the curve of his back. I can feel the fear and tension drain from his body as he sags down. I kiss him again, this time more open mouth. I repeat the process as I make my way toward his core. Toward a place I'm pretty confident no one has ever been. I pull back, situating myself, and I lick my finger again while I rub along his lower back and down onto the cheeks of his glorious ass. He tenses again as my hand draws ever closer to my goal.

"It's alright," Talon says and then his hand is stroking through Kyle's hair. I smile as Kyle relaxes yet again. I nod at Talon and he continues stroking as Kyle continues sucking. Once he is back in a rhythm, I take my chance. I lean down and with a wet, languid tongue I find that happy spot just under his balls, exposed to me because of his position. His balls tighten, his cock jumps and he moans around Talon.

I gradually move my tongue higher, drawing closer to the tight ring of where I want to be the most. Kyle's body quakes with tension and pleasure. Then I reach it. I stroke a very wet, fat tongue across his entrance and he shudders, moaning loud and hard against Talon. I see Talon's hand grip into Kyle's hair, holding him, guiding him. I let some spit fall down my tongue and again Kyle trembles, need pouring out from his body. I pull back then slide my finger along the outside of his entrance, toying with him.

His hips begin to thrust, his cock bouncing. I look at Talon, raise an eyebrow then look pointedly at Kyle. Talon nods and his eyes roll back into his head, and his muscles clamp down hard.

I gently push my finger into Kyle while I grip his cock in my other hand, stroking downward. Talon's cock pops free as he grunts out the last of his orgasm.

Kyle explodes. "Ahh! Fuck. Shit," Kyle screams out. I milk out his orgasm with my hand. It wasn't quite the reaction I expected, but, it's better and I can't help but smile and look over Kyle's backside and meet Talon's eyes. He has his own little satisfied smile on his face.

"I think it's her turn," Talon says, raising an eyebrow at me. I gently extract my finger, what little of it made it in, and watch as Kyle sinks into the mattress, curling into a turtle on the bed.

"That was fucking intense," he breathes against Talon's thigh. "I need a minute."

"Mind if I have at her?" I roll my eyes at Talon's question.

"Nuh uh," Kyle groans and slides himself off of Talon's leg so that Talon can move.

Talon wastes no time sliding off the bed and picking me up. I squeal as he throws me down on the bed next to Kyle. He forcibly spreads my legs and before I can catch my breath from the toss, my clit is in his mouth and he is sucking hard and nibbling. Sending an orgasm rocking through me as I shatter into millions of pieces and scream Talon's name.

That brings Kyle around and he rears up on his elbows so that we are face to face. "You're fucking gorgeous, one of a kind and you are fearless." He kisses me, once, twice, three times, and finally on the fourth he doesn't pull back. His lips and tongue go to work on my mouth and I feel Talon sliding a finger inside my core. Twisting and swirling it against my g-spot until I come unglued again.

Talon pulls off of me and then goes in search of something, condoms I'm assuming, but he's back quickly.

"Kyle, you got any...?" He doesn't finish and Kyle groans, not in a good way.

"No, I thought you had some."

"Fuck, I did, or so I thought. Fuck, fuck."

"It's alright," I say.

"Damn, baby, I'm sorry," Talon says, disappointment in his eyes and tone.

"No, I mean, it's alright."

He cocks his head at me. "Angel, I've never not worn a wrapper." I watch him run his hand through his hair.

"I can go downstairs. See if they..." Kyle says and I stop him.

"No. It's alright."

"What if... are you on birth control?" Talon asks.

"Yes, but it wouldn't matter to me if I wasn't. I need you, both of you. I've waited so long, I don't want to wait any longer and damn it, I don't care. I fucking need you." I feel like bursting into tears but somehow I manage to hold them back.

Talon slowly slides his way up my body. "Are you sure?" he asks me. He's terrified. Almost more terrified of this than he was of what Kyle was going to do with him.

I stroke his hair and run my fingers through his messy beard. "Why are you so scared?"

"Because I fucking need this. I need you," he says with sincerity and emotion is pouring out of every inch of his body.

"Take me. Damn it, take me, I'm here. I'm yours. I'm both of yours and nothing can take that away from me. I need you more than I need oxygen in my lungs or blood in my veins. Take me, Talon, mark me. Make me yours."

Talon leans down, planting his lips against mine in a warm passionate kiss just as he starts to slide inside me. His bare cock is bumpy and soft over hard steel as he slides inside. I moan, pulling back from our kiss. His cock feels so good. Deep seated pleasure blossoms from within my core, radiating outward so hard and fast that my whole body quakes in response. I watch as Talon leans sideways slightly and puts his forehead between Kyle's shoulder blades.

"Fuck," he moans as he picks up his pace, thrusting and rolling his hips, the head of his cock kissing my cervix driving my need higher. My breathing becomes highly erratic. "You're so tight, you feel so fucking good." He slides in faster and then he starts to slide in and out in short bursts. Kyle shifts, bringing Talon off of his back.

Kyle rolls onto his back, leaning up on his elbow looking at Talon. He sits up enough so that he can pull Talon down to his lips. I watch them kiss and feel Talon's hard cock slow momentarily then pick up, faster and harder than before. Pounding into me. My orgasm is climbing higher and more intense the longer they kiss. The longer they're joined by the lips and Talon and I are joined where it matters most, the more my heart fills with love for these two men.

My eyes roll up and my whole body trembles. "I can't, fuck me, Talon, fuck me. I'm..." Talon's pace increases, thrusting in and out of me harder and faster and I shatter once again into millions of pieces.

"Fuck. I'm, damn it, I have to pull out..."

"No. Don't," I beg as Talon begins to growl against Kyle's lips. Finally he pulls back, pumping once, twice and on the third time he explodes inside me. Feeling him pour into me forces me to explode once more.

chapter 40

Now before you freak out and think that I left Kyle hanging, I promise you I didn't. I was just too exhausted to recount the amazing orgasms brought on by him. After the day of crazy horniness and then finally finding my release with Talon, every orgasm I receive from Kyle was just that much sweeter. Believe me when I tell you that he passed out first.

I learned one thing last night and it was equal time for all of us will make this easier for everyone. When both the guys were having their own moments of unbridled passion between them, I wasn't jealous, hell no, I was fucking turned on like nobody's business. I enjoyed every minute of it. Though I took comfort in the fact that they took reassurances from me and even more comfort in the fact that they did it for me. I didn't realize until last night that I have a voyeuristic side to me and I like it. A lot!

I felt a little left out at first; before I let the horniness override rational thought and embraced the gift they were offering me with each kiss, each caress they gave one another. When Kyle sought me to help and comfort him through his nerves, I knew that being with Talon alone was something he really would have never done. I just hope I didn't push them into doing something they weren't ready for. I guess it's something to talk about later.

I'd spent a good portion of yesterday afternoon and evening horny as hell, compliments of their denying me orgasms because I wouldn't discuss the conversation with Cami and Tristan in the dressing room. So when it came to me finally being sated, despite Talon providing some seriously amazing orgasms, I didn't feel fully satisfied until Kyle marked me as his.

When I finally thought I was sated, for the time being, there was still a slow achy burn, but a slow burn I can handle, for now.

We passed out much like we did the night before, the only difference this time is the fact that I'm actually aware of it, not already passed out. Oh, and the fact that we're all naked under the covers.

I am nestled against Kyle, my leg is thrown over his hip and my back is twisted just enough so that I can hold Talon to me. I can feel every inch of their erections pressing against my body and I do the near impossible by ignoring them.

This wild and crazy 12 Week - 25 City - 39 Show adventure is only getting started and I can't wait to see what tomorrow brings. Our first day off and nothing but each other to hold us together. It is with that thought that I clear my mind and fall into the most restful sleep I've had in a very long time.

Monday dawns with a new light in my eyes. Last night was amazing and what's more amazing is that I am still surrounded by the two men who make my life wonderful. Last night I was claimed spectacularly by two beautiful, gorgeous, and sexy as hell men. One is the lead singer of 69 Bottles and the other, their manager. It brings a shiver of excitement every time I think about it.

Today is our first day off since kicking off this tour last Thursday. Now working Thursday through Sunday might sound like a dream job, but since Thursday I have been in Los Angeles, San Diego, Las Vegas, and now I am waking up in Phoenix, Arizona. Thank god, I'm not the tourist type because the idea of getting out of bed for anything but a shower is unthinkable.

Tomorrow is another story. Tomorrow night we have a party, a party at my boss's house here in Phoenix. Now I've had so much shit happen in the last four days, that having dinner and drinks with my boss and her husband, who just so happen to be one of Hollywood's hottest celebrities, seems like old news and regular business. What I didn't expect was last night's concert, getting pulled on stage by Talon and then, just because I love the song I started to sing along with him. Then the next thing I knew, I was taking over the show. I roll my eyes. Yeah, I've always known I could sing, or at least everyone made sure to tell me that, plus four years in the church choir and solo after solo is a pretty good indication but now Cami, my boss, has offered me the chance of a lifetime.

Sign with Bold. The idea sends thousands of spiders crawling across my skin. Don't get me wrong, I think in the back of everyone's mind at some point in their life, they dream of being a celebrity, of being famous or at least getting their fifteen minutes of fame. I have a feeling my fifteen minutes are about to start knocking on my doorstep.

Now to disentangle from this massive pile of arms, legs, bodies and oh yes, morning wood. I shiver in anticipation, wondering what today will bring with the men surrounding me.

I don't know how I manage it, but I do. I slide through them and off of the bed. Duty calls. I decide to take a shower and put on some clothes and order breakfast. That is until I get a glimpse at the clock. Fuck me, it's after one in the afternoon. Then again, I vaguely remember catching the clock at one point before passing out and it was after six in the morning. I go looking for my stuff and find that my suitcase is the only one in the room and I cock my head.

Then I smile. The boys gave me the biggest room in the suite, again. I don't remember much of what the suite looks like because I was too wrapped up in these two hotties but I seem to remember a desk just outside the door. I tug my suitcase and my messenger bag out into the main suite. They deserve to sleep. They've worked hard these last few days. So I find a lamp and turn it on before laying down my suitcase and putting my messenger on the desk I saw. I go digging for a pair of pj pants and a tank top. I find it, find my toiletries and quickly pad back into the room.

Once in the shower I turn the water up to as hot as I can tolerate it. I have aches and pains in various places and the water is soothing. I also vow to myself that at some point while we're here, to take advantage of the monster tub in the bathroom. Actually, the three of us could fit in the thing and it gives me more than a few ideas and a new shot of arousal right in my pussy. My clit is sore. I can feel its tenderness with each wave of arousal that pulses through it. In all honesty, it's not unpleasant.

When my hair is coated in shampoo and my loofah is lathered, the door behind me opens. I squeak and turn around to find Kyle with a wolfish grin on his face. "Good morning, panda girl."

"Hi, there. How are you feeling?"

He looks down at his erection. "Horny."

"Oh for pete's..." I don't get to finish when Kyle slams into me, pressing me against the wall. His lips are on mine with ardor and I melt into his body. His hard body holds mine hostage against the wall as his hands make an assault on my body. His hands slide up and down my ribcage, holding my hips tighter to him and pinning his erection between us.

"I need to be inside you. I can't take it another minute," he growls in my ear. His desperation spurs me, and after finding balance on my feet, I lift one of my legs in invitation. He hisses through his teeth and begins kissing my neck as his hands wrap around my thighs, lifting me up and spreading me wide, opening me to take his cock.

He lifts me up just a little more, lining himself up and slamming home. He lets out the most carnal noise I've ever heard as he takes a moment to settle himself. After a couple heartbeats, he starts to move, thrusting upward as his hands on my thighs hold me steady against the wall. His thrusts becoming desperate and needy, drawing me to my own release.

"So. Fucking. Beautiful," he growls, pounding into me. "Come for me, Addison." He moans and my whole body shutters with his command. The orgasm I was working toward boils to the surface and my clit is in the path of his assault on my core. The friction is too much and I explode. Biting my lip until Kyle's mouth crushes into mine, taking my cries of ecstasy and turning them into his own orgasm as he pours himself into me.

We stay like that for a few moments until he gradually lets me down. My legs are stiff and my hips ache as my legs come back together, but it is a delicious ache that I will take any way and any day so long as it is with him, or Talon.

Once Kyle sets me down, he goes about re-lathering my loofah and then he sets out to wash my body from head to toe. I don't argue with him because I enjoy his hands all over me.

That's the roughest Kyle has ever been with me; he's usually the gentler one between the two, but I'll take it. He was desperate and to be honest, so was I.

As he finishes washing me, I rinse off as he quickly washes himself. I can't take my eyes off his body, watching his muscles give and take as he flexes to wash himself. Watching him sends a new wave of arousal to my sex.

Kyle's tattooed body is skinny sexy, meaning that he works out, which is obvious in the muscle tone, but he's not stacked. At least not the way Talon and no doubt some of the other band members are. Despite being skinny, he isn't bony. Well, except for the erection he's still sporting.

"How do you do it?" I ask him.

He looks at me. "Do what, panda?"

I step closer to him and wrap my hand around his cock. "Fuck me, come like you do and then you still have this."

His eyes roll into the back of his head at my touch. "Baby girl, until you, I was a one and done kind of guy. But being around you, looking at you, constantly hard is my new middle name."

"Does it bother you?"

He tilts his head back soaking up my touch. "That he's never soft?" He smiles, "Not really. It got pretty painful yesterday, but it just makes it all the more sweeter when I do finally get to come. But when you walk out of the room, it's like he knows his favorite place to be is gone and he goes limp." He gives me a wink.

I laugh a little. "Is that even possible?"

He presses me against the wall, putting both hands on either side of my head. "Baby girl, with you, anything is possible."

With that, he kills the water, pulls his erection free of my hands and backs away. I pout. "I wasn't done with that."

He laughs and grabs a towel. "Come here." He winks at me. "I'm saving it for later." I give him a half smile and bat my eyes. He snorts. "Nice try. Now let me dry you off."

chapter 41

I'm dried off, dressed and partially sated. I am now sitting at the desk in the sitting room of the suite. Kyle took care of ordering some food for us and Talon is still passed out in the bedroom. Neither one of us had the heart to wake him up so we closed the door and came out here.

I am powering up my laptop when my phone chimes with an email, then it chimes again, and again and it is literally blowing up on the coffee table near Kyle. "A bit popular this morning, aren't we?"

I shrug and power up my computer. I can access that same email from here.

When my email finally loads it is going crazy with email after email. A lot of them are the various google alerts I have set up. Couple that with the fact that there are several from Trinity that appear to be forwards.

"What the fuck happened last night?" I growl at no one in particular. "Get me Mills, now," I all but shout at Kyle.

"What's going on?"

"I have no goddamn clue but I can only guess that someone has done or said something because whatever it was is blowing up like nobody's business."

"Shit," Kyle says and quickly heads for the door. I hear it open. "Rusty, get in here."

I can't hear any replies, but I'll be dammed if he doesn't get his ass in here now.

I hear them come back, they're chatting about something, though I can't make it out and my iMessage pops up.

Trinity: Call me, immediately.

"Fuck! Fuck! Fuck!" I turn around to face the two guys. "Rusty, what the fuck happened last night?"

He has a completely dumbstruck expression on his face. "Nothing out of the ordinary, why?"

"Really? Because I have a demand from my boss to call her and my email is exploding with something that's hitting the news outlets."

"If something happened, it happened behind closed doors. Nothing, and I mean nothing, happened at the club or in transit from the club to here. If something had happened, we'd have been in here immediately."

Just then the front door opens and Mills walks in. He rounds the corner to find Kyle, Rusty and myself. "We have a situation."

"I'll say, but before I get into my email, care to enlighten me?"

"Video," he says and all he has to say.

"Who?"

"Dex."

"Get his fucking ass in here right now!" I shout. "I don't care if his dick is stuck, or he's butt fucking naked. Get him in here..."

"What's going on?" Talon says from behind me and Mills and Rusty cover their eyes and turn around. Kyle on the other hand is staring.

I don't turn around. "Get dressed, and get out here. Mills, get me Mouse and Peacock too. This is not going to be pretty. You have five fucking minutes." I am so goddamn pissed off. We had this fucking conversation not four damn days ago.

I walk to the coffee table and grab my phone, pull up Trinity's number and hit send. "Jesus, what the hell happened last night?" she greets me.

"I am working it out right now, my phone just started blowing up not three minutes ago. I haven't even opened a single of the hundred plus littering my inbox. I'm certain I have a pretty good idea and I will take care of it here on my end and then get to work with it on the public side," I tell Trinity.

"This, darlin', is where you will make the big bucks. Oh, and by the way..."

"What?" I try not to snap.

"Not all those alerts are regarding your drummer boy. It seems we have a star in the making." I can tell she's smiling just by the sound of her voice. Leave it to Trinity to get to the point and move past it quickly. I snort a laugh. "Don't be so quick to judge. From my understanding, Cami wants her hands on you pretty bad."

"We can talk about that later," I tell her.

She laughs. "You bet your ass we will. Listen, I'm out of the office for the day, on business. I am supposed to take off for New York around six. Call my cell if you need me."

"Will do. Thanks, Trinity."

"Anytime." The call is disconnected and I sit down at my computer. I go for one of the Google alerts. 'Who's the mystery woman on stage with hot 69 Bottles lead singer Talon Carver and when will we see her again?' That headline is followed immediately by a still image of Talon and I face to face on stage. I want to cry.

The next email says, '69 Bottles drummer Dex Harrison gives into the rocker mentality. Sex, drugs and rock n' roll.' The headline is followed up with several images of Dex with women draped all over him. With countless bottles of alcohol on the table, and a mirror with several white lines.

The door to the suite opens. "You could have at least let me get some clothes on," Dex protests with whichever bodyguard had the pleasure of waking his ass up. When he rounds the corner he is naked as the day he was born. "Well hello, sweetheart, call for a little action did ya? Your boys not enough, you need more?" He provocatively swizzles his hips causing his semi to bounce wildly. I charge toward him, ready to smack him stupid when Kyle's hands come around my waist. Fine! I growl in my head.

"I'm surprised you could get it up after last night."

Dex looks around the room at the entourage gathering. The door swings open again and in come Mouse and Peacock, both fully clothed with Beck and Rusty hot on their heels. "Where's Leroy?" I ask.

Beck looks at me. "He's playing bodyguard outside Dex's room. There are more than a couple passed out in there."

"Are they all alive and breathing?"

Beck gives me a smile. "Yes, and we've managed to find their phones. We're extracting what we can from the unlocked ones, and we will do what we can to get anything off of the locked ones."

"Good. Thanks. Now someone, anyone, get him a fucking towel or a blanket. I don't need to see his shit."

"What the fuck is your problem?" Dex asks me.

I step a few steps closer to him. "You're my fucking problem, in fact, right now you're about to become everyone's problem." I pick up my iPad off of the coffee table and open my email. I pull up the same article that I saw and open the picture and shove it in his face. "Care to explain this?"

"I was just having a good time. Besides, the coke wasn't for me, they were doing it."

"You need to get a better fucking poker face, Dex, because you suck at it. Oh and next time, wipe your fucking nose." His hand goes to his nose and he wipes, his hand comes away with white powder still attached to it. "Now, care to try that again?"

Dex slumps onto the couch and Beck throws a blanket over him. I nod my thanks and Beck steps back. "Not four days ago I sat on that bus and explained the rules. Did I not?" Dex and the rest of the guys nod. "What was my biggest rule?"

"No cameras," Mouse says.

"No god damn cameras or phones." I look to the three bodyguards. "Care to explain to me how you're just now extracting cell phones from these chicks?"

Mills steps forward. "Confiscating cell phones is not our job, Addison. As much as we should make it ours, it's not. The guys are responsible for keeping their heads and they've done a damn good job of it so far."

"Until now," I say as Talon comes storming into the room, looking around he sees Dex plopped on the couch. Mills, Beck and Rusty stand with their legs spread and hands clasped in front. Mouse and Peacock are sitting stoic in chairs opposite Dex and Kyle is leaning against the wall.

"What the hell happened?" Talon asks. I hand him my iPad with the picture. He looks at it, looks at Dex then back to the picture. He calmly hands the iPad back to me and walks right up to Dex and punches him in the jaw. "You fucking idiot, what the hell were you thinking?"

"Fuck, Tal, that shit hurts. I wasn't thinking, obviously."

"How long you been back on coke?" Talon asks him.

"I haven't, that was the first time last night. I got really drunk, then came back to the hotel and got drunker with a couple chicks. Nothing more than normal. One of them pulled out a bag and, fuck!" Dex says as he lets his head fall back on the couch.

"Do you need to go to treatment?" Talon asks him seriously.

"No," Dex moans. "It was a weak moment. I was drunk, horny, too drunk to get it up, so... Fuck, they pulled out the coke. I did a couple lines and then the next thing I remember is waking up to Mills pulling my ass from the bed."

"You're restricted," Talon says to him then looks at Mills. "Twenty-four seven while we're here." Mills nods and Talon turns back to Dex. "This isn't middle of nowhere PA, brother. You've got no choice but to watch your six, you get me?"

"Yeah. Fuck, I'm sorry."

"I'm not the one you owe an apology to." I watch as Dex looks at Talon, confused. "You owe an apology to her." Talon jerks his head in my direction. "She's the one that has to clean up this mess. I'd start kissing her ass if I were you."

chapter 42

Dex doesn't apologize to me and I hate to admit it but I agree with Talon. This is my job and this is why I get paid the big bucks and while it is a challenge, it's not something I can't handle.

"I need you guys to go get the women up, get cell phones, pass codes, the whole nine yards. If there are more pictures, videos or anything else, I need it all. Also, do we know if the chick who put these out is still here?" I look at Rusty because he was on door duty when I called them in.

"No one's left his suite since I took over around six this morning. Beck was there first." Rusty turns to Beck.

Mouse and Peacock look a little ashamed when Beck answers. "Mouse and Peacock's girls left from their respective suites, but that's it."

So something really did happen between Peacock and Jess, because he'd been a good boy until last night. I just might have to talk to him about that, another time.

"Alright. Let's get to finding out who sold the pictures and the story and get them in here, now." The bodyguards go to work with their task, quickly leaving the suite and I turn to Mouse and Peacock. "I'm not trying to be a bitch, but do you guys now understand why this was so important on the bus? It is important because one member of the band, or the crew, can ruin the reputation for everyone else. This is something I can and will overcome and with the scheduling and tickets going on sale for the added shows today, we really could have ruined that for everyone." I take a deep breath. "You all already have a natural preconceived idea of what and who you are. The whole sex, drugs and rock 'n roll thing has been around since rock 'n roll began. Let's not play into it. Please?"

Mouse, Dex and Peacock all nod their understanding and agreement to what I've just said and to see Dex rather dejected is a bit heartwarming. My phone rings.

Sam... FUCK, FUCK, FUCK!!! "I fucking knew this would happen." I send her to voicemail and she immediately calls back. I silence her call and my phone. "Mouse and Peacock, you can go. If you decide to go anywhere today, you do it with two guards, and you speak to no one, do you understand me?"

"Yes," they both say in unison.

"If it isn't urgent, please stay in?" I ask them both and they huff. "I'm not you're mother and you're not five, but this story is hot right now and if you're seen, you will be bombarded. Just be forewarned and let the bodyguards do their jobs."

"Guys, I'm sorry," Dex says. "I lost my head, it won't happen again." The apology is for Mouse and Peacock.

"Seriously? Because this isn't the first time," Mouse says to Dex and then turns to me. "From now on, I'll keep a closer eye on him."

I frown at him. "It's not your responsibility, Mouse. It's Dex's. Look, I'm not telling you guys you can't have women and booze or even drugs for that matter. I am simply telling you that your celebrity status makes people crazy, case in point is what's happening today. It's not fair to keep you locked up and stop you from having a good time, and I won't do it. I refuse. But keeping a clear head is important and necessary so that stuff like this doesn't happen."

"Understood and maybe it took something like this for us to see that," Peacock says.

"Sometimes it takes a two by four. The band's reputation will not be ruined by this, in fact, it just might make you guys that much higher in the hierarchy of celebrities. But gaining a reputation for being a man-whore or a drug addict or an alcoholic can have lasting effects for future relationships. Don't let one night completely ruin you, but keep it in the back of your mind. Imagine how Dex is feeling right now and decide whether or not it's worth feeling like this." I smile. "Now get out of here." They both laugh and leave.

I turn to Dex who is still looking pretty dejected, severely hung over and ready to pass out. "I am going to fix this any way I can. But, Dex?"

His eyes open and he looks at me. "Yeah, love?" he says with a half smile.

"Do it again and I'll have your balls for breakfast."

He smirks. "I lost my head, too much chewing on me at once and I caved. I won't let it happen again. Thank you for doing what you do best and I'm sorry," he says sincerely.

I give him half a smile. "Kyle, can you take him to Mouse or Peacock's room, let him get some sleep, sleep it off. I have work to do and he needs to sober up." Kyle nods, smiles and goes to help Dex up. After some adjustment Dex gets the blanket wrapped around his naked ass and Kyle escorts him out the door.

When I turn around to my computer I see Talon standing in the doorway to the bedroom we shared last night. He's leaning into it with his shoulder, arms crossed over his naked chest and his legs crossed at the ankles. "You're one seriously amazing woman, you know that?"

I snort. "Hardly, Talon, I'm just doing my job."

He smiles. "And you're amazingly good at it. Dex doesn't deserve your help, not after the way he treats you."

I smile. "He may not deserve it, but it is my job to protect his reputation, along with yours and everyone else's. In all honesty, not commenting on what happened last night, or this morning, is probably our best course of action. The media are vultures and today is a slow news day. They will find something else in about an hour and Dex's escapade will slide to a tiny blip in the entertainment section of the newspaper and nobody will care." I laugh, "And those that do are the ones that envy him far too much. Like Sam."

He cocks his head. "Sam, why her?"

I frown. "Dex slept with her in San Diego, even after Dex and I both told her not to. She did it anyway. I told her that if she went through with it that I didn't want to hear about it, ever."

"Why would you not want to know?" he asks, honest curiosity in his voice.

I shrug. "A few reasons. One, he's Dex. I knew from the moment he first saw me, hit on me, and made an ass out of himself that he was a man-whore. A different woman in his bed every night and never the same woman twice. And two, well, anyone who sticks their dick in Sam is destined to be 'the one' and she 'falls in love' and becomes obsessed about it. Whether or not Dex handed her his phone number or not, I have no clue, but I do know that she's kept her distance from me, until today." I look at my phone. "She's called eight times in the last ten minutes. She's seen the news and no doubt wants to know if it's true. She's hitting 'obsession' mode now."

He raises an eyebrow. "Did you warn Dex?"

I roll my eyes. "I tried, he agreed with everything I told Sam in the back of that club. But I doubt he took the warning to heart. He's Dex. He doesn't care."

"What about your other friend? What's her name, Jessie, Jessica?"

I smile. "Jess?" He nods. "I got the impression from Kyle that she slept with Peacock that night, which wasn't anything that was normal in Jess's MO so I didn't think to say anything to her. Though Eric kept to himself afterward, at least until tonight. Kyle, again, was under the impression that there may have been something more between the two."

"Eric's a pretty faithful kind of guy. If he slept with her and had any feelings for her, he wouldn't have slept with someone else. My guess is maybe something happened between him and your friend, which is why he had someone else."

I smile. "You're pretty insightful when you first wake up."

He smiles. "Join me for a shower?"

I giggle. "I've already had one, thank you, and I need to deal with the picture wielding bimbo and I've got to eat something. You go, be quick and join us."

He winks, shoves off from the door frame and stalks toward me before wrapping me up in his arms. "You're amazing." He kisses me once, twice and then slips his tongue in on the third and my knees give out and his arms tighten around me.

I can barely breathe as he assaults my mouth. Then he pulls back. "You sure about that shower?"

I smile, "I'm sure, for now." I wink at him and then he kisses me chastely three more times and ducks into the bedroom, closing the French doors. I fall into my chair at the desk, completely distracted as I start clicking through emails.

Guilt washes over me when I realize that only about twenty percent of the emails pertain to Dex's escapade. Apparently his little headline is small potatoes compared to mine. I am the real hot topic of conversation today and my headlines are burying Dex.

chapter 43

I put my head in my hands. I fucking knew this would happen, especially after Cami approached me so quickly before the concert was even over. She didn't even give it a second thought. She just made the offer and tried to get me to run away with it. Then again, I think she knew deep down that it wasn't necessarily the life for me.

"What's that?" I hear Kyle behind me and I scramble to close it.

"It's nothing."

"You certainly don't look like it's nothing. Come on, panda girl." He pulls on the ear of my hoodie, "Talk to me?"

"It's nothing, really."

He cocks his head at me. "You realize that the only way this is going to work between the three of us is if we communicate. We've got to be open and honest with each other."

I stare at him. Such a profound statement that is ridiculously true on so many levels. "I know, it's, damn. I just jumped the gun on Dex a little too hard and far too quickly than I should have."

"No, you did exactly what needed to be done. But regardless of that, what's making headlines that has you so upset?"

"It's..." The suite door slams shut and Beck comes in with an either still drunk or extremely hungover blonde. "Talon's in the shower," I whisper to Kyle. "Go, keep him in there. I don't need more drama." Kyle looks from me to the chick standing next to Beck and then to the bedroom door and nods before he ducks into the room.

"So, you're the one responsible for this mess?" I ask her.

"What mess? Who the hell are you?" she snaps and I can see Beck's jaw tighten.

"Where's your phone?" Beck holds it up. "Did we get what we needed off of there?" He nods. "Good. Now, how much money did you get for the pictures?"

"Excuse me?" Her lip twitches.

"Who did you sell the pictures to?"

"What pictures?" She has a shit eating grin on her face and I want to slap it off of her.

"What pictures? Oh, let's see the ones we found on your phone that are all over the internet this morning. Tell me, Blondie, who paid you for those pictures?"

"Nobody paid me for the pictures. I got paid to sleep with him and send proof."

I close my eyes and count to ten. By the time I get around to opening them, I'm no calmer. "So, you're a prostitute?"

"What?" She scowls, looks from me to Beck and back again. "No, I'm not a prostitute."

"Well, obviously you are because someone paid you to sleep with Dex and provide them with proof. How much did they pay you?"

"Five hundred dollars."

I laugh. "Was it worth it?" I ask, curious more than anything.

She visibly melts. "Oh yeah, totally worth it."

"Good, because you got screwed, in more ways than one. Whoever you sent those pictures to sold them to every news outlet in North America and more than likely walked away with about fifty-grand for the hottest story on 69 Bottles." I tell her and I watch as her face turns red.

"What are you talking about?"

Oh my god, is she really this fucking dumb? "Whoever it was that asked you to sleep with Dex Harrison and send him proof, turned around and sold that proof to the media. Given the number of outlets running the big 'Dex is a man-whore, coke head' story, I would wager to guess that the person on the receiving end of those pictures paid you a lousy five hundred dollars while they got at least fifty thousand dollars for the story. So you, my dear, got scammed while getting laid."

"You're kidding me, right?" she says.

"Oh my god, no chickie pooh, I'm not. Who was it that wanted the pictures?"

"Some short awkward chick who I met at the bar last night. She said that she'd pay me five hundred dollars to sleep with Dex and to send her proof. She also provided me with the coke."

"What did she look like?" I ask.

"She was short, like five five, brown hair, very awkward and completely uncomfortable. When she was talking to me she was really jumpy, I didn't take her serious at first but then she handed me three hundred and said I'd get the rest once the pictures were delivered to her."

I look at Beck. "Get the phone number or email address she sent them to off of that phone."

"Can I go now?" Blondie asks.

I smile. "Absolutely."

"I have the number," Beck says and he rattles it off to me. "Text messages."

"Thanks. Oh, Blondie, one more thing. Where are you supposed to meet this chick for the rest of your money?"

"Like right now, in the bar downstairs," she says.

I look at Beck who nods in understanding. "Bring her up here after the exchange. Make sure Blondie gets her money." Beck nods and ushers her out the door.

Fuck me fucking sideways.

I turn for the bedroom, swing the doors open wide and stop dead in my tracks. "That's one way to keep him busy." I smirk and Talon's eyes land on mine with a wide smile spreading across his lips while Kyle's head bobs up and down. I clear my throat and Kyle jumps.

He laughs. "You said keep him in here." I bust out laughing and Kyle and Talon join in.

"So fucking hot," I mumble. "I really hate to break up the party but we have a bigger problem."

"What?" Talon asks and I'm looking at Kyle.

"Does this sound familiar." I repeat the number Beck rattled off to me and Kyle cocks his head. "Not really, no. Should I know it?"

"I think it's time for you both to get dressed and take a seat. It's gonna be a long day."

Within ten minutes Talon and Kyle come out of the bedroom, both in jeans and t-shirts, no shoes, no socks and fuck, they're hot. It takes everything I have to not jump them but we need to deal with the problem at hand. "Kyle, grab your phone. Let's cross check and make sure this number isn't in your address book."

"Uh, okay?" he says hesitantly and goes to the coffee table, grabbing his phone as I recite the number. "Six, five," he says before I can call out the last two digits.

"So my theory is correct, it's her. Isn't it?"

Talon perks up, "Who?"

Kyle and I say in unison, "Kate."

chapter 44

So much for a day off. "When this day is over, I want a hot bath and a massage and a very, very large bottle of wine."

"You got it, angel," Talon says. "Come here."

I go to Talon and sit down on his lap. I notice just now that in a public type situation, I am Talon's and Kyle doesn't hesitate to back away, or to stay someplace other than near me and I wonder why that is. Not that it's a big deal, but I wonder idly if it is Talon and Kyle separating our relationship for the masses. But I don't dwell on it, for now.

Talon begins stroking his hand along my hair and down my back. I look at Kyle but ask neither for an answer to my thoughts. "Of all the things to do, why do that? Why to Dex? Why not Talon?"

"Talon is off limits," Kyle says automatically.

"Meaning?" I notice that Talon sits up a little straighter when I ask for more.

Kyle takes a deep breath. "Meaning, Talon doesn't generally bring chicks back to his room, at least not alone.

In the past, he's usually taken them in the club or backstage. Never in his room. Case in point, our first night in Vegas. When Talon came back to the room, he had Dex with him. I was there already. I told Talon right away that you were missing and he stopped what he was doing, rallied the troops, leaving Dex alone. Then when things went south with his 'dates' he called for bodyguard reinforcements to throw them out."

"I later realized that after you'd come back I was just looking for a reason to throw them out. I didn't want to be with them at all, let alone after that debacle and they provided the excuse. You see, angel, a lot of times, while I take pleasure from the bimbos, it's never meant anything to me. It was a place to get off." Yeah, this conversation is making me feel better. "They were women of convenience and well, I am a guy so it's an inevitable fact. Most girls throw themselves at me because they want the fantasy of a rock god between their legs and that certainly strokes a man's ego. You, on the other hand, didn't want a rock god between her legs, so you posed a challenge, which is why Dex is the way he is with you. No one says no to Dex, no one except you. You said no to me, and that was when I realized that you were something more than a disposable Barbie doll who wants a rock god between her legs."

I don't know whether to laugh, cry or scream at him. "You certainly have a way with words," I mutter.

He shrugs.

"So the bottom line is, Talon is off limits to random chippies because he doesn't let them get to him that way and it drives the chicks nuts." Kyle smiles as he sits next to Talon. "Soak it up because you are the first who's ever crawled under his skin like you have."

Talon nudges his shoulder against Kyle's. "She's not the only one," Talon says and then there is a moment of shock that passes between the two of them but dwelling on it is something I don't get to do because the suite door slams shut once again and Mills, Beck, Rusty and Leroy are all surrounding one absolutely petrified production assistant.

"Did Blondie get paid?" I asked Beck.

"She did. Then she slapped Kate. It was great," Beck laughs but Kate fumes.

"I'd tell you to go get Dex, but I imagine he's sleeping off his god awful night." The door shuts again.

"Nope, I'm wide fucking awake," Dex says as he comes storming into the room oblivious to the circle of bodyguards and what in the middle of them. "Look Addison, I'm really fucking sorry about what I did last night. I promise it won't happen again."

"Dex?"

"Yeah."

"Breathe. You were set up last night."

"Fuck me! How so?"

"Well, one of your little blonde bimbos was approached and offered five hundred dollars to seduce you, drug you and then finally fuck you."

"Five hundred? That's the going rate for rock star sex these days?" He laughs.

I can't help but laugh too. "Well, see, the person doing the paying said that she needed proof or Blondie wasn't going to get paid. So I'm guessing sometime after you passed out, Blondie did her job and sent out the pictures to her point of contact and that person then turned around and sold the story to news outlets across the country, or maybe it was just one, we're not sure yet. But anyway, they pocket the cash, scamming not only you, but the Blondie as well. I'm guessing those pictures grossed, maybe fifty grand." I look at Kate who mouths fifty grand and looks ridiculously disappointed. Oh, talk about a backfire. "If the contact was smart that is. Now here's the real kicker, the point of contact could have and probably should have used an anonymous email so that we couldn't trace the pictures. But the middle man wasn't that smart."

"Well, what the fuck?" Dex says. "I've never in my life…well, fuck. I don't even know…shit." A speechless Dex is rather interesting and he turns around running his hand through his hair. "What's she doin' here?"

I smirk. "Dex, meet the point of contact. Who I'm guessing is pretty pissed because she didn't get fifty g's for the pictures."

"Fucking hell."

"So Kate, how much did you get for the pictures? You know, for curiosity's sake."

She doesn't answer and Dex takes a few steps in her direction. "I know you. Why do I know you? Why did I never see it before?"

"Because you're too busy sticking your dick into some bitches cunt," Kate snarls and even I take a step back. Awkward Kate is pretty pissed the fuck off about something and I can't even begin to imagine what it is.

"Well now, aren't we feisty? So tell me, darlin', what exactly have I done to you to make you want to pull a stunt like this?" Dex asks her and I just sit back wondering idly what the hell could have possessed her to do something like this. The only things that come to mind are…

"No way, Dex, you didn't fuck her, did you?"

"Hell if I know," Dex says with such nonchalance that I almost want to laugh.

Kate starts to openly sob and the entire room goes still. "What on earth would make you want to do something like this, Kate?" Kyle stands up from the couch walking toward her. He doesn't go all the way to her because I don't want to go near her either.

"He..." She weeps, "He's responsible for my sister. He's the reason she tried to commit suicide. He's the reason she's gone crazy."

"What?" Dex says with genuine shock.

"Stacy, do you remember her, asshole? Do you remember what you did to her? She was my sister and you fucking dumped her so that you could go off whoring around with whoever you wanted. It's all your fault," she sobs.

Dex stops dead in his tracks. Frozen in place. "She understood, she said she fucking understood. Now you show up here, trying to blackmail me, she said she fucking understood." Dex is nearly shouting.

"She wasn't enough for you. She was never enough, you always wanted more than her, and yet she stood by you, was there for you every night then you just dumped her like yesterday's garbage."

"How much, Kate? How much did you get for the pictures?" Dex asks her.

"I needed money. I need money to pay for her hospital. I fucking need to save her," she sobs more.

"How much, Kate?" he asks her again.

"Ten grand," Kate blurts.

I almost want to be pissed off at this chick for what she's done, but now I admire her for her spirit. Protecting her sister.

"I didn't know, Kate. Honest to god, I didn't know." Dex's voice is soft, unlike anything I've ever heard from him before.

"If you cared about her at all, you would have never left her like you did, you would have never put her in the position she's in."

"So you decide to use me to get money for her? Did it ever occur to you that I just might actually help her?" Dex says and Kate looks at him with eyes as wide as saucers.

"She doesn't need your fucking money, Dex. She needed you."

I step in between the two of them and look at Dex. "This is no longer my concern, or anyone else's for that matter. If you want to continue talking to Kate, that's your choice, and I highly recommend it. But at this point, I think you need to take it to a private location. Without the audience." I look to Kate who still looks petrified and turn back to Dex. I lean in and whisper to him. "Keep one of the guys with you, for safety, they won't judge you. But you really should talk to her. Talk to her before this turns into something bigger than it needs to be. This is personal and private, try and keep it that way."

Dex nods and looks at Kate. "Will you come with me? Talk to me some more?"

"I have nothing left to say," she says snottily.

I walk over to her. "You wanted his attention, you got it."

"She was supposed to leave before sending me the pictures so this wouldn't have come out," Kate says to me.

"Well it did, and I'm sure I speak for Kyle and the label when I tell you that you're fired. This might be your last chance to talk to him. Give him details on your sister and her condition. Believe it or not, I really do believe he had no idea and that he wants to help. Let him talk to you."

"Fuck you," she says to me.

"Listen here, Kate, I am not your enemy. I feel sorry for your sister, honestly I do, but this is no way to help her. You got ten grand now, but what about when you need more money, what next? Talk to him, work it out with him. Pinning this on him isn't fair."

She finally nods and Dex takes that as his cue. He and Beck escort her from the room. I turn to Mills. "Make sure she gets her stuff off the bus and out of her hotel room. Get her on a plane to wherever she needs to go and get her away from the band. We don't need another incident like this popping up, at least not like this."

"Agreed," he says with a half-smile. "Peacock and Mouse want to get ink. Are they okay to leave?" Oh new ink, now that sounds like an amazing idea.

"They are, just remind them to keep their mouths shut. What happened in here, stays in here, unless Dex decides to tell them. All they know is that Dex got drunk, got high and had pictures taken. Leave it at that. I'll handle it publicly with a press release."

"Sounds good," Mills says.

"Oh, and if their ink shop checks out, let me know." I wink and he smiles. Mills, Rusty and Leroy leave the suite, leaving me to Talon and Kyle.

"Well, I certainly didn't see that one coming," Talon says as he leans forward, putting his elbows on his knees. Then he runs his hand over his chin.

"You can say that again," Kyle retorts as he sits back down next to Talon.

"You guys knew this Stacy, right?" They both nod. "So what happened between them?" I ask, honestly curious.

"Dex didn't want to grow up," Talon says.

"That doesn't sound like a good enough reason to dump someone," I counter.

"No, it's certainly not. Dex didn't think that Stacy was road material. Thought that she'd make a better mom and a housewife than a rocker's wife. She was insanely jealous but a good person. I liked her a lot and was pretty pissed when Dex dumped her. I think it only took Dex a couple of weeks to realize the mistake he made. What he did with that realization is beyond me. Other than the fact that he turned into what he is today." Talon's eyes are sad as he talks about Dex and Stacy. "She was good for him, but like I said about rock gods, he wanted to be one of them."

"Well, I feel sorry for Kate. But it is obvious to me that Dex feels pretty bad about it. So maybe now they can make it right. Handle it in the right way," I say and sit down in front of my computer.

"Hopefully," Talon says.

"I don't know how to handle this, publicly. The story is already buried," I say looking at my screen and my email.

"With what?" Talon asks.

"Me."

chapter 45

"Why you?" Kyle asks and I pull up the video I found from last night on YouTube and press play, turning up the volume.

"Oh shit." I look at Talon who is grinning from ear to ear as the video from last night's concert plays. The sound quality is awful but it is a very close shot.

"Oh, it gets better." I look at them. "Come see for yourself."

They both look at each other and then stand up in unison. Their bulky bodies stalking towards me is a rather amazing sight to see. But I stand up and move out of their way. They look at the computer, so that they can see what I'm talking about.

"Holy SHIT!" Talon shouts. "Four fucking million views." He snaps his head around to look at me.

"Refresh the page, that's over a million more since the last time I looked at it. And that is only one video, there are at least fifty of them on YouTube by different users." I take a seat on the couch behind me and just watch as my boys watch the video. When it's over I can see one of them hit refresh and the number jumps by over six hundred thousand views. "So my conversation with Cami backstage last night?" The both look at me. "The one you were trying to coax out of me with kissing and orgasms and fucking me."

"Yeeahhh," Talon says in a 'get on with it' kinda way.

"She wants to sign me to Bold."

"No fucking way," they both say in unison.

"What did you tell her?" Talon asks me.

"Nothing, she really didn't give me a chance to say yes or no. She told me to think about it and that we would talk after the tour was over. But I am pretty sure that's going to change now." I lean back into the couch. "It's never been anything I've thought about before."

Talon laughs. "It's usually something that happens when you least expect it. Trust me, I know and now I see why it takes those who want it so bad as long as it does." He chuckles. "You have to not want it to get what you want."

"Your logic baffles me," Kyle says to Talon and they both laugh. "So baby girl, what do you want to do?"

I snort. "Right now, get through my emails so that the two of you can take my mind off of everything."

"We can do that, but I was talking about Cami's offer."

"Hell if I know. I have never, in my entire life, sung in front of an audience bigger than a small Kansas City congregation. Let alone what I did last night. Fuck, I didn't even plan that and to be honest, I didn't even realize I was singing out loud. It was all, fuck, I don't know, it was a damn adrenaline rush." I smile.

"Welcome to my world, panda," Talon says and he sits on the coffee table in front of me, putting his legs on either side of mine. Kyle comes around the back of the sofa and puts his hands on my shoulders. He begins rubbing them softly and I get goosebumps all over my skin and my nipples turn to pebbles beneath my tank top. Talon is quick to notice and he smirks. "So, since you have until the end of the tour to make up your mind, I'd like you to sing with me at every concert."

"No way," I say shaking my head. Kyle's hands dip lower, working their way into my tank top. "Not fair, Kyle," I grumble. These two can get me to agree to just about anything when they're touching me.

Kyle's fingers slide past the top band of my tank top and I shiver in anticipation of his fingers brushing my nipples. He continues pushing his hands further south, he's almost there.

"Yes way, angel. You're amazing and obviously the crowd loves you."

"No." Kyle's fingers reach my nipples. "Ahh!" I moan and he slides them back.

"Let's try that again, shall we, angel? Are you going to sing with me?"

I can't answer because Kyle's hands slide down right across my nipples at the same time Talon's hand begins tracing circles between my legs, right over my clit. "Ahh."

"Come on, angel, what do you say? You and me, singing your favorite song."

"Not fair," I groan as they continue their assault. Kyle's hands push my tank top down, exposing my breasts to the cool air and Talon's waiting tongue.

"What. Do. You. Say?" Each word is punctuated by the flick of his tongue on my nipple. Before I can respond, he sucks it into his mouth and sucks like his life depends on it.

"Yes!" I moan as my body convulses with need, a hot desperate need to come.

And just like that, all hands and mouths are gone. I am left panting on the couch. "That's my angel."

"What? Oh seriously. No fucking way, get your tongue back here."

"Maybe later, you have work to do." He stands and side steps me toward the computer where he plops down and starts to play the video again.

"So not fucking fair. You know there is always a thing called payback," I mumble.

"Oh that is payback for pulling Kyle off my dick earlier," Talon says with a laugh and Kyle is smiling like a Cheshire cat.

"Hmph!" I pick up my iPad and get to work on my emails.

chapter 46

Two hours later and I have finally filtered through all of my emails, with no help from the boys, mind you. They've been watching that damn video on repeat since they saw it the first time. Which is okay, except for the fact that I blush like a teenager every time I hear my voice.

It's now just after six in the evening and while there were a lot of new outlets reporting the Dex issue, it wasn't anything derogatory. Not to mention the fact that those same news outlets were covering my performance of the concert.

I received an email from Cami that I put off sharing with the boys because I don't want to distract myself from finishing my task at hand. I also email Trinity letting her know that the band is not going to return comments regarding the pictures of Dex for reasons that we now understand who was behind it and the reasons for it. Out of respect for all parties involved I've decided it's best not to engage the animals. She replied quickly with a "good call" email and reminded me of her travel plans this evening, but that she would be available via email if necessary.

I'm not a Facebook person, never really have been. I have an account, but rarely use it. I decide, given the fact that I now seem to be a major celebrity that I might want to visit the social media world.

"Holy hell. How the hell did they figure it out so damn fast?" I mutter.

"Figure out what, panda girl?"

"Who I am. From the video."

"What makes you say that?" Talon turns to look at me. I flip my iPad around and show him my Facebook profile. He squints, stands and comes to sit next to me. I point to the upper right hand corner.

"Three thousand, four hundred and forty-nine friend requests. Seventeen hundred notifications. And over seven hundred messages," I say out loud so Kyle is in the loop and I groan. A message window pops up and I recognize the image. It's Sam's. "Where is my phone?" I ask no one in particular as I look around the room.

"Right here," Kyle says and brings it over, taking a seat on the other side of me from Talon.

I press the button on the bottom. "I'm gonna fucking kill her," I groan as I see over a hundred missed calls. The only ones that I truly care about are the one from Cami, with respective voicemail, the one from my mom, hers too has a voicemail and the rest are all from Sam with countless voicemails. "I can't deal with her." Just as I say that my phone starts ringing.

"You know what, I'll deal with this," Talon says, taking my phone from me.

"Talon, don't..."

"Where's the fire, Sam?"

I can't hear the other end of the conversation. "It's Talon." He pulls the phone away from his ear and puts it on speaker.

Sam is going on and on. "I need to talk to Addie, put her on the phone, Talon."

"I'm sorry, Sam, I can't do that right now. She's in the middle of working."

"Bullshit, she's been ignoring my calls all afternoon, tell her to get over her shit and answer the fucking phone."

I gape at Talon and he's turning bright red. "Why are you calling her like this? What's so fucking important that you're blowing up her phone?"

"That's none of your damn business. I know she's there, give her the fucking phone."

I hold my hand out for the phone but Talon refuses. "I am not going to let you talk to her that way. I cannot imagine anything she could have done to warrant such an attitude from you. Now why don't you tell me what your problem is and I'll decide if it's worth her time."

"What are you? Her fucking secretary?"

"No, I'm her boss among other things."

"Bullshit, she doesn't work for you."

I can tell Sam is losing steam and Talon is winning. I try to give him a smile and some encouragement.

"Oh, on the contrary, Sam, she does and I pay her damn good money to do her job, which she is busy doing, so I suggest you tell me what is so fucking important that you've called her over a hundred times."

"I don't want to discuss it with you," she mutters through the phone.

"Does this have anything to do with Dex?" Talon asks and I hear her huff on the other end of the phone. "Because I'm pretty sure Dex made it very clear to you what you were to him and more importantly, I am pretty sure she told you not to discuss it with her, ever. So if you're trying to use your quote-un-quote friendship with her in order to try and get to Dex, I will have her number changed so fast you'll never be able to talk to her."

"Sorry for you, I'm staying in her house," she counters back to him and I roll my eyes.

"Has her house burned down?" Talon asks her a little sarcastically

"No," she snaps back.

He shrugs. "Then I can't imagine a valid reason for you to be blowing up her phone. And believe me, I'm sure we could make it so that you never talk to her again. Since you've been blowing up her phone since the story started popping up all over the place, I'm pretty sure you're pissed off because you think you mean something to Dex. Am I getting warmer?"

There is no reply.

"Then let us continue with the fact that Addison warned you that Dex would fuck you and leave you and without a doubt have another woman in his bed the next night. Did she not?"

Again no response, but I can hear her on the other end of the phone.

"I'll take your silence as confirmation. With that in mind, Addison has had a very trying day compliments of Dex, among other things, and I am here to remind you that you willingly slept with a man who told you himself that it was a one night stand and now you're all lovey dovey thinking he's prince fucking charming and you're pissed off because he stuck his dick into another chick. Seriously, Sam? Enough already. When you decide not to be a lunatic about this, call Addison again, leave her a voicemail telling her you're sorry and then maybe she will talk to you again.

For now, call this phone again and I'll have you charged with harassment. Good night, Sam."

"Uh..." I hear her on the other end of the phone as Talon hangs up. I am completely shocked by what Talon just did and a little in awe too.

"Thank you," I scowl. "I think."

Kyle and Talon bust out laughing. "She was pissing me off. I can't believe, no wait, I can believe it. It happens all the time." Talon gives me a half smile. "Sorry, panda."

I raise an eyebrow at him. "For putting you in the middle of Dex's not so secret love life. Putting you between your friend, making you put up with all of this."

I pout. "You want to know something?" I ask softly.

"Always," Talon and Kyle say together.

"I don't know if I really have friends. Not solid ones anyway. After Dan, I made acquaintances with people, including Sam and Jess. Yes, Sam and I are close, but sometimes I just keep her at arm's length. She comes around when it suits her most. Which of course, annoys the crap out of me. Plus even when I don't have mega rock stars requiring my services for twelve weeks, I always made up excuses to ditch the girl outings. I'm not that much of a girlie girl and spending that much time with people gives me the willies."

Talon cocks his head at me. "But you're spending twelve weeks on a tour bus, with people no less."

I smile. "That's different. This is different."

"How so?" Kyle asks me.

"Because, when I climbed on board the bus, I was a business woman. Here to do business and nothing else."

Talon comes to sit on the coffee table in front of me like before. "Are you still just a businesswoman?" he asks softly, afraid of my answer.

I put my iPad down, lean forward and take his hands in mine. "No," I say seriously. "A lot has changed since I boarded that bus on Thursday. I've changed a lot too." I look over at Kyle. "I've come to understand that there is more to life than working all day." I look back at my hands in Talon's. "When it was taken from me, when Dan died, throwing myself into work was easy because I didn't have anyone anymore. After the funeral, nobody cared, except for my mom, but she's my mom. So not having anyone made it easier to survive. To make a name for myself. Everything has changed because I finally see how stupid I've been for secluding myself from people. But I also see how that seclusion has helped shape me." I take a deep breath. "I see now that secluding myself brought me to that bus, and brought me here."

chapter 47

"Alright, enough of the heavy stuff," I say after a couple of minutes of silence. "What are we doing tonight?" I ask just as my phone chimes with a text. "Oh, it's Mills." I read the text aloud.

Mills: Shop is good, clean, guys are gonna get inked, will be here a while. Secluded and private. Said they will shut down shop if T, K, D, and you want to come for ink. Let me know.

"I vote ink," I say with a laugh.

"Then let's go," Kyle says.

"EEK!" I squeal and lean over and kiss Kyle on the cheek and I whisper in his ear. "You had your fun this morning. We will all be together tonight. Let me have him."

"Of course," he says out loud, standing from the couch. "I'll get in touch with Mills, go talk to D and figure out dinner."

Talon looks at both of us, confusion in his eyes. "I need a shower," I say looking straight at Talon with a mischievous grin on my face.

He looks at Kyle. "You sure?"

Kyle smiles down at Talon then lifts his hand to Talon's cheek, cupping it. Talon leans into it and kisses his palm. "Absolutely." They both smile at each other. "Besides, we have tonight." He winks and I stand, wrapping my arms around Kyle, kissing him once, twice and on the third, I slide my tongue inside, seeking his. He kisses me back. "So. Not. Fair," he says between kisses and I laugh.

"You had your fun earlier. It's his turn."

"Wait, what fun?" Talon stands, nearly knocking me over until his arms come around me, holding me to him. I look at him.

"Kyle woke up before you did and attacked me in the shower."

"Oh." Talon smirks. "Okay then, buh bye." He sticks his tongue out at Kyle and the three of us laugh.

Kyle kisses me on the head and then Talon pulls Kyle in for his own kiss before he goes.

"Fuck!" I breathe and watch as they both smile through their kiss.

I manage to slide out from between them and start walking toward the bedroom. I pull off my tank top and slide down my pj bottoms as I go.

"Fuck!" I hear both of them say and then I can hear one of them running up behind me, lifting me and spinning me around as he tosses me on the bed and just as fast as I was tossed, I am mounted by Talon, kissing me and thrusting his denim covered erection between my legs and then I hear the click of the door as it closes.

"All mine," he growls kissing me again.

"All yours," I reply to him with heat in my eyes. "I've had a very shitty day. Make me forget it." And with that, he pins my hands above my head, rubbing his cock against my slit. Though still covered in denim the friction is almost too much. He starts kissing and biting down my jaw to my neck. "Faster, Talon." I urge and he bites into my breast. I cry out from the pain and pleasure as it makes my entire body shake with need.

Then just like that, his mouth is lapping at my nipple. Sucking and tugging. I am pinned by his hands and his hips and I need him naked. I need him inside of me.

"Take me, Talon. Fuck me. God, I need you," I sigh and he doesn't hesitate. He readjusts so that my hands stay bound above my head and he pulls back so that he can unbutton his pants, freeing his erection from the confines of his jeans before sliding them down so that his balls have room to move.

"Lift your legs, angel."

I comply with his soft command. As soon my knees are up and I'm fully exposed to him he slams into me. Skyrocketing my orgasm and I shatter. Coming unglued at the seams. He slows his pace, but continues pounding into me, building another orgasm faster than should be natural. He swirls his hips, forcing his cock to hit me in all the right places.

I close my eyes and arch my back. His mouth is on my other nipple, licking and sucking it like a starved child.

I need this. He needs this. He doesn't relent, he only drives deeper and deeper building me to a fever that I can no longer control.

"Fuck! Ahh! I'm, fuck, Talon…" I scream as my orgasm explodes. My screams are only matched by his cries as he pours himself into me. His entire body is trembling with his release as I fall into the clouds of bliss, forgetting anything and everything but him and me and where our bodies are connected. A small twinge of guilt fills me, just like this morning when I realize Kyle isn't here to watch, or to help.

"He would have said no if it wasn't okay," Talon says against my chest where he is resting his head. Our breathing finally slows to normal rates. "We talked about it earlier, talked about how we can't always expect you to service both of us every time. How we are two people and you're only one. Believe me, we both want you so bad, with or without the other, but with the other, it's a million times better," he says. "We will do anything for you, angel. Anything at all."

I can't stop the overwhelming emotions and they boil over, tears seeping down my cheeks. Everything from today, opening up to these guys, the fact that I've never felt so comforted and protected. Add to that the fact that these two men are more than any one woman could hope for.

"Angel?" Talon whispers. "What's wrong?"

I don't answer him; I just try desperately to stop the tears. This is so stupid. I shouldn't be reacting like this, not over something like what Talon had to say. Why am I reacting this way? I shake my head back and forth.

"Oh no, we talk about things, remember?"

"I know, it's just, damn it. It's so stupid."

I feel his quiet chuckle. "Nothing you feel is ever stupid."

"Oh, believe me, this is."

"Do I need to get Kyle?" he asks and I shake my head. "Then talk to me, please."

"It's just...I don't know how to say this because it makes no sense in my head," I whine.

"Start at the beginning. What did I say?" He lifts his head to look at me better.

"The fact that you guys talked about all this. I feel so confused. I feel like I need to like one of you better than the other, but I just can't."

"Oh no, neither of us are asking for you to choose, we can't do that to you. One, it's not fair to you because we both have pursued you and two, well, frankly I can't picture you without him and vice versa," he says softly. "This whole thing is new to all of us, we're going to have some serious growing pains and I have no doubt that jealousy will come into play at some point, but the more honest and open we are with each other, the easier talking about this will become. Rome wasn't built in a day."

"Dammit, now I want to cry again," I say quietly. One minute, I want just a physical relationship with these two and then something sweet happens and I feel myself falling into their trap. Falling for them, and damn, I don't know if I'm ready for that.

"Don't, because there is no reason to. We're all overwhelmed. Trust me, hitting Dex was more of a release for me than I realized." He smiles. "In other words, it felt really good. Tonight, with you, raw like this is amazing. So I was helping you forget while you were helping me let go."

I smile. I'm not any less confused than I was when I started crying, but I will take it and absorb it. He pulls away from me and slides forward a little bit, when he does this I realize that he's still buried inside of me. I moan and he freezes.

"I didn't mean…shit, Addie, I'm sorry."

"What for?" I flick my hips at him and his eyes roll up. I lift my hips, trying to show him what I want and he rolls to his side. He slips out in the process but that's okay. "Kyle!" I holler as I climb on top of Talon and bury him inside me once again as I shiver. "Kyle!" I call out again and I start to grind myself against Talon's erection and he moans.

Seeing what I'm doing to him is working, I continue working his erection, grinding and sliding myself up and down. The thick crown of his cock is brushing that sweet spot inside causing my pleasure to rise higher, grinding harder.

The door opens. "What's...oh, what's wrong?"

"I need you," I moan as Talon thrust his hips.

chapter 48

"You didn't…"

I cry out. "I need you too."

Talon's hand slide up my thighs to my hips to help steady me so that he can pound himself into me. My body quivers watching Kyle strip out of his shirt and jeans. He kicks his shoes off before climbing onto the bed. I lick my lips.

"Come here, Kyle," Talon says and Kyle moves toward him. Talon lies back against the bed, opening his mouth.

"Oh fuck," I groan, flicking my hips against Talon's. With my clit rubbing against him, pleasure soars the moment Talon's lips kiss Kyle's cock. Talon isn't thinking twice about anything, he's going for it and I can't stop my cries of desperation. Talon swallows down Kyle's cock. "Fuck me. I…" I grind against him on his up thrust and he slinks back onto the bed allowing me to take over. I reach over and grab the back of Kyle's neck and pull him toward me. I need his mouth on mine since Talon has stolen his cock from me.

He comes willingly and I crush my lips to his. Talon's hand moves up my hip to my breast, stroking his thumb over my nipple and I moan into Kyle's mouth. Kyle's hand comes up to my other nipple and begins twisting and pulling.

Talon continues licking and sucking Kyle's cock. Breathlessness pulls me away from Kyle's kiss. I flick against Talon again, pulling in a deep breath. I grab Kyle's hand from my nipple and bring it to my mouth. I start licking his finger, sucking it in and out of my mouth. I settle onto Talon's cock, just holding him inside me while I blow Kyle's finger. Once I'm satisfied with the result, I lean forward onto Talon's chest and guide Kyle's hand toward the tight ring of my untapped entrance.

I plead with my eyes and his hand moves until his finger is just over my puckered hole. He begins to move his finger slowly in circles. I moan and begin to move against Talon's cock.

I help Talon with Kyle's erection, both of our tongues working along his shaft causing Kyle to groan and tremble. Talon and I start taking turns with Kyle's cock in our mouth. The combination of his cock in my mouth, Kyle's finger, my clit rubbing against Talon's pelvis and his cock sliding in and out of my core is too much. Talon's hand tweaks my nipple. The sharp burst of pleasure and pain sends me flying over the edge, my body trembles. Kyle slides his finger inside, past the tight band and I cry out as my orgasm erupts. "Fuck, Fuck!" I shout as I tremble along Talon's cock.

"Talon, I'm gonna…" I watch as Talon nods his head, sucking Kyle and stroking him as Kyle erupts down Talon's throat and at the same time I feel Talon jerk and explode deep inside of me.

I collapse onto Talon's chest and Kyle slowly extracts his finger from me and then Talon falls free of my body.

"Fuck that was... Damn, that was insane," Kyle groans as he plops down on the bed next to us.

I moan an incomprehensible agreement and both of them chuckle.

"Addie?" Talon asks me and I nod. His silent laugh shakes his chest. "Do you want to be able to take both of us at the same time?" I nod. They both laugh. "Can you talk?"

"Nuh uh," I grumble.

I feel both of Talon's hands wrap around me. Kyle shifts positions so that he can set his head on Talon's chest, he's looking at Talon when he says, "I think we need to go to the toy store."

"Huh?" I breathe.

He smiles. "Anal sex isn't something you can jump right into."

I pout and he laughs. "You're so fucking cute. But we can't just do it, okay? We need to work you up to it. Do you want to do that?"

"Yes," I say softly.

"Okay, baby girl. We'll work on it."

"Okay."

We stay that way for a couple minutes then I start to get up. Talon holds me to his chest. "Hang on, baby." He shifts his hips so that he falls out the last little bit. Two rounds of his orgasms combined with my own juices quickly slides out. "Oh shit," Talon's says with a laugh. When I sit up I see why he said that, our mixed fluids are sitting in a pool at the base of his semi-hard cock.

"God, that's... damn, that's a lot." I laugh, extracting myself, walking into the bathroom to clean up. I climb into the shower and I am quickly joined by my guys who help me clean up.

"So panda girl wants to go get inked?" Kyle says and my face lights up.

"It's been a long time," I say with a smile.

"Do you know what you want?" Talon asks me.

I shrug. "Sort of. Though it's not a one and done kind of thing. As you can tell, I'm not exactly known for that. But I have a couple of ideas that I could start with."

"Then let's go." Talon kisses my shoulder.

They finish washing me, then wrap me in a towel and dry me. There is something to be said for the way they take care of me. I don't know if this is going to be a good thing or not. But I am incapable of deciding one way or another right now. The only time I've ever seen anything like this has been in the books I love to read. Their actions tell me that I am dealing with two men who enjoy dominance and I think I'm kind of okay with that. For now.

We finish getting ready to go. "What do you guys want to do about dinner?" Kyle asks while I finish up my hair.

I look at my watch, it's almost eight. "Did you tell Mills we were coming?"

"Yeah, he said that Dex was on his way and that Peacock would be in the chair for a while and that if we were coming the shop had two more artists they could bring in for us."

"Wow, that's awfully accommodating."

He laughs. "It's not every day you get members of the biggest rock band in your store. They'll do just about anything."

"Are we sure it will be private?"

He nods. "Don't worry about it, baby girl. Mills knows what he's doing."

"Okay, it's just hard to let that part of me go. Not that getting ink should make national headlines, but you just never know."

"I know. It's all good. Also, at some point tonight or tomorrow we need to discuss Kate," Kyle says seriously.

I look at him. "What about her?"

"Oh don't worry, she's still fired. But the label wants to send a new assistant for me."

"And how do you feel about that?" I ask him.

"I told them I had one already."

I raise an eyebrow at him. "Who?" I ask when he doesn't take my silent hint.

He leans in and whispers, "You." Then kisses me on the cheek and runs away laughing. I on the other hand stand in front of the mirror with my jaw on the floor.

"Or for pete's sake. Kyle!" I shout.

"What?" he says innocently back to me.

"Why me?" I scowl at him.

"Because you're good at what you do, and you were already doing it the other day. Besides, between the two of us, we can do her job without any problems."

"Does this mean I have to move to the other bus?" I laugh.

"Yes," Talon and Kyle say together, laughing the whole time.

"Sorry, boys, you're not getting rid of me that easily."

"Damn!" Talon says. "I wanted Kyle all to myself."

I turn around to face him with my mouth wide open and notice he has a guitar strapped on his back. After I get over the whole 'why does he have that' I morph into an over exaggerated pouty face. Which of course makes him laugh harder. "Fine. He's all yours." I turn back to Kyle. "You better watch out, he's a damn animal in bed. Nothing is safe around him." Just then Talon slams into me, picking me up. I squeal. "Put me down, you ogre." I'm laughing so hard that I can hardly breathe.

"I'll show you an animal," he growls into my ear; sending shivers of excitement racing across my skin.

Kyle comes up, helping Talon hold me and they squish me. "You haven't seen animalistic yet," Kyle says and I throw my head back laughing.

"You guys are too much." They both sandwich my face in a kiss on my cheeks. "Can we go now? I wanna get tattooed," I whine and Talon carries me from the suite. Once we leave the room we find Rusty and Beck standing guard.

"Will you put me down?" I whine.

"No," Talon says deadpan.

"I'll scream and whine and throw a fit." I cross my arms and huff.

"Then I'll spank you or better yet, make you wait until Albuquerque for an orgasm."

I look at him, my jaw falling open. "You wouldn't dare."

"Oh, just push me and find out," he says sternly. His eyes scream for me to just try.

"You don't fight fair."

Kyle laughs behind us. "You can say that again."

Talon laughs and without warning he drops my legs and I squeak as he wraps his arms around me, holding me chest to chest. My feet dangle as we step into the elevator.

chapter 49

We have a Suburban to take us around town. It beats the town cars and at least this way we can all fit into one vehicle getting there. Coming back with everyone might be an issue, but we can deal with it later.

After a twenty minute drive we arrive at Incision Tattoo. It's a cute little shop but far from secluded, but I can tell, based on the drive, we're far from downtown. Couple that with the fact that there isn't a bar in sight.

When we walk in, two of the artists get a little too excited over Talon. It's crazy, I guess I've seen the girls go nuts, but never the guys. Talon is ever the gentleman and probably one of the nicest I've met when it comes to his fans. I think Talon has a great grasp on what fans really mean to what they do. They chat for a little bit and Talon introduces me and Kyle to the artists. Then we all get down to business.

"I know she wants something done," Talon tells one of the artists.

"Great. I'm Scott." He holds his hand out for me to take and I do. "What do you want to do?" I smile and take him over to the counter to show him my idea. I notice then that Kyle starts talking to the other guy about what he wants to do.

Talon comes to stand near me. "Aren't you gonna get something?" I ask him and he shakes his head. I raise an eyebrow. "Any particular reason?"

"I tend to get sick afterwards. I don't mind, but we have a lot going on, I can't run that risk."

"Aw crap, I didn't know."

"Shh," he says. "Don't worry about it. That's why I brought my guitar. I'm gonna work on a couple of ideas while you guys do your thing."

I smile. "Alright."

Talon watches over me as I discuss my plan with Scott and then he sets off to work on the drawing for me. "Where you gonna put it?" he asks.

I lift up my arm then run my fingers downward, wrapping around just under my left breast. He flinches. "That's gonna hurt, angel, you sure?"

I smile and nod. "I've been wanting to do it for a while now, might as well. Plus, I need some more color."

He smirks. "But black and grey looks amazing on you." His fingers trace along the line between my shoulder blades.

"I know, but I like the color on my arms and sometimes I think about coloring in parts of my back, but I'd hate to have another artist do it and I've lost track of the artist who did the work."

Talon and I don't talk too much more, we just kinda enjoy each other, it's weird, but kinda cool. Kyle returns, waiting just like me for a drawing. When he asks me what I'm doing, I tell him that he will just have to wait and see.

He calls me a tease and tells me that I can't see his until I show him mine.

After about twenty-five minutes, Scott returns with a drawing and it's perfect so we set off to his room to get started. "Addie," Talon says behind me and I turn back to him. "Take this. You might want it." I smile at his thoughtfulness and I take his hoodie from him. He bends down and gives me a kiss on the cheek.

Nearly two hours and a shit ton of pain later, I grit my teeth because Talon was right, I'm done. I've been topless for the last two hours and I am stiff from lying on my side. When Scott's done, he helps me sit up, which causes quite the head rush so I sit there for a couple of minutes before I finally make it to my feet for an inspection of his work.

"Wow," Talon says behind me. "You might want to lie back down and do the other side because, fuck me, that's hot." I smile so wide my cheeks hurt.

"I have a similar but different idea for the other side. And I don't know if I can lie here for another two hours."

Talon laughs. "You say that, but look at your back, how long did that take? Forty or fifty hours?"

"Sixty two."

He laughs, "And you don't want to sit here for another two hours for the other side?"

I look at Scott who shrugs. "I got nowhere else to be. You want it, you got it."

"Is this a conspiracy theory? Tattoo me up, force me to sit on my ass tomorrow? You know this one already ruins my plans to take advantage of that oversized bathtub in our suite tomorrow."

Talon shrugs a shoulder. "Peacock has at least another hour to go. Mouse is nearly done and Kyle is at least another ninety minutes. So it's up to you, sweetheart."

"How are you doing out there?"

He chuckles. "I am doing great. It's nice to have a night not on stage and I'd be lying if I said the creative juices don't flow in this place." He winks.

I finally stand up to inspect Scott's work and it's perfect. The design is a series of stars in various shades of blues and greens with black filigree just under my breast, a couple of the swirls come up to the bottom swell toward my nipple, giving it the effect of holding my breast in place. When I look at it as a whole, Talon is right; I should just do the other side. "If you're up for it, Scott, let's do the other side."

"Absolutely, Addison. What are we changing?"

"The stars to hearts and then the colors of the hearts I'd like in reds and oranges. A fire effect without actual fire." I pull my phone from the pocket of Talon's sweatshirt that I'm holding to my chest, keeping myself covered up. "I have an image idea for the coloring."

"Perfect."

Talon comes in and kisses me again. "I'll be out front."

"Thanks."

Scott comes around with plastic wrap and tape. After rubbing goo on his work, he then wraps up the ink job. "Why don't you stay up for a bit, I need to go redraw the design with the hearts."

"Okay, thanks, Scott." He leaves the room and I slip Talon's hoodie on, zipping it up.

I walk out of the room as a lull in the overhead music kicks in, giving me an eargasm of Talon strumming his guitar. I walk the twenty or so feet to the lobby area and lean against the wall watching Talon go to work on the notes for a new song. This one seems softer, like 'Your Eyes' is. He is humming the words, but I can't actually make them out. Regardless, watching him work is a major turn on and I lean against the wall with my shoulder holding me up and my head resting against the wall.

Watching his fingers move is hypnotic and before I know it, Scott is tapping me on the shoulder, gesturing for me to follow him back to his room.

I have to ditch the hoodie completely so that he can line up the sketch with the other one. I have to give him some serious credit because he is extremely professional, or gay, either works because he easily goes about business despite my nakedness.

Holy crap, lying down on fresh ink is a bitch. Scott adjusts the chair and I'm finally able to get comfortable, putting my ear buds back in and closing my eyes.

At least now I know what to expect, but it doesn't mean it is any less painful.

chapter50

Everyone finishes up before I do, but it isn't fifteen minutes before I'm done. I manage to keep it from Kyle. He can see it later. Talon finished writing his song. Who knew four hours was all you needed to write a song. I teased him about it, but he just said he was inspired. I can't even begin to imagine by what but he promises to play it for me in a couple of days.

Once we're all done and the artists are paid, it's almost midnight. "Let's go get some drinks," Mouse suggests and I shrug, though it hurts to do that now. The guys make the decision to hit a bar close to the hotel, not knowing the area it's probably best if we stay close.

When we arrive there is no fanfare, no paparazzi, no cameras and no reporters. It's kind of nice.

We step inside, the bar is packed and the music is being provided by karaoke singers. I roll my eyes but say nothing. Hopefully none of these guys will get the idea to start singing. Nothing like drawing attention to themselves.

We find a table big enough for Talon, Kyle, Dex, Mouse, Peacock and myself. I'm sandwiched between Talon and Kyle, of course. Our four bodyguards are in their places around the bar, within earshot and fighting distance, if it comes to that. The waiter, who happens to be a chick - of course- comes over and starts flirting immediately with Talon and Kyle, but rather than be irritated, I find it arousing. Not that some chick is hitting on them, but the fact that out of all the men at the table, she picks my two guys. At least until she moves down the line and gets to the rest of the gang. She's equally flirtatious with them and for the first time since I met him, Dex is on his best behavior.

We order our drinks and the guys kick off with conversations about this and that. It's nice to watch so I just kind of sit back and listen.

They talk about everything, but mainly about the tour and some changes to the line-up in the set. They also talk about adding the song that Talon wrote tonight into the mix. Everyone but me seems to know about this song and now I'm really curious.

"So what's the deal with this song?" I finally pipe up. "Everyone is in on this gig except me," I pout.

Talon laughs. "That's because it will only work if I have someone to sing it with."

I raise an eyebrow at him. "Isn't Mouse your backup vocals?"

Talon smirks. "Not that kind of singer." His eyes grow sultry. "The sexy redheaded female kind."

"Good thing I'm dying my hair purple."

The entire table erupts into laughter. "Fine then, a sexy purple haired female kind." He wiggles his eyebrows at me. "What do you say, angel? Wanna sing a real duet with me?"

I put my head in my hands. "You can't be serious."

"As a heart attack." He turns to the guys. "Do you guys know who was at last night's show?" There is a collective "no" or a shake of the head. "Cami and Tristan came to the show again last night."

"Oh nice," Peacock says. "But we didn't see 'em."

"That's because they ducked out before the crowd came back. I don't think they planned on coming back, but before our show was over, they were backstage talking to Addison."

"About what?" Mouse asks.

"Oh, just the little fact that Cami wants to sign Addison to Bold as an artist."

They erupt into a chorus of "no ways", "hell yeahs" and "nice" and I blush as red as a cherry.

"Seriously, one performance and they want her? That's pretty fucking intense. What are you gonna do, Addison?" Dex asks me.

"I have no fucking clue. She said she wanted me to think about it until after the tour was over. But after what happened today..."

"What, with me?" Dex points at himself.

I shake my head. "No, Dex, you were not the only one making headlines today."

"Four and half million hits on YouTube, dude. Someone, even though the quality of the sound sucked, got it all on video and uploaded it and by the time I saw it for the first time, it had more than four million hits. When I was done watching it for like the thirtieth time, it had gone up to over six million," Talon brags.

"What?" I say. "You never told me that?"

He laughs, "You didn't need to hear it again, besides I was on cloud fricken' nine about it. Hence the song."

"You wrote an entire song, music and lyrics in four hours because of that video? Seriously, dude, that's..."

"No, silly girl. I'd been working on the song for a long time, but it just never felt right. Until I found the right woman to sing it with me." He smiles sweetly at me. "Don't forget, you've already agreed to 'Your Eyes', every concert."

The guys laugh and I blush. He wouldn't. Would he?

"Oh, he would," Kyle says. Damn it. I said that out loud.

"So not fair. Maybe you should hear the song before you judge and jump to conclusions, angel."

I want to cross my arms to pout, but as I do the tattoo pain radiates causing Talon to smirk. "I think I like that new tattoo of yours." I stick my tongue out at him.

The waiter finally returns with our drinks and we have at it. We keep talking and order some food, thank god, because I'm starving.

This, by far has been the longest day ever. But being surrounded by these guys makes it feel like family and home. The prospect of that idea is both good and bad...I'm starting to feel like I actually belong somewhere for once in my life.

chapter 51

The rest of the night in the bar went without incident. I had to hold the guys back from taking over the karaoke stage after a string of really bad, really drunk singers. Then they all tried their hardest to get me to do it. I laughed and told them hell no. They even went so far as to tell me that it was good practice for Albuquerque and I told them to stick it. We stayed in the bar until it closed.

Talon is really keeping me to my near orgasm agreement to perform 'Your Eyes' with him for the rest of the tour. Hell, the man went and wrote a duet for the two of us. Now, I am no rock star and certainly, singing with the alternative likes of 69 Bottles is far from what I'd imagined doing.

But the idea excites me on some level. Seriously, it's like the idea of singing in front of thousands of people is terrifying but it is thrilling none the less.

When we got back to the hotel, it was amazing having my two guys so close to me, making me feel like the most important person in the world. Okay, maybe just their world, but a world none the less. I'm blown away by how comfortable they both seem to be getting with each other and in such a short period of time. I would have never imagined it would happen ever, let alone like this.

Though I was the center of attention last night and I soaked up every minute of it until we all passed out.

Kyle loved my new ink. He said he can't wait for it to heal so he can kiss it. Kyle's new ink was adding two stars to his chest on his right side. They're two toned, black, one with red and the other with blue. I'm assuming there is some symbolism behind them, but I don't press, it's none of my business and if he wants to make it mine, he'll tell me.

So now I am sitting in bed, alone. The guys have left me to run some errands, against my better judgment of course. I told them I'd come with them and they refused to let me go. Told me that I deserved a day in bed. So I am taking advantage of it. With my new ink, a hot bath is out of the question, especially considering the shower alone was enough to make my knees buckle. In all honesty, it feels more like my ribs or muscles are bruised than anything else.

Tonight is our big dinner party at Cami's and I have to say that I'm excited about it and even less excited about the fact that there is a good possibility my impending music career is going to be a big topic of conversation. Even still, today the headlines about me are blossoming and all favorable, for now.

My mom called again this morning; I didn't get to my phone in time and decide to wait to call her back.

"Hi Mom."

"Hi baby, how are you?"

Oh, isn't that a loaded question. "I'm great, finally have some down time. How about you?"

"Oh sweetie, why didn't you tell me?" she says into the phone.

"Tell you about what, mom?"

"That you wanted to sing for a living."

I roll my eyes. "Oh mom, seriously? Where did you get that?"

"Some article I read online. You're all over the place, they want to know who this mystery singer is and where can they buy her album." she says with such pride that it makes my heart soar.

"Oh seriously, mom, it was like a one-time thing, I got caught up in the moment and it just went from there. You know as well as I do that singing for a living isn't at the top of my list of priorities."

"Well, I think it should be. You sound amazing."

"Mom, how many times have you watched that video?"

She hesitates then says, "I lost count after about twenty times."

I laugh. "I don't know what to do about that. Cami, my boss, was at that show and she pulled me backstage afterward and told me that she wants to sign me with Bold. I was so shocked I didn't know what to think or what to say."

"Oh baby, that's amazing. You deserve it. You should do it."

"Mom!" I scold her. "You're joking, right?"

"No, sweetheart, I'm not. You're beautiful and you can do anything you want with your life. I think it would be an amazing opportunity for you."

"But what if I fail?"

"Oh nonsense, they love you already, there is no way you can fail."

Oh yes, there are several ways I can fail, but I don't need to tell her that now. "Mom, Hollywood is a tricky business. One minute you can be on top of the world and the next minute you're at the bottom of a barrel. I don't know if I'm ready for that kind of roller coaster."

"Oh sweetie, sometimes you just have to take a chance, live your life, be who you are, enjoy every minute of it."

I wipe a tear from my eye, listening to my mom rattle on and on about how I should throw caution to the wind and go for it. It could end up being the best thing that ever happened to me. Though I have to disagree with her, because Talon and Kyle feel like the best thing that's ever happened to me.

We move past the whole music career thing and begin talking about what's happening in Overland Park, Kansas and it's no surprise that it's uneventful.

"Mom, I will be in Kansas City next week. The band has a concert on Friday. I want you to come."

"Oh sweetie, that's not my kind of music."

"Mom, it's not for the music, I want you to come to see me. We won't be in town long. We have a show the night before in OKC and a show Saturday night in Des Moines. During the show is the only time I'll have and I need to be at the show."

"Oh, alright."

"YAY! I'll send you an email with the details and where to go to pick up your ticket."

"Alright, sweetheart. Where are you now?"

"I'm in Phoenix. I have a dinner party to attend at my boss's house here in Phoenix tonight, then we leave for Albuquerque and then onto Galveston and Dallas. I'll send you the itinerary when I email you about your tickets."

"Okay, sweetheart."

"Oh, and mom?"

"Yes."

"I love you."

"Oh, I love you too, baby. Miss you, and I can't wait to see you."

We wrap up our call a few minutes later and then just as I'm about to pick up my laptop to send her an email, Talon and Kyle come strolling into the suite.

"We told you no working," Talon scolds.

I scowl. "I'm not. I'm emailing my mom information on the Kansas City show."

"You're bringing your mom to our concert?" The look on Talon's face is amused.

"Yes, we're only in town for the show. I won't have time to see her otherwise while we're there. Besides, I think she'd like it and apparently I'm being held to my pre-orgasm promise of performing with you for the rest of the tour, so not being there poses a problem, wouldn't you say?"

"Oh, I'd let you off for your mom, but since she's coming, nah, you're on, baby." He smiles and bends down, kissing me on the cheek. That's when I notice the massive amount of bags the two of them are carrying.

"You guys shop more than girls. What is all that?"

They both give me Cheshire grins. "Oh baby girl, this isn't for us." Kyle wiggles his eyebrows.

"Oh for crying out loud, I don't need that much stuff," I scold.

"Well, it isn't all just for you, you know," Talon says and they set the bags down. "Time to model."

I roll my eyes and stand up, trying to see what's inside. "Oh no, you don't. We will decide what you try on first."

I cross my arms over my chest, pout and tap my foot. "Well then, let's get this over with."

chapter 52

"Do I even want to know how much money you two spent today?" I tease them as I finish trying on the last of the clothes they bought for me today. There are three pairs of shoes, a couple pairs of pants, some shirts, and a few more rock chick risqué outfits for shows.

"It doesn't matter. But since you'll be performing with us, you needed some clothes to wear." Talon grins. "Besides, we had a hell of a lot of fun doing it." Then he laughs.

"How am I going to take all this stuff with us? My suitcase is crammed full enough as it is. I can't fit this in those bags."

"Oh don't worry, we've got that covered too," Kyle says. "It's just not here yet." He smirks.

I point to one more bag on the floor, but I notice that inside that bag is another black plastic bag. "What's in there?"

Talon and Kyle look at each other. "That's something we can show you later."

I roll my eyes. "Why not now?"

"Because if we show you, we'll have to break them in and we don't have time for that." Kyle smiles a wicked, playful grin.

"You didn't?" I scoff.

"We didn't do anything," Talon counters but his grin only gets more devious.

"You went to a toy store, didn't you?" They both bust out laughing and I shake my head. "Seems I'm not the only one excited by the prospect of being taken by both of you at the same time."

They both laugh and the air grows heavy with sexual tension, but Kyle deflects it. "We have something for you to wear tonight," he says, then walks around the wall toward the door of the suite. When he comes back he is holding a black garment bag that has another plastic bag hanging from it. I watch as Kyle removes the bag and Talon steps over to him to pull down the zipper on the bag.

Inside is a deep purple halter top, though the halter aspect is basically spaghetti straps that go around the neck. There are two additional straps that fall down the backside of the hanger. Talon unhooks the hanger from the clasp inside the bag and pulls it out. He turns it around. The two straps hanging down the back of the halter connect to the sides of the top and then there is a deep cowl drop in the back that will showcase my entire back. The bottom of the top is tapered with elastic so that when it sits on my hips it will balloon out in the front.

"It's gorgeous," I say as I reach to take it from Talon.

"We bought two different bottoms for it. One is a matching skirt, so when you put it together it looks like a dress. The other is a pair of black jeans," Kyle informs me.

"So what's in the bag?" I point to what's in his hand and a wicked gleam dances in his eyes and he hands the bag over to me. I take it, pulling out the unmarked silver box from inside. The box is big so it is obviously shoes. I toss the bag aside and balance the box on my left hand and open the lid. I nearly drop the whole thing when I see what's inside. "No fucking way." I don't need an explanation on the designer. The signature red sole is enough of a dead giveaway. It's a pair of purple suede platform pumps with no less than a five inch heel.

I'm not a prude, and I've spent a good amount of money on shoes, but never in my life have I paid more than three or four hundred dollars. These shoes set them back no less than a thousand dollars. "This is way too much. I can't accept these." I try and hand the box over to Talon and he refuses to take it. "Seriously. This is too much, all of this is just way too much." I run a mental total in my head, not counting what's in the black bag and it has to be more than ten grand worth of stuff. "At least let me pay for all of this?"

Talon clenches his chest dramatically, but I can see it's in good fun. "We can't take it back, sorry." He shrugs.

I shake my head. "I mean it, guys, this is all way too much."

"You work hard and you deserve it," Kyle says.

"Kate worked hard too and look what happened," I bite back.

"That's not fair. That's different. This is different," Kyle argues.

"Why, because you're sleeping with me?" Both guys flinch and I immediately want to take back my words, but I don't. I have to stand my ground somehow.

"No," Talon growls at me, the look in his eyes is furious and I step back. My heart pounds in my chest. "We bought this stuff for you because you deserve something nice, something special, and something that is uniquely you and something we both know damn well you wouldn't do for yourself. Addison, it is obvious to both Kyle and I that you spend so much time taking care of everyone else, making sure that everyone else is taken care of that you barely recognize when it's time to do something for you."

I scoff. "I bought tattoos last night, those were for me."

I watch as Talon calms down a little bit with my words, but he's still furious. "Yes, but who outside of your tattoo artist is ever going to see those pieces of art? No one. You barely even show off the beautiful piece of art you have on your back and that, Addison, is a real piece of art and it should be shown off and displayed proudly."

Talk about whiplash. We went from them buying me clothes, to a pair of thousand dollar shoes, to attacking my character and insecurities. It's just all way too damn much.

"It's my body, it's my choice what I want to do with it, or how I want to show it off. Did it ever occur to you that I don't show it off because I don't like to be ogled by everyone? Did it ever occur to you that there are personal reasons behind why I don't show off my back tattoo? No, Talon, it didn't, because if those occurred to you, you wouldn't be standing here attacking me for something you don't understand. I take care of everyone else because I don't need someone taking care of me. I've been the one doing it for so long I don't know any other way to live my life. Taking care of people is part of my job and it's who I am. So when you're ready to get off of your damn high and mighty kick, you can pack it up and take it back. I don't need your clothes, I don't need your money and for god's sake, I don't need your fucking pity."

I throw the shoes down on the couch, pull off the top I'm wearing, and slide out of the jeans I have on as I stalk off toward the bedroom, leaving clothing crumbs in my path toward the bedroom doors. Reaching them, without turning around, I slam them shut, lock them and fall into a heap on the floor.

Fuck him and his cocky arrogance. I am not a prize, I am not someone who can be bought and god damn it; I don't need someone taking care of me.

There are flashes of the past few days that run through my mind. Kyle helping me dress with a migraine, Kyle holding me up while I waited for my boys to plant their kisses, Kyle feeding me, then Talon skipping out on the party to be with me while I slept. The way they pleasure me in bed and the aftercare they provide after they've had their way with me.

My heart shatters the moment I realize that there is a damn good possibility that I just completely screwed up anything I may have had with Talon. Kyle I don't see running from what just happened, but Talon has already said he's fragile and that he will fuck up, he asked for patience and I agreed to give it to him and this is how I treat him the first time he does something nice for me.

I begin to cry, upset and angry with myself for what I've done, what I've said. I want to take it all back. Then comes a knock at the door, "Angel?"

chapter 53

Just the nickname alone tells me that it's Talon who's come after me. Which, if I have a choice of the two, he is probably the better option since I just blew my cork at him, but I don't know if I'm ready to talk about this. "Come on, angel, please, open the door. I'm not mad and I'm sorry. Please?"

Fuck. He apologized to me, damn it. I reach my hand up and unlock the door. "Don't open it yet," I say. "Give me a minute." I get up and go for the bathrobe on the back of the door. Shedding my clothes out there means I'm nearly naked in here and this isn't the kind of conversation to have like that.

Once I have the robe on, I open the door. My red eyes meet his worried, almost petrified eyes. "Can I come in?" I nod and he steps inside, taking the door from me and closing it softly.

"Talon..."

"I'm sorry," we say together. "You first," he says with a smirk.

"I don't know what came over me. I'm so sorry." I wipe a stray tear from my cheek and he gives me a sad smile.

"This is all pretty overwhelming, isn't it?" I nod and take a seat on the bed. "We can take the stuff back."

"No, don't do that. It's just, Talon, I'm not used to this. I've spent so much time alone that having one is hard enough but having both of you has my mind in a tailspin. Please, tell me you understand that."

He nods, "I do understand it. I understand it because this is a first for me too. I don't..." He pauses, runs his hand over his messy facial hair and looks me square in the eye. "I don't do relationships, Addison, I never have. I never thought I wanted one, but all of that is changing with you and Kyle. I don't know what to do to make you happy."

My heart bleeds at his words. "Talon, you do make me happy, extremely happy. I don't need ten grand worth of clothes to make me happy. I need you and I need Kyle, and I need to be able to be me, too."

"I know, angel, and I forgot that and I'm sorry. I warned you I was going to screw up."

I shake my head. "Talon, you didn't screw up. If anyone did, it was me. Instead of being happy and thankful for your gifts, I threw them back in your face and for that I'm sorry, but you have to see where all of this makes me so confused. I don't know what I'm feeling or why I'm feeling this way, but I can't even begin to imagine feeling any differently than I do right now." I take a deep breath, "I nearly broke my own heart out there."

He comes to kneel in front of me. The gesture and the look in his eyes is so sweet and pleading that I almost want to cry again. He takes my hands in his. "Addison, this is the kind of stuff we need to talk about. I understand why you're upset, but this is minor and worth talking about, not screaming at each other. I bought you clothes because I wanted you to feel sexy, to feel the way I see you. Kyle bought you clothes because he wants you to be comfortable with receiving things from both of us, together or separate. Our buying you clothes wasn't meant to cut you down or break you apart. It was meant to lift you." He kisses my hands that are resting in his. "I want you to feel comfortable around us, to feel appreciated and admired because that is how Kyle and I feel about you. You're a strong, independent, amazing woman."

I blink back more tears. "Do you want to know why I do the things that I do for people?" He nods. "I do them because they make them happy and seeing them happy makes me happy. Is it selfish? Sure, in a way, but the person on the receiving end gets the glory, I get the reward. So buying all this stuff for me gives me the glory and it is not something I know how to handle very well. I've always been the girl in the shadows, the girl behind the scenes, hiding from the crowd because that is where I feel I belong. You and Kyle put me on a pedestal that I'm not ready to stand on. I don't wear clothing that shows off my ink because it puts me on that pedestal. I keep my ink to myself because it makes me appreciate a true piece of art, not because someone else enjoys it for a while and discards it like it was nothing. Which is how I've lived my life- in the discard pile. Ready when someone needs me and then back into the pile I go." I pull my hands free of his to wipe my eyes and take a shuddering breath. "You've got to give me time to grow, time to change a lifetime of habits, emotions and insecurities."

"I think it's time I told you a story," he says as he sits on the floor in front of me. "Do you know why I play the guitar?" I shake my head. He smiles, "Not many people do. But I am going to tell you. I started when I was five. I started because if I kept busy at something, I wouldn't get into trouble. Getting into trouble in my house meant getting your ass beat. Getting in trouble meant being put on display for the entire house to see, made fun of and paraded. It also meant a punishment far worse than any belt or wooden spoon could give you." He reaches for the back of his shirt and begins pulling it over his head. It dawns on me now that I've never actually looked at Talon's back, at least not like this.

He turns around on the floor and leans forward. Running along his spine is a series of tattoos that look like words but the design mimics that of a heart monitor reading where words flare into a triangle on one side of the invisible line and then to the other and back and forth.

It says

> Take
> My scars
> Hide them away
> Save me
> From
>
> The
> Man who
> Tries to take me
> Away from
> The
>
> Person
> I'm trying to
> Become. The man
> I want to be
> Desperate
> To be
> Free

When you get to Free it starts over again until it melts into a flat line.

T
O
B
E
F
R
E
E

It is then that the light catches just right and I see one scarred line, then another and another, now that I know what I'm seeing they're popping up everywhere. I break into a sob that I can no longer hold back.

"Addison," he says, his voice is a pain filled whisper. I slide onto the floor and wrap my arms around him, gently kissing his scars. "Angel, please, stop."

"I can't," I breathe.

"I was trapped by my father and my mother didn't stop him. She simply bought me things, got me things, snuck me candy and all the things my father would never let me have. She never said I love you to me, she never hugged me or held me when I would cry." I can hear the emotion in his voice. He's crying. "The only way I know how to show someone affection is to buy them things, give them things. Which is why sleeping with different woman, never getting attached, was easy for me; I don't know how to do it. I don't know any other way."

I squeeze him tighter, holding him to me while he cries. I've always known that musicians who write their own music find inspiration from life, not always the good, and many times it's the bad, and now something about the song he wrote last night hits me. Giving, giving is all he knows how to do, so he is giving me a song. 'Your Eyes' certainly wasn't written for me, but it was my favorite song. This song, his new song is a gift from him to me, his way of telling me how he feels. "I want to hear your song. The one you wrote last night." He stiffens in my arms. "I want to sing it with you."

"Addison, I..." He takes a breath, this time he's calming himself. "It's not ready."

A small smile spreads across my lips. "It's not ready or you're not ready?"

"I'm not."

I close my eyes slowly. "I'm ready to hear it, when you're ready to sing it." I kiss his back again and he turns around, breaking our contact. He wraps his arms around me. "Ow! Ow!"

"Shit, Addie, damn it, I forgot."

I start laughing because he is positively paranoid that he really hurt me. "So did I." I lean in and kiss him once, twice and then the third time he holds me to him. The pain in my ribs and the pain in his eyes forgotten, if only for a moment, this moment, right here.

*chapter*54

"I want you to meet her."

"Who? Your mother?"

"Yes, my mother." I hesitate to respond, I don't know how I feel about that. "She's not that woman anymore, Addison. Trust me."

"If your mother never stopped your father from hitting you, how can you not hate her?"

His eyes grow weary. "Because, for every time he didn't hit me, he hit her ten times harder. She put herself between him and me and when he would get to me, it was usually after he already beat her and he wasn't satisfied with just that."

"How did you get out?" I breathe.

"We lived in a small town, so everybody knew what went on. The doctors at the clinic had finally had enough when my father broke her cheekbone and jaw, and I ended up with a broken wrist. They'd had enough. Child services was called and because she was a victim, they told her to get out or they'd take me away. So she did." He rubs at his left wrist; I'm guessing that's the one his father broke. "We lived on the streets. I'd sing and play guitar to make money for food. After a couple of years she finally had enough and figured out her shit and got us off of the streets. After that I went back to school. I decided that I would make something of myself and I graduated with academic honors in high school and was awarded a full scholarship to Penn State. That's where I met Kyle. We got to talking one night and I picked up my guitar, a random act I would do when things got too intense, and he saw what he thought he'd seen when he met me. He said he knew a couple of guys who were looking for a lead singer. I went, auditioned and after sixty-nine bottles of beer, we had a name for ourselves and the rest is history, or so they say."

With one conversation I've gone from being a blubbering mess over my own shit to crying over Talon's. From hating his mom one second and to completely in love with her by the end. "Yes," I say, "I'd love to meet your mother."

He smiles. "She's the reason we're staying in Philly for a couple of days. That's where she lives. When we signed with the label, I gave her a choice of where she wanted to live. She chose Philly, so I built her a house."

I smile and laugh. "I think that's what all rock stars do when they get their first check. It's not a guitar or a house or a big fancy car, they buy a house for their mother." I kiss him on the cheek. "Well, Talon Carver, you're certainly one of a kind. Now if you don't mind, I have a party to get ready for." He kisses me quick then stands, pulling me with him. "Thank you for sharing your story with me."

He gives me a half smile. "Believe me, it wasn't my intent, but it was warranted. Not that I wouldn't have told you eventually, it just seemed appropriate today." He slips his t-shirt back over his head.

"I couldn't agree more. Now go." I swat him on the ass.

"Yes, ma'am." I scowl and he laughs as he opens the door, leaving me to get ready for tonight.

kyle

"Hey, she doing better?"

He nods. "I think we hashed it out."

"So what was that all about?" I ask. I wanted to go in after her, but he said that this was his mistake and he needed to make it right.

"She feels overwhelmed, rightfully so, about you and me, us. All the clothes, and buying of stuff just made it that much harder for her to handle so she lost it. We talked, she explained where she is coming from in regards to the gifts and it boiled down to her independence and her own insecurities regarding relationships. Then I told her my story."

"Which part?"

"The part about my mom, how she used to sneak me stuff and never said she loved me. It seemed appropriate because I know deep down that's why I did what I did today. I have no other point of reference to telling someone that I care about them."

I slouch back on the couch and Talon comes to sit next to me. He puts his hand on my leg and I shiver with excitement. "So, did you do this because you love her?" I ask him. I'm surprised when he doesn't flinch or deny it.

"Honestly, I don't know what I'm feeling, but it's strange and euphoric in a way. Being with her and you, it's like everything else melts away. The drama with the band, life in general, it just doesn't seem to matter to me anymore, you know?"

I sigh, "Yeah, Talon, I do."

"What about you?" he asks me.

I pop my head up off of the couch. "I think so," I breathe. "I've never met anyone like her before. I want nothing more than to get to know her better, you know? But yet I'm scared to death of pushing her too far. Pushing you too far and then this whole thing just pops and fizzles out. I guess being afraid is a good thing, it means something, right?"

I feel Talon's hand squeeze on my thigh and I look at it. Talon and I have been close before, sometimes too close, but this is something else entirely. Knowing what I know now about my feelings for Addison, I understand better why Talon was always so important to me before all this craziness. There has always been something about him, something that drew me in without a second thought. But it wasn't love or lust or even a desire to be with him, but something was always there, under the surface and now, I think I know what it was.

"Do you ever feel like destiny is taking over your life?" I ask, letting my head fall back on the couch.

Talon laughs, as I expected him to. "Depends on what you mean."

"Without sounding like a total sap? I'm not sure that's possible."

"Try me," he says, completely serious.

"When I met you back in college, something drew me to you. Now before you go all 'you've had the hots for me for years' that's not what I mean."

"I know what you mean without all the 'hots for you' shit," he says, still serious but there is a lightness in his tone.

"I thought that my meeting you was just to get you and Dex together to form a band; to take it on the road, kick ass and take some names. But now I'm starting to wonder if that was just a step in the ladder of this journey."

"Yeah, you totally sound like a sap." I feel the couch shift and I look at him. He looks at me. "But I agree with you."

We're so close and the drive to kiss him spikes, but I refrain. Despite all the touchy feely between the three of us, especially between Talon and I, I'm not quite sure how he feels about it all. Sometimes I wonder if my excitement has pushed him too far too fast, and then he does things like last night where he just starts sucking my cock out of nowhere. Then I often wonder if it's Addison's doing.

"She's a very courageous woman," I say.

"What makes you say that?"

"Well, think about it. She's like a magnet. She pulled us into her, both of us. Then you and I decide, without even knowing what could have happened, that we couldn't fight over her. We equally decided that not making her choose meant that we had to find a way to make it work with the three of us. Sure, sexually wouldn't have been an issue, we've shared chicks before, but it's one thing to share one chick for one night. We've found it within ourselves to make this work. Top that off with the fact that she puts up with us and our shit. Then she goes about encouraging us in ways neither of us ever thought or expected to find we were capable of. I mean, hell, we would not have bought some of the shit we bought today without her encouragement whether she was there or not." I sit up and turn toward him. "I mean it. She's the one bringing us together and I'm sorry, that takes guts."

Talon laughs. "I think, eventually, something like this might have happened between us, with or without a woman."

I cock my head at him. "What do you mean?"

"Oh come on, how many woman have we shared without touching each other? How many times have we done stupid shit like that and not thought about doing something to the other." I try and follow his logic and he catches my confusion. "You mean to tell me, with all the chicks we've shared, you've never once thought about what my dick would feel like in your mouth or up your ass?" And just like that, crass ass Talon is back.

"No, I've thought about it more times than I care to count," I grumble.

"Me too," he says with such conviction that it's almost scary. In truth, I think we've reached a point between Talon and I that all bets are off. Things will continue to change between him and me as we wrap Addison up in the cocoon of what we have to offer her. She wants it, she craves it just like we do, she just has the balls to step forward and make it happen.

"I don't think I can ever give you or her up," Talon whispers. "We've claimed her and I never intend to let her go."

I settle back against the couch, taking a deep breath that for the first time makes me feel freer than I've ever felt in my entire life. We've claimed her as our own, and in the process, we're claiming each other. "With her, the world is brighter, the colors more vibrant. She's ours," I breathe.

chapter 55
kyle

It's about an hour and a half later and nearly time to go when Addison finally comes out of the bedroom. Talon and I took the liberty of getting dressed in our respective bedrooms, though we haven't slept in them since our arrival Sunday night. Talon is wearing his usual get up of jeans, shit kickers, and a leather vest. Only difference, he's wearing black instead of white for his t-shirt but like always, he looks hot.

I am wearing jeans, a royal blue button down, open at the collar, sleeves rolled up to my elbows and a black undershirt.

"Why aren't you dressed?" I hear Talon ask Addison. I turn around to see her hair and make-up are done very nicely. Her hair is pulled back, but it's curly in the back. Her make-up is lighter than she normally wears it, but all she is wearing is a robe.

She laughs. "You never brought in my clothes for tonight. Where's my outfit?" She pouts at him, I laugh and point to the wall behind her. Hanging there is her new purple top and the black skinny jeans, on the floor below it are the Louboutin shoes we got to match. "Oh. Okay, give me five minutes and I'll be ready to go."

"About time," I tease and she turns around sticking her tongue out at me.

"You can't rush perfection, you know."

Be still my beating heart. "Honey, you were perfect an hour and half ago, now you're just fucking gorgeous," I tell her and she blushes.

"Now move," Talon teases her and she scoots into the bedroom, closing the door behind her. Talon turns to me. "Did you know she'd take this long?"

I snort. "Don't all women?"

He shrugs. "Probably, they're usually all done up when I get around to 'em."

I nod. "This is true. You look great, by the way."

He looks at me and gives me that sultry look that makes Addison's panties melt. "So do you," he says.

"I'm not the one you need to be seducing, you know?"

He laughs. "Is it working?"

"Uh yeah!" I tell him and go back to checking my emails. "It's official," I say and he looks at me.

"What's that?"

"As far as the label is concerned, Addison is my new 'assistant'-" Yes, I used the air quotes, don't judge me "-which basically means that we don't have to bring in another unknown. They said they'd rather deal with her as an assistant than run the risk of another incident, which they're pissed about by the way."

"Did you explain the circumstances?"

"I did, but you know David, it doesn't matter. At first he was pissed at Addison for what happened, assumed that she didn't do her job. Which of course I explained, anyway, the point is, she's my new assistant as well as doing the job she came here to do."

"Is that gonna be too much on her?" he asks.

I snort. "No, she's already doing it and what little Kate did on show nights can honestly be covered either by myself or by Eddie. It's not a big deal, though Eddie might want more money." I laugh.

"We don't pay Eddie now."

"That's my point. Thought it might be something to discuss with the guys. Eddie busts his ass around the venues. Might want to make it official."

"Yeah, okay, I'll think about it. Anything else?" he asks, which is what I was waiting for.

"I don't know whether to tell you now or wait for Addison."

He gives me that look like I've lost my mind and I know I have because that's hot. "Well, you seem to be better at convincing her than I can. So I'll tell you then you can tell her."

"Tell me what." Busted.

"Nothing." I look up and fall to my knees, yes, I'm being dramatic, but fuck me.

"Fuck me!" Talon breathes harshly.

Addison blushes but does a twirl around and I blink rapidly.

"You're damn lucky we have to go," I growl at her.

She's wearing the open back purple number, skin tight black skinny jeans accented by the purple Louboutins. "Come on, it's not that..."

"Shut up," Talon growls playfully at her. "You're fucking gorgeous." He turns to me. "We need to get out of here before we rip that off of her."

"Down, boys," she says very commandingly and something about the way she does it is very settling to me.

Talon too. "So what are you not telling me?" She looks very pointedly at me.

I can't deny her anything. "They want 69 Bottles in New York the day after the Boston show."

"We're already going to be there for a week." She scrunches her eyebrows at me, puzzled.

"Yes, but we have Sunday through the first show on Thursday as down time, it is the only significant down time we have until the tenth week. Which is being cut short by Denver."

"So why New York?" Talon asks, moving me along.

"Because they refuse to wait any longer than that to put the two of you in the studio for 'Your Eyes'."

"No fucking way," Talon balks with excitement.

Addison rolls her eyes. "They're never going to give up, are they?"

"Hey, you should be lucky they're letting you wait that long."

"Why?" She asks.

"Because 'Your Eyes' is currently sitting at number one on Billboard," I say with a big ass fucking grin on my face. Talon on the other hand is stunned stiff. Addison collapses onto the couch in front of her desk.

"I bet they're disappointed it's only Talon singing," she teases.

I smile. "Probably, which is why the label wants you in the studio as soon as possible. They're emailing a contract to Cami, I have no doubt that she will discuss it with you tonight." She nods her understanding and we both stare at Talon who hasn't moved.

"Hey, big man." Addison says getting up from the couch and going to stand in front of him. "Hey there," she says when she falls into his line of sight. "You with me?" She waits for a reply and doesn't get one. "Talon, baby, look at me." I watch his eyes shift. "Hi there, big guy. How you doing?"

"I, fuck, did he really just say what I thought he said?" Talon squeezes out on one breath.

"Which part, baby? The recording or the Billboard ranking?"

"Billboard."

"Yes, Talon. 69 Bottles has a number one hit."

Just like that he unfreezes, scooping her up into his arms, wrapping them tightly around her midsection. She winces in pain because he's got her right on the ribs. "Ow! Baby, you're amazing and I'm so proud of you, but ow."

"Shit shit shit, I'm sorry, I, fuck, are you okay?" He looks so flustered, a first for Talon.

She laughs. "I'm fine. Let's go tell the boys."

She tugs him toward the door. "No." He stops her. "I'll clear it with Cami, but I want to tell them tonight at dinner."

She nods. "Well then, let's go." He pulls her back, wraps his arm around her back and kisses the top of her head.

"I love the shoes," he says. "I don't have to lean over so far to kiss you."

She smacks him playfully. "I'm not that short."

Talon and I both huff together and she busts out laughing.

We leave the suite to find the bodyguards, Peacock and Mouse. After a few heartbeats, Dex comes out of his room. He looks beat up. No doubt the last couple of days have been tough on him. I put my arm around his shoulders.

"You alright?" I ask.

"Yeah, mate. I'll be alright."

Mills goes over our plan for tonight. Since we're all going together, Mills has agreed to let us stay in the hotel for tonight, but without exception everyone has to be downstairs ready for the cars to take us to the buses at five a.m.

Everyone agrees and we set off for the dinner party with Cami and Tristan. With excellent news in our hands, I refuse to share the bad news I've just received today. It's too good of a day to bring down the high.

ARE YOU READY FOR BOOK 2?

Craving Talon
Available February 17th, 2015

Her is a look at Chapter On1e

chapter 1
addison

Sandwiched in between a sexy as hell rock god and his equally sexy and sweet manager...yup that's where I sit right now. We're on our way to a dinner party. In a Suburban, packed with the members of the band 69 Bottles, along with their manager, and four - yes I said four - members of their bodyguard staff. I feel bad for Dex - the band's drummer; Eric, also known as Peacock - the band's bassist and Calvin, better known as Mouse - the bands lead guitarist - because the three of them are sandwiched more than I am between Talon and Kyle, the band's manager. They're some big guys and well, it's a Suburban. In the middle seat, behind me, are Beck and Rusty, two of the four body guards, and sitting in the front passenger seat is Leroy, the dude is frickin' huge, and Mills, lead bodyguard extraordinaire is behind the wheel.

We're on our way to Cami and Tristan Michaels' house for a dinner party that is promised to be not only us, but a few of their friends as well. Which should be great, a chance to be normal, sort of.

Normal is hardly in my vocabulary anymore. Not since five days ago.

Five days ago I stepped onto a tour bus that belongs to America's hottest alternative rock band, 69 Bottles. And five days ago, everything I thought I knew about myself has been turned upside down.

I hit that bus with a fierce determination to be professional, to do my job, and to have a good time doing it. But what I didn't expect was the hotness that would surround me. Dex, the drummer, he's a dick, but still very attractive, living up to the rock god name in every stretch of the imagination possible.

Then there is Mouse, why do we call him Mouse? Well for his size, he has a tiny ass voice that resembles Mickey Mouse in a strange way. Though when he sings backup for Talon, he actually has a very low register. It's kinda strange to watch.

And finally we have Peacock, who is aptly named for his wild hair color choices and his mad mohawk skills. His hair is colored to be hawked, so on nights like this, when it's pulled back, it looks like a mosaic of color. He's very good looking too, little on the heavier side when compared to the guys, but he's solid underneath.

Ironically, I've yet to see any of them use the gym, so how they keep their figures is way beyond me.

My hotness meter landed on Talon, the bands lead singer. He's just all around yummy to look at with his shaggy light brown hair and the sexiest scruffiest beard worn by any one man. Now before you go all, ewe beard, or OhMyGod beard on me, it's scruffy, short, and deliciously perfect. He basically just looks like he hasn't shaved in a week. He keeps it that way and it's fucking delectable. He has these vibrant green eyes. Similar to my own, though mine are blue and bright, Talon's nearly glow. Just thinking about them when he looks at me with sex on his mind makes my entire body vibrate with sexual promise.

On my other side is Kyle, the band's manager, who is equally as sexy as Talon is, in a much softer kind of way. He's built and tall, not quite as tall as Talon is, but close. Kyle has beautiful blue-green eyes that open straight into his soul. Though he isn't an open book, he's incapable of hiding who it is that he is on the inside. Which is one of the reasons why I love is passion. He has dirty blond hair that has a little length to it, but he's more of the pretty boy between him and Talon. He keeps his go-t trimmed and he has that small, perfectly shaved line of hair that runs along his very strong, masculine jawline. Tonight he's wearing a dress shirt, boots and jeans. All he needs is a cowboy hat and he'd make the perfect country specimen. But he's far from that, though cowboy seems like an appropriate nickname for him.

Just this last Sunday morning, waking up in Vegas, Talon, Kyle and I crossed a line that I never intended to cross, but was unable to resist any longer. They refuse to make me choose between the two of them, which is a good thing, because there is no way that I could have. They're the perfect balance of salty and sweet. Talon's rough around the edges, a little crass at times, and loves taking control and taking me roughly. I shiver. Reminded of not so long ago, when he took me, hard, fast and rough. It was the perfect antidote to the shit day I'd had. He pushed me to let go, to surrender my body to him, thus taking my mind off of everything else. It was amazing.

Then you have Kyle, who is the polar opposite of Talon. Though not at all bashful about speaking his mind, he's softer and more controlled and very passionate about me and things in general. I don't think he realizes just how sweet he really is.

With the two of them, it's the perfect balance. Good and evil. Salty and sweet. Loud and quiet. Hard and soft. And I am sandwiched in the middle of both of them. Engulfed with their own personal need to be near me, to hold me and to have me.

They've claimed me as theirs and I wouldn't change it for the world. They're proving to be everything I need all rolled up into two nicely kept packages for me to unwrap at any time of my choosing.

Made in the USA
Monee, IL
06 September 2022

13407164R00194